The Forest of Fate

Paddy Stubbs

To Isaac,
with best wishes.
Hope you have as much
fun reading this as I
had writing it.
    Paddy
    23/4/2016

The Forest of Improbable Fate

Text © 2014/16 Paddy (Patrick) Stubbs

First published in ebook format by Kindle, October 2014
First published in paperback by Createspace, February 2016

Cover image:

Enchanted forest background

ID 19182587 © Ellerslie77 | Dreamstime.com

Cover image text added by author in Corel Paintshop Pro X8

This novel is a work of fiction. The characters, events, names and places contained herein are either products of the author's imagination or employed in a fictitious manner. Any resemblance to actual persons, living or dead, or actual events or locations, is purely coincidental.

Dedicated to my Mother, Mrs Dorothy Stubbs, without whose endless encouragement, wit and wisdom this novel would not have been written.

PROLOGUE

Are you weary of the world as it is, my friend? Then lay down your burdens, sit here beside me and I shall tell you of the world as it was, in a time before Time was recorded, in a land long forgotten by the makers of charts and maps. Put aside your fear of mounting credit card bills, dwindling pension pots, worthless savings accounts and useless lottery tickets, for there was once a time when the old Gods still held the earth in their thrall, and a mortal could sup ten flagons of real mead, scoff a boar and gravy pie, enjoy a couple of hours of rampant lust and still have three derans left out of a dunc.

Yes, those were the days, my friend, when the blade was still mightier than the pen, and the cosmic furnace of a sunset was a glimpse of the fate that awaited any warrior who failed to die with a sword in his hand. Theirs was an age of warlocks and wizards, swordplay and sorcery, compulsory alliteration and terrible puns; halcyon days, now shrouded in the mists of antiquity, when mythical beasts were as real as the terror they inspired, and Good and Evil were the poles of existence.

Hark unto me then my newfound friend, for I sense your longing for that lost world, where the tellers of tales around the campfires, and from whom your humble servant is descended, earned their meat and mead by their ability to conjure visions (occasionally, without the aid of magic mushrooms) in the minds of those who dared to listen. Theirs was a world where the strong and fearless might pursue their destiny, even unto the ends of the earth, and thereby carve their names upon the swelling trunk of History.

So, let us set aside the tiresome baggage of the present as we return to an age of myth, magic and uncomplicated sex, in a world long forgotten by all but a handful of dreamers, whose timeless task it is to cast themselves adrift upon the twilight sea betwixt wakefulness and sleeping and recall the ancient memories of their race.

CHAPTER 1

A lone magpie perched on the bloodied hand protruding from the carpet of mist that had settled over the valley floor. The bird shuffled nervously from foot to foot as it scanned its silent surroundings. Nothing moved amongst the smouldering, fire-blackened remains of the settlement, save for an occasional wisp of acrid smoke; it was as though Nature had attempted to sweep all evidence of the raid under the carpet, but had missed a bit here and there. A shadow passed over the magpie and the bird tilted its gaze beyond the gathered carrion crows to the buzzards and a lone golden eagle, circling slowly on the thermals drifting up from the sacked settlement, impatient for the unveiling of the feast.

Ignorant of the violent drama enacted in its absence, the sun eased itself above the rim of the eastern hills, inadvertently catching the burnished surface of the ring on the finger beneath the magpie's feet. Dazzled by the sudden brilliance of the gold, the bird opened its beak momentarily, toppled backwards from its macabre perch and was swallowed soundlessly by the mist. The goose-feathered flight of the arrow protruding from the magpie's breast offered the only clue to the unfortunate creature's final resting place.

"Cor!" said the largest of the crows, impressed by this display of marksmanship, and wasted no time in flapping its way to a height it assumed would be sufficient to ensure its immunity from feathered death. Death, of the aforementioned variety, in the shape of the eagle, thudded into the coal-black scavenger a split second later, sending dislodged feathers flying in all directions and proving unequivocally that one should never assume anything in this life.

Crouched in the shadow of the pines that descended almost to the valley floor, the slayer of magpies fitted another arrow to the drawstring of his bow, lest any of the mounted marauders had lingered in the vicinity to pick off escapees returning to the village. His instincts told him this was a forlorn hope and that he was the sole survivor of the massacre, but an admission of the fact would have left him with no refuge from the tide of guilt threatening to engulf him. Although just sixteen years of age, the youth was already almost as tall and broad as the average man (a traveling codpiece salesman named Grunk), but on his father's command had hidden in the forest all night, where he had been tortured by the terrible screams of the butchered and dying. From his hiding place he had watched others try to make it to the safety of the trees, women and children mostly, while the ill prepared and poorly armed menfolk had attempted to protect their escape. Fighting from horseback and armed to the teeth, the rampaging marauders had shown the settlers no mercy; all had been cut down and slain, brutally.

Young Gorm, lean and tanned, blue of eye and blond of hair, waited two more hours before venturing in to the open and pulling off his sleeveless leather jerkin and linen shirt to set about digging a great pit, into which he would eventually drag the bodies and limbs that had not already been devoured by scavengers or Kolyn the Cannibal. The ashen skinned, but immensely strong troglodyte inhabited the darkest recesses of a limestone cave on Fani Hill by day, but was wont to prowl the outskirts of the local settlements by night, surprising courting couples by gnawing their legs off. He actually preferred their tender young flesh to that of the sinewy elders, but was not averse to an armoured takeaway in the aftermath of a battle. Having satisfied his initial hunger pangs amongst the overcooked former residents of the devastated settlement, Kolyn had scoured the edge of the woods in search of fresh meat, but had been unable to sink his teeth in to the young archer on account of the hail of arrows that had met his every attempt, and had finally dragged less belligerent prey (butchered corpses were renowned for their lack of spirited resistance) off to his lair, instead.

Finally, towards dusk, drained of tears, pity and mutterings about the obesity of some of his former neighbours, Gorm stood wearily atop the burial mound, thrust his arms towards the heavens and cried:

"Mighty Grun, I am a young and inexperienced son of a farmer, though I have heard it said...by my father, mostly...that he was a great warrior, once upon a time. I am without home or family now, but if you will guide my feet, strengthen my arms and sharpen my wits, I shall avenge the terrible things that were done here, though it take me to the end of my days. All I ask is a sign, to set me on the path that I must follow."

As if in answer to his prayer, the earth beneath Gorm's booted feet began to tremble. As his legs buckled beneath him, with fright as much as anything, a pallid hand thrust up from the freshly dug earth between them, gripped his left ankle and began to pull him down.

"Aaaaiiiaaarrrggghhhh!"

Still screaming, Gorm kicked out viciously with his unencumbered leg, but the zombie continued to cling to him with the tenacity of a limpet.

"Gorm, you turnip headed excuse for a farmer's son! What are you trying to do, bury me alive?" a strangely familiar voice demanded to know.

The youth dropped on to his backside in astonishment and sat there open-mouthed as the unmistakeable bulk of Blunt, the village blacksmith and fashioner of swords and other potentially lethal weaponry, rose from the grave, spitting earth. His jerkin, coarse shirt and torn leggings were liberally spattered with dried blood, though most of it turned out not to be his own.

"But...but I thought you were dead!" the bewildered and not a little relieved lad exclaimed.

"I was playing dead and hoping the bastards would tire of dismembering the corpses before they got to me." the balding and unsurprisingly disheveled blacksmith admitted, as he brushed the earth from his soiled clothing with equally soiled hands and finger-combed the earthworms from his extravagant sideburns (a vain attempt to distract attention from his nearly naked pate).

"Not very noble, I grant you, but when it became obvious that we were going to be annihilated no matter how hard we fought, I decided it was the only way I was likely to survive the night in one piece."

"A coward's way!" snapped Gorm, thankful for the opportunity to shift the crushing weight of blame for the slaughter on to someone else.

"If you like," the big man agreed with a shrug of his shoulders, "but dead heroes cannot avenge their butchered loved ones. Your father knew the outcome was inevitable and was prepared to sacrifice his own life, because he knew that if you escaped the sword and numerous other implements of unpleasant death you would swear to avenge him. A very moving speech it was too, if I may say so."

Gorm frowned at the inescapability of the blacksmith's logic.

"I suppose you're right. Anyway, it's reassuring to know there are two of us, now."

Blunt blanched and cleared his throat.

"Err...well...not exactly. I mean, I'd like to help, but I've never been one for all that macho hacking other people to bits for the heck of it stuff. I can see the attraction, of course, but I can also see that, come the day when you meet the fellow who can wield a sword more lethally than you, the attraction is likely to pall rather rapidly."

Gorm stared at Blunt in disbelief.

"So that's it? You're just going to leave me, a sixteen years old boy, single-handedly to hunt down and attempt to slaughter eighty or ninety fully-grown, heavily armed professional killers?"

"Thirty."

"Eh?"

"There were thirty of them. I counted."

"You had time to count them?" Gorm asked, scarcely able to believe his ears.

Blunt stared shame-facedly at his feet for a moment (he hadn't washed them in days), before lifting his gaze to meet Gorm's own penetrating stare.

"Yes…but I *can* equip you with some pretty nifty weapons before you go hunting them down. You've already got that beautiful hunting bow your father made and the sword he had me forge for you, and with the assortment of other useful blades I can fashion, axes and daggers and suchlike, you should be in with a fighting chance."

"You think?"

Blunt turned his head away, lest the boy read his eyes instead of his lips.

"You can't fight that many seasoned killers with force, Gorm. You'd be Kolyn fodder before you even started, but what you *can* do is fight them with guile and cunning. Tail the buggers from a safe distance, watch them from the shadows, and pick them off one at a time; the more you slay, the more it will spook the ones who are left behind."

Gorm considered the blacksmith's advice and the more he thought about it the more sense it made.

"Okay, but I'd still feel happier if you were coming with me, Blunt. Odds of fifteen to one sound a lot better than thirty to one."

The youth knew that Blunt would be unable to dispute that fact, but the blacksmith's expression suggested he would still not be averse to giving it a shot.

"You wouldn't even have to do any fighting, if you really didn't want to...just keep me in lethal weapons," he added, by way of enticement. Apparently, the suggestion was still not quite enticing enough.

Blunt shook his head.

"You're a Delirian, young Gorm, and warfare is in your blood. A hunger for the dubious thrill of battle is cast in your bones. You knew your Father as a farmer and leader of a peaceful community, but I remember him as a fearsome mercenary who sold his mighty sword-arm to the highest bidder. He settled down when he met your mother, but sometimes he would get that look in his eye and I just knew he was itching for a blood-curdling scrap against seemingly overwhelming odds. Well, he finally got what he wanted, poor sod."

Gorm picked up a handful of scorched earth and sifted it slowly through his fingers as he gazed around the sorry remains of his home.

"You think this was what he wanted?" he asked, incredulously.

"The destruction of everything he had worked for, everything he'd built?"

Blunt shivered as a raven walked over his grave.

"No, I wouldn't go that far, but the old ways die hard for all of us, Gorm. You may not be aware of this, but although I have lived much of my adult life in this beautiful valley of yours, I was actually born in to a family of Lumbeygan artisans. We were, are and always will be a peace-loving people, never happier than when we are working with our hands, and if some of the things we fashion with those hands happen to be instruments of violence, we are simply providing a service, meeting a demand that somebody else would profit from if we turned down the work; it does not make us warriors."

Gorm eased himself to his feet and regarded the blacksmith with a pitying look.

"Perhaps, but I wouldn't want to be what it does make you, Blunt. I would rather break my back in the fields than place a sword or a battle axe in to the hand of a man who would use it to populate a burial mound with women and children. Where is the honour in that?"

After a moment of reflection, the average man-sized youth added: "I am glad for you that you survived the carnage, but I would hate to live out my life beneath the burden of the yoke of guilt on your shoulders. So, I will take my leave of you now. My quarry has a good start on me and the longer I leave it the colder the trail will get."

The raven commenced hopping up and down on Blunt's grave, squawking loudly and flapping its wings, as if clamouring for attention.

"Raven lunatic!" muttered the blacksmith, hurling a rock in the general direction of the mocking bird, although he was careful not to aim too precisely. Every man knew that to kill a raven brought an unnatural amount of bad luck, whether it be in the form of a dried up well, diseased cattle, erectile dysfunction or marriage.

Ignoring the altercation, young Gorm pulled on his shirt and jerkin, gathered up the leather water-pouches he had filled at the stream, buckled on his sword, shouldered his bow, leather pouch full of arrows and the bag of over-cooked food scraps and small flagons of mead he had salvaged from the burned out dwellings and set off towards the neck of the valley without a single backwards glance.

"Grun go with you, Gorm." Blunt called after the tall, tanned, muscular, golden haired youth as he was spotlighted by a single ray of sunshine piercing the thickening cloud cover, but the lad was already too busy plotting the grisly demise of his first victim to even acknowledge the blacksmith's farewell.

CHAPTER 2

Malroth the Malevolent woke with a start and stared at the roof of his yurt, where the wooden ribs met the circular bracing frame supporting the stretched and stitched hides that comprised the wall. The naked woman beside him stirred briefly in her sleep, but did not wake. She lay on her belly, head turned away from him, dark hair spread across the abundant, down stuffed cushions that served as pillows. Malroth's right hand rested in the cleft between her buttocks and cupped the hemisphere of her right cheek. Somewhere outside and not too far away a lone wolf howled and was answered within moments by another, more distant member of the pack. So far so good, so what had woken him, the marauder wondered? As if in answer, a savage pain exploded suddenly from a decaying tooth at the back of his lower jaw on the left side of his face, raced along his jawbone, up in to the roof of his mouth and erupted in his head like a long extinct volcano blasting in to life.

"Aaaaaarrrggghhhhh!" he cried in anguish.

"Fuhkk muhh!"

"Again, my lord?"

Startled from her slumbers by her bedfellow's loud exclamation, the woman assumed it to be an order to perform the function he had assigned her. Still somewhat chafed after Malroth's earlier excesses in celebration of his sacking of another settlement, she was less than enthusiastic about the prospect of resuming their coupling, especially in view of his preferred method of entry.

"Nuh, nut yuh, yuh stupud butch!" he snarled in temper, clutching at his swelling face as if trying to hold in something struggling to get out, which in a sense he was.

The entrance flap of the yurt flew open and Norvul, his tall, loose-limbed second-in-command, burst through in dramatic fashion, followed by two armed guards of the camp watch, the mail of their rust flecked hauberks rustling, like metallic curtains. Norvul wore no hauberk, but his thick, leather, fleece-padded jerkin was peppered with raised, metal studs designed to deflect the tip or edge of a sword. Alarmed by the intrusion, the woman scrambled to her feet, drew a large fur around her body and retreated to the far side of the yurt. Norvul, sword drawn in readiness and an expression of alarm disfiguring his heavily pox scarred and somewhat less than handsome features, cast a swift glance around the unusually large dwelling, before addressing himself to his leader, a contrastingly good looking, dark haired and heavily bearded giant of a man with a great barrel chest, bulging biceps and a temper to equal his enormous physique.

"We heard you call out in anguish lord and thought perhaps it was an ambush or attempt at assassination."

He stared pointedly at the woman crouching in the shadows. She stuck out her tongue at him and, with arms crossed over her breasts, drew the fur tighter around her body.

Malroth, whose left cheek had already taken on the appearance of a swollen leather bladder beneath the less than medicinal pressure of his hand, laughed sarcastically.

"Wod, hur? Duh muh a favvur!"

"What's that you say, my lord?" Norvul enquired, unwisely.

Malroth's fury at his second-in-command's inability to understand his scarcely intelligible speech was instantaneous.

"Urr yuh deff?" he exploded, drenching the nearest guard in spittle. Anxious not to enrage his leader further, the man did not even flinch, but allowed the saliva to dribble down his face and on to his hauberk. The second guard stifled a snigger (in preference to having his throat cut, it has to be said).

Norvul turned to him, abruptly.

"Fetch me a lighted torch."

"And you," he addressed the spittle flecked member of the watch, "get out!"

The men nodded and left the yurt, the second one returning moments later with a stout, lighted torch, fashioned from the wood of a Dewrahsel tree. Snatching it from him, Norvul jerked his head towards the door flap. The guard needed no second bidding.

"My lord, please, sit here beside the table and allow me to inspect your face."

He glanced again at the woman. The glance, though misinterpreted, did not go unnoticed by Malroth.

"Shuh steyhs. Uh guttah huv sumthnk tuh tuk mah mand urf the pen."

"Absolutely, my lord." Agreed Norvul, without knowing quite

13

what he was agreeing to, but having a sneaking suspicion it had something to do with the woman, who had by now relaxed sufficiently for her to rearrange the fur so that it revealed an expansive length of her naked flank. He assumed this was for his benefit, an assumption borne out by the woman's salacious wink.

Ignorant of this unspoken exchange, Malroth, resplendent in a recently liberated (by the garrotting of its former owner), shin length, crimson shirt, intricately embroidered with gold thread, got up and seated himself on the pile of silk cushions beside the low, wooden table. Somewhat reluctantly, he removed his hand from the side of his face and saw Norvul's eyes widen in horror.

"Thut bud, huh?"

Norvul chose his words carefully.

"There is considerable swelling, lord…and it looks a trifle…inflamed." He answered as he held the torch closer to inspect the extent of the infection.

"Owwwww! Yuh fukn idyut!"

"Sorry, Lord Malroth!"

Norvul drew the torch away sharply and tried to extinguish the tiny brazier of burning beard below his leader's chin with a flapping hand that served only to fan the flames. In a panic, he sheathed his sword, grabbed a wooden goblet from the table and pretended to trip, flinging the contents in to Malroth's beard and soaking the long, crimson shirt the marauder was wearing over the protective leather vest hammered out for him on a lapstone by the armourer.

"Yuh clumseh twut!" exclaimed Malroth, leaping to his feet and coughing profusely as the miniature inferno doused by the contents of the goblet commenced billowing smoke and a curious fusion of singed hair and mulled wine. Norvul, in an extremely rare, none-battlefield example of thinking on his feet, decided the best way to play this and remain attached to his genitals was to act as if nothing had happened.

"I'm no expert, but it's my guess you have an infected tooth."

Malroth rolled his eyes in the general direction of the apex of his yurt.

"Wull, ted oud uh ted fuh ubserfashun, Nurvl."

"Er, next Wednesday, I think." guessed Norvul, nervously,

clutching at the smouldering straws protruding from Malroth's beard.

Malroth, who had been caught off balance (metaphorically speaking) and sat down again, leapt to his feet once more in renewed and amplified rage, scattering cushions and kicking the table over in his pain and frustration. His features now bore more than a passing resemblance to the Elephant Man (but that's another story) and his bed partner of a few minutes earlier was beginning to wonder what she had ever seen in him, apart from wealth, power and a huge prick. After a moments deliberation she decided that winning combination still outweighed his continuing metamorphosis, shrugged off the fur and slipped back beneath the rest of the bedding.

'Nice arse.' Norvul noted appreciatively to himself, before being distracted by Malroth yanking him off his feet by gripping the thick material of his jerkin beneath his armpits.

"Arghh, wud the fug iss rug wid yuh? Ged oud…ged oud ud leeb mih in pus!"

CHAPTER 3

To Gorm's considerable relief the raiding party had not proved too difficult to follow at first, the thirty or so horses they were riding having deposited a convenient trail of turds to accompany their hoof prints, but the speed at which they were moving was proving something of a problem for the youngster. Like most Delirian lads his age he was possessed of considerable stamina and could boast an impressive turn of speed over a short distance, but he had rarely ventured further than the confines of his own valley and was unaccustomed to both the variety of terrain and the sheer distance imposed upon him by his quarry. Nevertheless, he burned with a fierce and unquenchable thirst for revenge (and the skin on the back of his shoulders, having left his shirt and jerkin off for longer than his mother would have permitted) and it was this that drove him on. Yet it was another six days, during which the midday sun beat down mercilessly upon him and the freezing night air chilled him to the bone, before he reached the sandy, rock strewn plain of Haemorrhoyde, where the tracks of the horses' hooves simply vanished in to the landscape.

Gorm eased his buttocks on to a large boulder and yelped as they made contact with the superheated surface. Leaping to his feet, he spread his jerkin over the top of the rock, sat down again and stared across the barren vista in dismay. A fierce heat had hammered the scorched air to a trembling membrane that now rippled above the desert like a liquid; a liquid in which were suspended huge, irregular outcrops of indistinct, wavering sandstone. As the anguished youth swept his gaze from right to left and back again beneath the protective edge of his right hand, one outcrop in particular seduced his attention, but for several moments he was unsure what aberration had distinguished it from all the others.

The mystified youth screwed up his eyes in an attempt to focus and decided there was something…or someone…perched on top of this particular rock. As he continued to stare he became certain he could detect an occasional movement; something startlingly white appeared to be billowing gently in a breeze his scorched skin longed for but was unable to feel. Sweat ran in to his eyes and he turned away from the glare of the sun and wiped his forearm across them to clear his blurred vision. When he looked again, Gorm was astonished to note the enormous outcrop of rock had taken on definition, was considerably closer than he had first estimated, and that the figure on top of it was undoubtedly an all white clad female of the sultry variety.

His curiosity (and at least one element of his anatomy) aroused, the young Delirian slid off the boulder and picked his way towards the increasingly solid looking natural edifice with extreme care, lest he stumble and twist an ankle, break a leg or give any indication that he was prone to youthful clumsiness. The woman atop the outcrop, the shadow of which he was now entering, regarded the young warrior's progress intently through dark eyes made darker by the application of strange (possibly Avonnian) make-up, but made no movement, nor any attempt to hail him. Her hair, which was the colour of the jet jewelry his mother had liked to wear to clan gatherings and mead mornings at the great longhouse, swayed lazily about her head in the breeze. Strangely, despite the fact that he was now just yards away, that enviable, cooling breeze still eluded the heavily perspiring youth. Pushing this somewhat unsettling fact to the back of his mind, Gorm studied the occupant of the rock with what had yet to become practiced eyes.

The woman wore a simple white, ankle length dress divided in a tapering V from neck to waist, expensive looking leather sandals, an elegant necklace and matching waistband of gold inset with lapis lazuli, and wrist and ankle bands of ornately fashioned amber. Her sculpted features were strikingly beautiful, her breasts full beneath the gossamer material of her dress, her skin pale as honeyed milk and her body clearly one for which she would be envied in female company and lusted after in the company of men. Her slender legs were tucked beneath her, but her dainty, sandaled feet protruded from beneath the hem of her dress. All this young Gorm took in appreciatively as he approached the base of the rock and peered up to meet her unflinching gaze, some twenty feet above him.

"Good day to you, mistress. Are you not uncomfortably hot up there, exposed to the ferocity of the sun?"

The woman laughed and her voice charmed him, instantly (at his age it wasn't difficult).

"I am accustomed to it. Apparently, you are not."

Ignoring her thinly veiled reference to the pink, peeling areas of his recently exposed skin, Gorm was unable to keep the taint of scepticism from his tone as he asked her:

"Then you often sit up there on rock baked hard and hot, still cool even in the fiercest cauldron of the day?"

Aided by the physical reminder of his own, recently tenderized buttocks, the lad could not help wondering if the buttocks he was trying desperately to envisage were clad in some form of flame proof apparel.

"Indeed, I do…but it is such lonely work. Would you care to climb up here and sit with me awhile?"

Gorm had been studying her immaculate teeth as she spoke, but could detect no evidence of fangs, so she was clearly not a vampire. Nevertheless, he remained cautious, for his father had often warned him that demons were inclined to take the form of a beautiful woman, in an effort to lure unsuspecting warriors to their doom. The beautiful woman brushed the hair back from her brow with a winning movement and smiled warmly at the unsuspecting warrior as she shifted her position slightly, revealing even more of her breasts as the narrow cleft in her dress eased wider still, accentuating the pressure of her nipples on the flimsy fabric.

"I won't bite, you know." She added, still smiling.

Confused by the prickling sensation creeping like hundreds of tiny feelers across his skin, the tightness in his chest and the urgent throbbing in his breeches, Gorm attempted to change the subject.

"You said it is lonely work up there. It didn't look to me like you were doing any work."

"Looks can be deceptive…and besides, my work is done, for you are here."

"Eh?" muttered the lad, advertising his increasing confusion.

The woman leaned forward, enabling the slit in her dress to widen to a seemingly impossible to sustain degree, though to Gorm's dismay it succeeded. Unaware that his mouth was hanging open, the young Delirian struggled unsuccessfully to concentrate his gaze upon her face as she addressed him once more.

"I have been waiting here for *you*, Gorm of Deliria."

Gorm was on his guard again almost immediately, as he considered the unlikelihood of this statement.

"How do you, a complete stranger to me, know my name, mistress…and *why* were *you* waiting *here* for *me*?"

Answering a question with a question, the mysterious woman was curious to know:

"Do you always sprinkle your speech with italics?"

"You started it!" he retorted, indignantly, adding:

"And you still haven't answered my question."

She tossed her head back and laughed, an entrancing sound that disarmed the lad once more, despite his misgivings.

"Ah, so suspicious for one so young…and yet wise beyond your years, too. Did you not seek divine assistance, young Gorm, to hunt down and slay the evil men who butchered your family and sacked your village?"

The youth was astonished.

"You know of this?"

"Indeed, I do."

"And do you also know the names of the vile men responsible for those despicable deeds and of their present whereabouts?"

The woman ran her tongue seductively around her lips, which glistened red as rubies against the contrast of her skin.

"The one you seek is known, most aptly in my humble opinion, as Malroth the Malevolent. It was he and his band of wicked cut throats and rapists who perpetrated those terrible crimes in the valley of Grath."

Gorm's eyes widened and he dropped to his knees, trembling of a sudden, though whether from fear, dehydration, exhaustion or a sudden influx of raging testosterone it was difficult to surmise.

"Then you are a Goddess?"

She shook her head and a curious smile played about her lips, like a fleeting glimpse of another personality.

"Not quite. I am a sorceress, Gorm and, as such, privy to things lesser mortals may not discern."

Gorm, whose knowledge of the world (despite frequent parental warnings on a whole host of topics) was severely limited, was inclined to accept her reply as a perfectly reasonable explanation, especially in view of his assumption that he must necessarily be one of the lesser mortals in question.

"I see. And as you already know mine, may I ask what is your name, mistress?"

"My name is Fluctuah…but my fondest friends just call me Fluc. You may do so…if you wish."

"I am honoured, mistress." Replied the gullible youngster.

"Then climb up here beside me, Gorm of Deliria, for you will have need of rest before you venture in to the Forest of Improbable Fate."

Gorm was shocked. Unsettling rumours concerning the great forest that covered much of the Darklands far to the North abounded. Some said that the very earth from which it had spawned was cursed, others that even the Gods feared the nameless and unspeakable things that haunted the poisonous gloom of its vast, uncharted interior.

"The Forest of Improbable Fate! But why should I venture there? They say that nothing but demons, vampires, warlocks, werewolves and tax inspectors inhabit the Darklands and its environs."

"So it is said, but it is also because of such rampant superstitions that Malroth has chosen the forested heart of the Darklands for his hideaway, for who would dare follow him to such a supposedly evil place? And who is to say he did not start the rumours himself…or, at the very least, exaggerate and spread them far and wide?"

Who indeed, thought Gorm, who was by nature incredibly superstitious and already beginning to have doubts about the absolute necessity for his relentless pursuit of Malroth and his marauders at this particular moment in time? It had been an oft-observed fact amongst the inhabitants of his village that Grun worked in mysterious ways, and there was consequently every likelihood Gorm's own and Malroth's paths would cross again at some future date, and in circumstances more favourable for the exacting of vengeance of a particularly brutal nature. Besides, if Grun and his fellow gods had a shred of decency they would strike the marauders dead with thunderbolts (or whatever they happened to have to hand) and consign them all to the eternal flames of

Haletosys, anyway.

"But have no fear, young warrior, for I shall gift you a powerful talisman that should protect you against all of the dark forces that shall be ranged against you in the days to come."

"It should...they will?"

The unexpected reference to potentially malevolent dark forces caught the youth completely off guard. Battling bloodthirsty raiders was one thing, confronting evil entities from the netherworld quite another and he began to wonder if he might not be straying out of his depth, here. There again, a talisman provided by a beautiful sorceress was no bad thing to have in one's possession, surely?

"Most certainly, for the talisman is possessed of powerful magic. So, come, lie here beside me and I shall first soothe your aching limbs with gentle massaging, for I sense your great weariness."

Despite his great weariness Gorm needed no further bidding and scaled the rock in what would have been record time, had anyone who had been bothered to consult a stop dial at the appropriate moment been present for the ascent. On reaching the summit and divesting himself of sword, arrow bag and bow, the excited lad settled down beside her and was astonished to note that, contrary to his expectation, Fluctuah was even more beautiful than she had appeared from the base of the rock. Her eyes, hair, teeth, features, skin and body were all flawless and, for one fleeting moment, it occurred to him that she was almost too perfect, as though her image had been conjured from his own, youthful fancies and expectations. Sadly, the moment passed unheeded as she laid her head against his firm shoulder and slid her left hand lightly over the top of his equally firm right thigh, until the edge of her little finger was resting ever so gently against the unsurprisingly firm bulge of his nearest testicle.

"Oh, Fluc!" exclaimed young Gorm.

CHAPTER 4

Blunt sat alone in the Ailing Parrot tavern and watched his tankard sliding slowly across the tilting tabletop for the umpteenth time. He had spent a rumbustious night with Aleetha, the tavern's mead maid, who was renowned locally for serving up far more than watered down alcoholic beverages provided the price was right, and had been mightily impressed by the size of his purse (amongst other things). At the crack of noon he had left her sleeping off their excesses and ventured downstairs for a belated breakfast of stale bread, hard Rumbugger cheese and a tankard of liquid that passed for strong ale. The blacksmith caught the brimful vessel an instant before it toppled to the floor. Still nothing wrong with his reflexes, he mused.

"Want me to put somfin' under the shorter leg, mate?" Tobias Jugg, the swarthy, one-eyed landlord called to him from beneath the shadow of his as yet unfashionable tricorn hat.

Blunt shook his head and gulped down half the contents of the tankard in one, great draught.

"S'fine." He answered, wiping a grimy shirt sleeve of coarse linen across his mouth and setting the tankard down at the highest edge of the table, to renew its slow traverse to the dropping off point.

'If the boy wants to commit suicide,' he thought to himself, 'what business is it of mine? We're not related…Haletosys, we're not even the same nationality!'

He glanced out of the window at the crossroads the tavern had been established to serve. A decaying, maggot ridden corpse swung gently below one arm of the signpost and bore grisly testimony to the wooden erection's dual function, but offered no clue as to where this latest, unexpected phase of his life should take him. He nodded in the direction of the well hung deceased.

"Customer of yours?"

Jugg spat in to the tankard he was cleaning and commenced scouring the interior with a filthy rag, but did not look up. Blunt currently being the sole occupant of the other side of the counter, it was obvious to whom his bleary eyed patron was referring.

"Was."

"And the poor fellow's crime?"

Jugg spat again and resumed his half hearted polishing.

"Blackguard tried to sneak orf wivout payin'."

Blunt glanced again at the occupant of the noose. The empty eye sockets of the tilted skull, to which shreds of rancid flesh and a pathetic ginger beard still clung, appeared to be staring pointedly in his direction, as if expecting him to come to its defence.

"Dastardly behaviour, I grant you, but the punishment still seems a trifle excessive."

Jugg looked up at him in surprise.

"Listen mate, you let one bugger get away wiv it and all the other tight arsed bastards'll be trying it on, so our suspended friend out there's a deterrent as much as anyfing. I'm runnin' a business, not a fuckin' charity."

Blunt studied the corpse again and noted that in life it had probably been significantly smaller than Jugg in both build and stature, which suggested to him the distinct possibility that the landlord was a cove of somewhat cowardly disposition who had opted to pick on the client least able to stand up to him, but right now the deceased dangler was the least of his own problems.

As far as the blacksmith could see, upon exit from the tavern he could leave in any one of five possible directions. To the North lay mighty Maleryha, rich in ore, minerals, hard men and feisty women, and beyond its northernmost border the region known as the Darklands, much of which was covered by a vast tract of ancient woodland; the notorious Forest of Improbable Fate. Throughout the four kingdoms it was rumoured that the forest was populated solely by goblins, demons and the wandering ghosts of long dead tyrants and sorcerers; a fearful, terrible place, shunned by man and beast.

To the South and just beyond the horizon visible from the lofty cliffs lay the glittering island queendom of Anthraks, home of the Anthraksians, ferocious female warriors whose legendary beauty was matched only by their ruthlessness, blood lust in battle and rampant nymphomania (the latter being largely wishful thinking on the part of their captives, passing sailors and pubescent schoolboys). In fact, theirs was a disciplined and insular society, forged upon the ruthless exploitation of men captured in battle, although their vast fleet of merchant ships, protected by the powerful Anthraksian navy, traded successfully with every corner of the known world.

Not too far to the East, Blunt's homeland, the famously scenic kingdom of Lumbeygoe, bore the dubious distinction of being the most conquered nation on Earth, but was equally famed for the quality of workmanship of its craftsmen, the skill of its boat-builders and seamen, the richness of its soil, the strength of its ale and the reluctance of its inhabitants to take to arms, despite the fact that they were known to forge the finest weapons in existence.

To the South-West and easily overlooked lurked the tiny kingdom of Scroffular, an isolated sliver of largely inhospitable land so small and perpetually insignificant it had never been considered worthy of mention as the fifth kingdom by anybody, with the possible exception of a handful of ardent and regularly inebriated nationalists. Referring to themselves, somewhat optimistically, as the Free Scroffulese Army, this meagre band of eternal optimists and conspiracy theorists met regularly at the Legless Newt to discuss tactics for the overthrow of their shadowy foreign oppressors, but were invariably too drunk to ever come up with a cohesive plan of action.

Finally, to the West nestled the recently sacked settlement of Nurk in the valley of Grath, and the fertile lands of Deliria, populated by a number of perpetually feuding warrior clans whose individual fighters made the best mercenaries gold (or anything even remotely valuable) could buy, but who also made their living off the land in the lean times between blood feuds, border disputes, wars and election campaigns. The Delirian warriors' ferocity and love of battle were admired grudgingly by the Anthraksians and feared by just about everyone else, including the bloodthirsty potentates who hired them, and none had been feared more in their heyday than Garok, Gorm's formidable father.

Yes, there was no doubt about it, young Gorm came from the finest fighting stock, but Blunt suspected he was already as good as dead, for Malroth the Malevolent was not known as the Butcher of Belbaran for nothing; the landscape was littered with the corpses of those who had dared to oppose him, and even more of those who had not. Blunt's gaze returned wistfully to the road to the East. He was just six miles from the Lumbeygan border and could be home before knightfall, when picking one's way between the armoured inebriates littering the highway virtually doubled the time it took to make the journey.

The blacksmith finished his ale, stood up and shouldered his bags as his tankard slid to the floor. Taking hold of the table, he turned it upside down and drew his sword.

"Ere, wot you fink you're doin', mate?" yelled Jugg, reaching surreptitiously beneath the countertop for his lead-studded, closing time comforter.

With a speed that dazzled the eye and deceived the mind, Blunt made three swift passes with his blade and three pieces of table-leg toppled to the floor, returning the furniture to an equilibrium it had not possessed in many a year… and possibly ever, judging by the lack of craftsmanship involved in its construction.

"You got a problem with that…mate?"

The landlord shook his head emphatically and relaxed his grip on the hidden cudgel.

"Err…no."

"Good."

Blunt sheathed his sword, squatted on his haunches and tried to shake the table, but it would not budge from its unaccustomed plane.

"There, steady as a rock, good as new. You can get your table dancer back in now."

"Thanks, I will…soon as her leg's been set."

CHAPTER 5

Gorm closed his eyes, luxuriating in the welter of new sensations already threatening to overwhelm his eager young mind and youthful extremities. He sensed rather than felt Fluctuah's hand move skilfully from his thigh to the center of his chest and push him down gently to the sun-baked rock, before slipping surreptitiously beneath the waistband of his breeches. Despite his delight at this unexpected turn of events, he felt things were happening just a little too quickly for comfort. He wanted to savour the entire experience a little longer and was about to open his eyes and give voice to his reservation when he was overtaken by yet another, most unusual impression. He realized with a start that he could no longer feel the rock beneath him, nor Fluctuah's delicate hand in his breeches, but was instead experiencing an extraordinary sensation of…of…well, it was not quite weightlessness, for he was aware of cooling air moving around him, as though he was descending gently, like a feather. Yes, that was it; he had experienced this sensation once before, several years previously, when he had toppled from the topmost branches of a great pine he had been climbing in search of a buzzard's nest. He was falling…falling…fal...

"Ooooooofffffff!"

CHAPTER 6

Blunt, a broad-brimmed, floppy hat protecting his balding pate from the ferocity of the sun, sat astride the horse he had just spent thirty minutes haggling over with the innkeeper. A thoroughbred the brute most definitely was not, but it boasted four legs to his two and seemed not in the least perturbed by the weight of its new owner and his bulging satchel of tools. Tavern and crossroads lay a mere thirty yards behind them as man and beast regarded the highway East, wavering in the shimmering heat haze.

Gorm was probably dead already, Blunt reflected ruefully, victim of the elements, wild animals (there is still fierce debate as to whether Kolyn should be included in the latter group) or Malroth and his bloodthirsty marauders. He flicked the reins and his horse resumed its leisurely progress along the road to Lumbeygoe, but after less than a minute the blacksmith reined the animal in again and peered back over his left shoulder. The boy was a Delirian, he reminded himself, orphaned only son of a legendary warrior. As such, native cunning, a propensity for extreme violence, love of savage battle against ludicrous odds and a murderous thirst for vengeance coursed through the lad's veins like infected blood.

The blacksmith heaved a great sigh, tugged the reins to one side and turned his mount around. The raiding party had been headed North to where the hardy and resourceful inhabitants of a handful of palisaded settlements traded with the least objectionable of the inhabitants of the Darklands; a risky business by all accounts, but affording considerable wealth to any settlers barbaric enough themselves to survive the encounters. Perhaps he could catch up with the youth at one of those isolated outposts in what passed for civilization at the rim of the known world.

Both Malroth and Gorm had a head start on him, but Blunt knew of a shortcut once used by redoubtable Lumbeygan explorers in search of a North West passage that might open up trading potential. The route had long since fallen in to disuse on account of the number of lives it had claimed each season, but it was still there, as treacherous, tempestuous and potentially lethal as it had been in the old times, he suspected. Bisecting the continent like a

gouge carved in flesh by a sword, the mighty and turbulent River Twai could reduce the time required to cross the landscape by two thirds, but demanded the price of the traveller's life for the privilege more often than not. Far more often.
"Hmm, why not kill two birds with a single stone, eh? Set off in hot pursuit, while still enjoying all the health benefits of a relaxing river cruise; it makes perfect sense." Blunt reasoned aloud, with all the conviction of a one-legged tightrope walker traversing the Fukkyndiep Gorge in a fierce crosswind. His horse maintained a diplomatic silence.

CHAPTER 7

Jerking his eyes open at the involuntary emptying of his lungs and the crushing sensation down the entire length of his spine, Gorm gave voice to a shrill and most unmanly scream. The demonic creatures leering over him were the stuff of nightmares, but judging by the all too real pain in his back, he wasn't having one of those right now. In response to his shriek, his observers peeled back thick, bulging lips to reveal jaws stretching snake-like over teeth that bore not the slightest resemblance to anything even remotely human. There were sixteen of the repulsive entities and the outlines of their ugly heads, arranged in a semi-circle above Gorm's own, were framed by the narrow opening to the sky far, far above them. The monstrosity at the centre of the semi-circle was considerably larger than its odious companions, whom the spreadeagled youth estimated to be no more than two and a half feet tall, and it was this creature that addressed him in a rasping, mocking voice:

"Did your daddy never warn you about demons, boy?"

Still struggling to control his terror, Gorm yelled at the creature:

"Who are you, monster…and what have you done with Fluctuah? If you have harmed just one delicate hair of her head I'll…"

"You'll what?"

Before Gorm could think of a suitable reply, the demon continued in unnervingly perfect mimicry of Fluctuah's dulcet tone:

"Seems to me you're in no position to be making idle threats, wouldn't you agree, guys?"

The little demons nodded, chuckling fiendishly in the finest tradition of demonic entities the nether world over.

Realising the hopelessness of his present situation, flat on his back at the bottom of a deep shaft and bereft of weapons, save for the dagger tucked into a neat little sheath in the boot on his right foot, Gorm sought to engage the creatures in further conversation, until he had had time to recover from his astonishment, recoup his breath and consider a strategy for escape or a winning plea for clemency.

"You still haven't told me who you really are. Goblins, perhaps?"

"Goblins? Goblins! You're not so much Gorm as gormless…which is what we'll be once we've devoured you alive, eh guys?"

The 'guys' indulged themselves in a little more fiendish chuckling, until they were cut short by a scything motion of the larger demon's left arm.

"I…" he paused here, presumably for dramatic effect, " am Bahber!"

"You're the demon, Bahber? I've heard of you." Gorm lied, quite convincingly for one so young.

"You have?" queried Bahber in surprise, uncoiling his grotesque, misshapen torso to stand approximately erect. Stood thus, Gorm estimated the repulsive creature to be at least seven feet tall. His arms and legs were long, boney and corded with sinew, the extremities more claw-like than hands and feet. His green tinged, leathery skin was warted like a toad's and ribbed with an apparently haphazard network of pulsing veins, and his breath stank of terminal decay, convincing the young Delirian that Bahber did probably not figure highly on anyone's list of hot dates. Worst nightmares, possibly, but suitor material he most definitely was not.

"Absolutely!" Gorm continued, playing for more time as befitted a captive in his unenviable situation.

"A lot of the folk in our village worshipped *you*, rather than…well, you know who."

As he spoke Gorm's eyes continued to wander surreptitiously about the rock strewn floor of the stinking pit. He had fallen in to a nest of sorts, comprised of intertwined branches and human and animal bones, all bound together with dried clay and faeces. The pit itself was at least thirty feet deep and the vertical surface appeared virtually unscaleable, although there did appear to be a number of potential handholds at more than twice the height of a man, but testing that impression would have to wait. Unarmed, he would have to come up with a cunning stratagem to overpower his captors, but right now Grun alone knew how he was going to go about accomplishing such an unlikely feat. He had to keep them talking and hope that inspiration would come to him.

"Worshipped *me*, eh? Well, I must admit that hardly comes as a surprise." Bahber fibbed, boastfully, completely oblivious to his captive's tortuous mental machinations.

"But what of your diminutive companions? I know naught of them."

"I call them the Demonettes. Cute, huh?"

"Wasn't the word that sprang immediately to mind." Gorm admitted, regarding the entities in question with something akin to abhorrence.

"Hmm," murmured Bahber, "well, that's the social niceties over and done with. So, if there's nothing else, we're going to eat you, now. Guys, tuck in."

The guys clearly needed no second bidding and pounced on the young Delirian with relish (possibly tomato, although I couldn't swear to it).

"Wait!" screamed Gorm, in a very real panic.

The Demonettes paused momentarily in surprise.

"What is it, now?" snapped Bahber, irritably.

"Surely you're not going to eat me raw?" Gorm improvised, playing for just that little bit more thinking time.

"And why not, may I ask? It is our custom, after all."

"Because everybody knows humans taste much better when they're roasted."

"They do?" queried the demons in unison.

"Mmmm." Gorm nodded, still thinking at unaccustomed speed.

"And which prize idiot told you that?"

"Kolyn the Cannibal."

Bahber raised the bony ridges that served for his eyebrows in a fair to middling attempt at an expression of astonishment.

"*You* know Kolyn the Cannibal? How can that be? He eats everyone he meets."

"Very true…but only when he meets them individually. I was playing with three friends when I met him. Luckily for me, he ate my friends first, by which time he was full to bursting and in the mood for a little after dinner conversation. I made my escape later, while he was sleeping them off."

"I see. And just how did he…prepare…your unfortunate friends before devouring them?"

A plan was beginning to form in Gorm's mind; it had been a long time in coming, but he was hopeful that it just might work. He got awkwardly to his feet, hands raised before him in a gesture of submission.

"Allow me to show you, Bahber."

"And just why would you feel inclined to do that?" enquired the demon, suspiciously."

"If you guys are really going to eat me, I'd rather be dead than alive when it happens."

"Fair point." The larger demon admitted, before suggesting:

"So, Gormless, you'd better show us how it's done."

CHAPTER 8

"You sure this thing is watertight?" Blunt, one foot still clinging desperately to the riverbank, enquired of the ancient mariner.

"Ohh, arr."

"And is there the slightest possibility that we could converse in an intelligible tongue before I finally take my leave of you and head up river?"

The grizzled old sailor scratched furiously at the stiff (with potage, mostly), grey stubble on his chin as he considered this request. A long clay pipe, from whence issued a pathetic wisp of pungent smoke, dangled precariously from his near toothless gums and rendered most of what he said virtually unintelligible.

"Praably."

"What?"

"Oh, never mind." Blunt added resignedly, withdrew his foot and sat down on the narrow, splintered cross-plank that served as the oarsman's seat, before the little vessel could overbalance and deposit him in to the sluggish (at this particular point in the landscape) murk of the Twai.

"As I have just been at pains to explain to you, my destination is the Forest of Improbable Fate in the distant Darklands. Have you any idea how long my journey is likely to take?"

The boatman sniffed the air, removed the pipe from his mouth, licked a filthy finger and held it up to the landward breeze before reinserting the pipe.

"Har, ee'll be there dreckly."

"Oh, for goodness sake! It was a simple enough question, you know."

Blunt eased the oars, worn smooth at the grips by decades of use, in to the heavily corroded iron rowlocks, planted his feet firmly either side of the leather baling bucket floating in the shallow water that had seeped between the planks in the time it had taken him to sit down, and called out to the boatman.

"Now cast off, if you please, my good man. If the gods be willing, I shall return anon with your stout vessel and retrieve the excessive deposit you extracted from me when I was in my cups."

"S'not my faalt 'e be pissartust."

The old sailor, still sucking furiously at the clay pipe hanging from his lips, bent from the waist with a suppleness that belied his years and unhitched the painter from the iron stake protruding from the earth, several feet back from the riverbank.

"'Sides, if 'e be t'ward Durklnds, 'e nar be cumunbaack, hence larrgj deepasit."

"Grun give me fucking strength!" Swore Blunt, as he struggled to extricate his starboard oar from a tangle of what he took initially to be drifting weed. On closer inspection it turned out to be the bloated corpse of a man of about his own age who had become enmeshed in the aquatic vegetation. Appalled by the empty eye sockets, the blacksmith rolled the fish-eaten obscenity over and noted the two, black feather flighted arrows protruding from the cadaver's back, and the ugly stumps at the ends of the arms where its hands should have been. As bad omens go, it was going to take some beating.

"Praaper jaab." Commented Blunt's one-man audience, in grudging appreciation of his body-rolling dexterity with the oar. Blunt assumed the man had switched to a different language in a forlorn attempt to communicate more effectively. Pointing to the corpse, now drifting south at increasing speed, he asked:

"Is that kind of thing a regular occurrence in these Grun forsaken parts?"

"Aye, reglur as sundialwurk. Grunbewithee." Mumbled the old river dog, more in hope than expectation. This was the seventeenth boat in forty years he had hired to as many intrepid souls determined to risk life and limb on an expedition to the Darklands. As yet, not one of the vessels had ever been returned, nor the increasingly extortionate deposits been reclaimed from his account in a canvass bag beneath his bed.

"There's no need for that kind of language." Blunt shouted from the little boat, as he finally began to make some limited headway against the current.

CHAPTER 9

"I'll need the assistance of the Demonettes, if you've no objection? We need to build a pyre."

Gorm was banking on the fact that, with his escape from the pit seeming all but impossible, Bahber would have no logical reason to refuse his request. Whether demons reasoned in a logical fashion, like human beings, or were irrational and unpredictable, like human beings, the lad had no way of knowing in advance. Denied that vital knowledge, he prayed silently to Grun and the spirit of his father for assistance or, at the very least, some recognisable sign that despite all appearances to the contrary, he had not been abandoned in this Haletosys hole.

Bahber considered the youth's request at some length.

"No problem," he declared, after what seemed to Gorm like an eternity.

"My little treasures are going to need plenty of practice if pit roasts are to become a regular feature of our diet. There's a lot hingeing on this experiment, y'know. "

Gorm nodded in agreement before indicating the nest in which they all stood with a sweep of one hand.

"I'm afraid they'll have to dismantle some of the nest, though. We're going to need a large, sturdy, circular base to support the construction, if we're to do this properly. These bones will be ideal."

Bahber shrugged his misshapen, skeletal shoulders.

"You're the expert."

"But if they start just yanking them out indiscriminately, there's going to be a lot of dust and mess, what with all the dried shit."

Bahber nodded in agreement.

"Stands to reason."

He turned aside and addressed the little demons:

"You heard what the kid said. We need a large, circular base of bones. Six of you start dismantling the nest, but carefully. Once the base has been laid you can start building the pyre with branches and twigs, sturdiest at the bottom so they can support the weight above them."

Gorm nodded, apparently fired with a similar enthusiasm.

"You've got the idea now, Bhabs. You're organising it like a pro. I'm impressed."

Bahber's facial skin flushed a filthy colour as he blushed at the unaccustomed praise.

"And lay the majority of the turds at the back there against the wall, but keep a few as tinder, together with some of this straw."

He kicked at the debris littering the floor of the pit.

"Stack them carefully, so we can use them again. Then pile the stripped wood next to where you're going to build the pyre, so we can feed the flames easily to keep it going once it's alight. The rest of you can start building the base as they hand you the bones. The sooner we get this show on the road the sooner we get to eat. Savvy?"

Already drooling at the prospect of a cooked meal, the Demonettes needed no second bidding and set to with a will and a song.

"And you can cut out the 'Hi ho, hi ho stuff!" Bahber snapped, irritably.
"I can't abide seeing anyone happy in their work."

Throughout the operation Gorm wandered back and forth around the pit, offering instruction as the Demonettes toiled on the construction of his funeral pyre. Finally, after some twenty minutes, during which Bahber had begun to regard their industry with all the interest of a warlock watching woad dry, the young warrior pronounced the edifice complete.

"Excellent!"

Bahber regarded the great cone of bones, wood, twigs, straw and excrement towering some fifteen feet above him with a somewhat dubious eye.

"Only…only…and forgive me if I'm being a trifle naive here, only shouldn't you be tethered to a stake at the center of all that stuff, preferably somewhere near the top? Isn't that how it works?"

"Absolutely!" Gorm nodded in agreement.

"Unfortunately, as you may already have noticed, we don't actually have a stake of sufficient length, so I've had to improvise."

"Improvise?"

"Yes. As I'm sure you are well aware, all the finest chefs insist that for meat to be cooked properly, the flames have to reach a certain intensity before the food can actually be added to them."

Bahber eyed the youngster warily.

"They do?"

"They do, indeed." Gorm reassured him, confidence now issuing from every pore.

"Yes…of course, they do, don't they?"

"So, we need to light the fire and let it burn down to approximately half its present height, by which time the heat at its core will be sufficient to sear my skin and produce some fine crackling, whilst keeping all the moisture of my bodily fluids essential for the correct roasting of my flesh locked in. Rest assured, the end result will make for spectacularly good eating."

Bahber wiped away the saliva dribbling from either side of his mouth with a forearm, all suspicions quelled.

"Sounds good to me, Gorm; we're so lucky we ran in to you today. But how are we to light the fire? Alas, we have no dragon."

Gorm smiled him a winning smile of such warmth the demon was almost saddened that he would shortly be making a meal of the lad.

"Fear not, Bahber, for I always carry a couple of flints in my pouch for making a campfire. We shall have a roaring blaze in no time…and on that thought, may I suggest that the Demonettes retreat to the far side of the pyre. I would not want them to be singed by the flames as it catches alight."

"Very wise. Well, you heard the lad, all of you over there against the wall on the far side of the pyre."

"Might be as well to have them cover their eyes with their hands as well, for a few moments. The initial flames are bound to generate a lot of smoke." Gorm added.

The Demonettes traipsed dutifully to the far side of the pit beyond the pyre, rubbing their claw-like hands together in expectation before placing them over their eyes, and were soon hidden behind the enormous bonfire.

"No peeking now." Gorm called to them as he gathered up a fistful of straw from the ground, took the flints from his pouch and commenced napping them against the bone-dry fibres of dead vegetation. Within seconds the straw was alight and he pushed it quickly in to the base of the pyre and stepped back to stand beside Bahber. Moments later the wood began to smoulder and the young Delirian turned to face his captor. Above the loud crackling now issuing from the base of the pyre and echoing about the pit, he gestured with a crooked finger for the demon to lean closer.

"Before you eat me, there is an old Delirian pre-feast custom I would like to observe, if you have no objection?"

"Oh. And what might that be?"

"A prayer to mighty Grun, for what you are about to receive."

Bahber pulled thoughtfully at his excuse for a chin.

"Hmm, given your commendable youthful exuberance it may have escaped your notice, but demons rarely feel compelled to offer up groveling thanks to the big G."

"No doubt, but I could adapt it for you to suit the current situation. Imagine the big G's chagrin at your mockery."

Bahber imagined it and an odious smile infused his repulsive features.

"Let me teach you how it goes." Gorm whispered, beckoning with the same summoning finger for Bahber to lean in closer in conspiratorial fashion.

"For what you are about to receive…"

Bending forward and slightly off balance, the startled demon paused uncertainly for one fraction of a second too long, allowing Gorm to lunge forward with astonishing speed, reach up and grab the pointed, leathery ears and use the demonic creature's weight to bring his own forehead crashing with sickening force on to the bridge of its incredibly ugly nose. Bahber toppled backwards to the floor of the pit, shrieking in agony as he clutched at his shattered face, from whence a dark and foul smelling gunge was pumping at a truly astonishing rate.

"Ooooooowwwwww, dads by dose! Youb brokun by fuckid dose, you liddle shid!"

"Yeah? Well, I haven't finished with you yet." Gorm yelled, adrenalin coursing through his veins now as he kicked the creature in the ribs, repeatedly and with all the force he could muster…which was quite a lot, what with all the adrenalin.

"Thought I'd prove an easy victim, did you, you sneaky, shape-shifting, flesh eating bastard?"

He cast around for a suitable implement for administering a coup de grace and spied a very large and heavy-looking lump of rock, not three feet from where he was standing.

Following his gaze nervously, the distraught and still spreadeagled demon eyed the rock with some trepidation.

"Wod youb pladding tuh do wid dat?"

Gorm chuckled evilly as he hefted the rock high above his head with both hands.

"Have a guess." He replied.

CHAPTER 10

After eight days of strenuous rowing, during which he estimated that he had navigated scarcely forty miles, Blunt sculled the little vessel to port and grounded it on a narrow beach of flood polished pebbles beneath a low, overhanging bank. When he had first hit on the idea of using the river to enter the Darklands, it had not occurred to him that he would be rowing against the current. Now however, physically exhausted and still more than sixty miles from his destination, he realized he was going to have to find another mode of transport. He could only assume the early explorers who had navigated the river must have had larger ships, sails and the advantage of wind power to aid them. Either that or fifty oarsmen, possibly slaves taken in battle, that could be encouraged with whip, cudgel and a barrage of colourful profanity befitting a seasoned helmsman. Without such aids or manpower, making the entire journey by river single-handed (although he had cheated and used both hands to row) was well nigh impossible.

The perspiring blacksmith clambered out of the boat, gathered up his belongings and hauled himself up the bank, before depositing his sore and heavily splintered rump on to the grass beneath the welcome shade of an overhanging willow. Below him, fat trout held station lazily in the river with no more effort than an occasional flick of the tail, making a mockery of his recent efforts to navigate the waterway. Exhaling a long, loud breath, Blunt leaned his bulk against the trunk of the sun warmed tree, slipped the satchel of tools from his shoulder and closed his eyes.

The blacksmith was woken some hours later by the rumbling of heavy cartwheels and the murmur of human voices, interspersed with coarse laughter. Looking up, he saw a train of half a dozen horse drawn carts trundling across the wild flower meadow not fifty yards from where he sat. His first thought was to remain hidden, but noting that the occupants of the vehicles appeared to be unarmed, he revised this decision, well aware that he was going to need assistance if he was to progress further. Struggling to his feet, he picked up his tools, slung the bag over his shoulder and started making his way towards the procession, one hand raised in greeting.

"What ho, friends!" he hailed the two, rough looking men seated on the first cart. The cut of their homemade, layered clothing suggested to Blunt that they were artisans or farmers, and the stubble on their chins that they had traveled for a couple of days or more. The semblance of beard about his own chin suggested a similar tale to the carters. They regarded him suspiciously for a moment before exchanging a glance.

"He a friend of yours?"

"Nope. Yours?"

"Never seen him before in me life."

The first man glanced back over his left shoulder and called to the other carters:

"Anyone recognize this geezer?"

"No!" they chorused.

By this time several of them, including the second man in the lead cart, had produced between them an assortment of brutal looking potential weapons ranging from billhooks to meat cleavers. Blunt decided he did not like the way this encounter was developing and paused, some twenty yards from the nearest vehicle.

"Gentlemen, I mean you no harm." He assured them with empty hands raised to shoulder height and stretched apart, in the hope that this more or less universally accepted gesture would signify he did not pose a threat.

"I am an itinerant blacksmith, en route to…the North…in search of paid work. Is there a village ahead where I might purchase a fast horse, do you know?"

The driver of the first cart halted his vehicle with a sharp flick of the reins and spat over the side in to the long grass before answering:

"There is a village not too far ahead, and you might purchase…a horse…there, for the right price."

Blunt relaxed, visibly; it appeared they were not about to butcher him, after all.

"And would this potential purchase be a swift and sturdy steed, do you suppose?" he enquired, recalling the indolent nag the proprietor of The Ailing Parrot had sold him.

"Depends how you would define swift and sturdy?" came the

cryptic reply.

Blunt nodded, and offered the following by way of explanation:

"I had intended to meet up with an old friend several days hence. He has his own business to attend to and if I am unable to make the rendezvous, he will be unable to wait and we shall not see each other for at least another twelve changes of the moon. In consequence, I am in need of a powerful animal, possessed of both speed and stamina."

The driver, a short, stocky man with thick, black hair, a broken nose and pockmarked cheeks, broke in to a broad grin for the first time in their encounter.

"I myself own such a creature, but horses are valuable commodities, and this particular horse is like no other you will find in these parts, nor any other part for that matter. My wife would never forgive me if I failed to obtain sufficient compensation for its loss."

"And you wouldn't want to upset *his* wife, believe me." One of the other drivers assured him, laughing.

"Ignore him, he's just jealous." Said the first driver, still grinning.

"I'm sure the two of you will get on famously…provided your fine boat on the shingle over there is included in the exchange, of course. I have need of such a 'swift and sturdy vessel' on occasion." He added, mischievously.

Blunt looked doubtful. If he agreed to the proposed deal he could wave goodbye to the hefty deposit he had left with the grizzled boatman. If he declined the deal, he was never likely to catch up with Gorm.

"Come on," the driver encouraged him, "hop on the back of the cart and I can promise you a belly full of good food and ale and a comfortable place to sleep. Seems the least I can do if you are determined to purchase my fine, but very expensive horse and head for the Forest of Improbable Fate at dawn. I can sell you the warmer clothes you're going to need, too; it gets pretty damned chilly in the Darklands and cold as the grave beyond them."

Blunt stared at the man in astonishment.

"Who said anything about the Forest of Improbable Fate?"

"You didn't have to. Any fool in these parts knows the only man

North of here who might have use for a skilled blacksmith would be Malroth the Malevolent. There is nothing North of his secret camp in the forests of the Darklands but a range of impassable mountains, beyond which lies a frozen, empty waste of snow and ice."

"Hmph, can't be much of a 'secret' camp if everyone knows about it." Blunt reasoned.

"And if the mountains are impassable, how do you know what's beyond them?"

The driver chose to ignore the obvious flaw in his description of the mountain range and concentrate on countering the blacksmith's ridiculing of the 'secret' encampment.

"We all know of the camp, but none of us speaks of it abroad. We're none of us too fond of the prospect of our internal organs being converted to the external variety. You'd be wise to take heed, blacksmith."

"Thanks for the advice. I shall, indeed." Replied Blunt, scrambling on to the back of the cart and settling himself in amongst the dozen squealing piglets he had just disturbed. The driver turned his head to look back at his newly acquired passenger as he made himself as comfortable as was possible amongst the heavily soiled clods of straw.

"One more thing..."

"Now why does that not surprise me?"

"When we get to my house, leave your sword and any other weapons you may be carrying at the door. My wife will not tolerate weapons beyond the threshold, and neither will I."

Blunt glanced down at the lethal blade at his hip and ran a hand along its scabbard-encased length as though he was stroking a woman's thigh.

"I forged this myself and it cannot easily be replaced."

The driver smiled, grimly.

"Have no fear, blacksmith. We chop off the hands of thieves in our village; it will be safe enough."

His tone left Blunt in no doubt that the statement was as much warning as reassurance. The statement itself refreshed the memory of his recent, watery encounter with the handless corpse. Clearly, the implied threat was not an idle one.

CHAPTER 11

Gorm pressed his back against the wall of the pit, sucked in as much of the rapidly diminishing oxygen as his lungs could accomodate and launched himself towards the pyre, the base of which was now blazing fiercely. Beyond the makeshift pyramid the Demonettes could be heard coughing and spluttering in foul fashion, still blissfully unaware of the grisly demise of their leader, who had been caught between a rock and a hard place. The young warrior who had put him there, concerned the diminutive demons would soon be forced to abandon their position, took a prodigious leap, cleared the partially obscured (by a large rock, mostly) figure of Bahber and literally raced up the burning structure, great, hot portions of which he could feel collapsing beneath his feet as he ran. Fired on by the flames already singeing the only recently acquired hairs on his legs, the young Delirian launched himself at the opposite wall of the pit and clung on for his life as the flaming pyre imploded, carpeting the floor of the pit in a thick layer of scalding ash and burning embers several feet deep. The roar of the implosion was deafening, but still not loud enough to drown out the horrible screams of the barbecued Demonettes.
"Well, that's one burning ambition fulfilled." Gorm muttered grimly, as he commenced the limb straining climb to the mouth of the pit. By the time he reached the surface night had fallen (a habit it was finding difficult to break) and, cooling quickly after his exertions, he crawled carefully around the undulating surface of the rock until he located his sword, bow, quiver and bag. Pulling out and donning his fleece-lined jerkin, he buckled on his sword, slung the arrows over his left shoulder, hunting bow over his right and quickly searched out a safe route down to the ground.

From the base of the rock Gorm could see a fiery glow from the opening at its summit, accompanied by a pillar of dense smoke and the unmistakeable stench of overcooked Demonettes and barbecued Bahber. Satisfied he would have no further trouble from his erstwhile captors, he glanced up at the night sky in search of the Pole Star. He located it swiftly and set off in the direction he hoped the marauders were still traveling, whistling softly (if not exactly tunefully) as he went. By dawn he was confident he had covered several miles, but he had also almost exhausted the last of the dried meat from his bag and water from his leather flagons and knew he would have to replenish his supplies soon or die here on the sandy, rock strewn plain of Haemorrhoyde; it was a sobering thought.

CHAPTER 12

Broos handed the reins to his tall and alarmingly thin cousin and co-driver Relf and climbed down from the cart.

"Follow me, Blacksmith. That bulging belly of yours is in for a treat."

Blunt lifted a piglet from his lap and eased himself down from the cart to the track, shouldered his bag once more and, with a nod to the other drivers, set off in pursuit of his host.

"Mind you take off your boots before you enter his home." Relf called after him.

"Lon is very house-proud…and she can swing an iron skillet like a battle axe!"

The big Lumbeygan fell in to step beside Broos and adjusted his stride accordingly.

"Lon is your house wife, I take it."

"Did you work that out all by yourself?"

Blunt was stung by the other man's sarcastic tone, but refused to rise to it for fear of jeopardising the offer of hot food, a bed for the night and a reliable horse for the morrow. Instead, he employed his lifelong defence of retaliatory humour.

"A simple process of deduction, my friend. Your name is not Lon, from the grime on your clothes you do not strike me as the type to be overly house-proud, and I doubt you spend much time practicing with a skillet."

Broos continued to maintain an even pace, but turned his head to glare at the blacksmith.

"Are you taking the piss, fatso?"

"Absolutely, short arse. Weren't you?"

Broos stopped in his tracks and stared up at the blacksmith in silence. Blunt paused too, wondering if he had underestimated the sting of his retort. Apparently not, for the driver suddenly broke in to a broad grin and extended his right hand. Blunt reciprocated in kind.

"Perhaps we're going to get along after all, blacksmith. I like a man who can take a jest and give as good as he gets, even if he is fat as a pig and twice as ugly."

"The name's Blunt."

"Ever thought of changing it to Sharp?"

Imppetigoh proved to be a much larger settlement than the blacksmith had been expecting. As the two men, still on foot, and the little caravan of rumbling carts reached the summit of a knoll, the village lay spread out before the carters and their erstwhile passenger, apparently secure behind its trio of stout defences. An outer earthwork some eight feet high and three feet wide sloped gently to an uneven, rubble strewn floor approximately fifteen paces from the inner earthwork, which was roughly half as tall and wide again as the first and fell almost vertically on its far side to a deep ditch of boggy looking ground. Like the killing ground between the first and second ramparts the ditch appeared to Blunt to be approximately fifteen paces in width. The opposing third earthwork rose some ten feet to a wooden palisade of stout stakes, each of which protruded a further six feet from the top of the mound and was sharpened to a point. This final defensive structure featured a walkway five feet below the tips of the stakes and ran around the palisade's entire inner circumference, completely encircling the settlement of assorted dwellings within.

By the time the little caravan had negotiated the narrow, staggered entrances through the heavy wooden gates, watched over by numerous, armed and fearsome looking guards, Blunt was beginning to worry he might have underestimated the savagery of the inhabitants of the forests of the Darklands these ramparts were intended to repulse. There was no time for him to reflect further however, for they had reached the long, low hut Broos called home. The dwelling was flat roofed with stout planks carpeted with a thick layer of moist, mossy peat to protect the dwelling from fire arrows. The two men were joking and laughing like old friends as they strode towards the building, but as they approached the front door the driver's mood changed and he became serious and defensive, indicating three pairs of what appeared to be children's boots standing beside the heavy frame of the equally heavy door with an inclination of his head.

"Relf wasn't kidding about the boots. She hates muddy footprints…and she doesn't approve of cursing or farting. Make sure you take off your hat, too…and don't spit, flick snot or winkle wax from your ears."

"Perhaps I should just stroll in naked." Blunt suggested.

For just a moment Broos looked truly horrified until he recognized the jest for what it was and laughed, his relief as much in evidence as his amusement. Blunt smiled as he divested himself of sword and dagger, laying the former on the earth beside the frame of the door and the latter leaning against the sturdy wooden wall. Broos clapped him on the shoulder with a companionable hand.

"One day, when I'm really, really drunk, I might just hide the skillet and kitchen knife and try that. Anyhow, come on in and I'll introduce you to the dragon...sorry, my wife."

The lengthy interior of the hut was warm, comfortable, and probably the most spotlessly clean abode Blunt had encountered in his entire life. The wooden floor was hidden almost in its entirety by heavy, woven rugs, the walls were draped with soft tapestries embroidered with intricate, abstract designs and the entire room lit subtly by obscured candles, placed strategically around the walls behind beaten copper reflectors, bathing everything in the property in a warm glow. A mezzanine at the far end of the room supported two wooden cots and a great, carved bed of dark wood, the like of which the much traveled blacksmith had never seen.

"Lon, I have brought a guest. Blunt the blacksmith, meet my wife, Lonellh."

Blunt dropped his gaze from the mezzanine and was staggered to be confronted by the very opposite of the buxom, opinionated Harpie he had been led to expect. Lon was short, petite and very pretty. Her strikingly blonde hair was plaited into a single pigtail draped across her left shoulder and falling to just below her small, but firm looking breasts. Her eyes were the blue of the sky at dusk and her thin, pink lips, which should have made her look shrewish, somehow managed to convey the impression of a naiad. She stood before him with her hands resting on her slim hips, thumbs splayed, and her head cocked slightly to one side, as though she was trying to decide whether or not she was going to like him. After such a long time without a woman, or any female company, he was certain he was going to like her, but thought it prudent not to stare for too long and glanced at Broos, as if waiting for further instructions.

"A blacksmith, eh? Well, if you wish to reward our hospitality before you leave us, I have a large skillet in need of repair."

She spoke matter-of-factly, but there was no denying the undertone of playful humour in her statement. Blunt decided there and then that he did like her, but was somewhat perturbed to feel himself becoming aroused by her earthy tone. Shifting his position slightly, he eased the hat he was still holding in his right hand around until certain it was covering the expanding bulge in his groin.

"I'm sure I can beat out the bonce-shaped dents, if nothing else, mistress. In the meantime, perhaps you can find me a temporary home for my tool bags; their contents weigh a tonne?"

Lon nodded and turned on her heel.

"I'll make a bed up for you beneath the hanging floor. You'll have to share it with the dogs, but they'll help keep you warm. They fart a lot, but I dare say you do, too. I brush them regularly to rid them of fleas, but its a losing battle, despite the cold. You can put your bags in the corner behind the guest palette."

She pointed to a straw filled wooden frame in the far left corner of the room as she walked towards it.

"Do you snore?"

"I sleep alone, most of the time, so I'm afraid I don't know. I tend not to when I'm awake, if that's any help."

Lon looked back at him, sharply.

"If you do, I'll peg your nose and bung your mouth. I'll not have you waking the children."

Blunt shrugged his big shoulders.

"Fair enough. How many do you have?"

"Two." She replied.

"Karelh and Nayah. They're five and seven summers before you ask, and right now they are asleep up there in their cots, so you had best not make any noise that might disturb them. They have a long day in the fields tomorrow. Here, set your bags down and I will fetch you a bowl of warm water."

"I prefer cool mead, if you have any." The blacksmith advised her.

"To wash in. You stink of pig."

And with that she turned away and headed for the cooking area, where an iron spit was suspended over a fire in a stone hearth on the far wall, below a small opening in the roof for the smoke and steam. The hole was lined with a tube of hollowed out bark, darkened and hardened by years of use. Blunt watched her in fascination. He was beginning to see how her reputation had originated. For all her undisputed feminine charms, Lon was clearly not a woman to be trifled with.

Later, after an excellent meal of roast pork and thick, freshly baked bread dunked in a broth of root vegetables, Blunt, Lon and Broos sat around the hearth on cushions filled with goose down and talked of the blacksmith's proposed journey to the Forest of Improbable Fate.

"He has need of a horse…a swift and sturdy steed, to quote his precise words. We have agreed a price. Also, he will need some warmer clothing." Broos suggested, hoping to distract his wife's attention from *his* provisional sale of *her* horse. Some hope.

"Agreed a price…on my horse?" Lon hissed, outraged by her husband's presumption. Blunt observed this exchange with some alarm and cast his gaze around in search of the skillet.

"To keep a mere rendezvous with an old acquaintance? Give me strength!"

Broos looked sheepish as he struggled to think of a suitable response, but Blunt saved him the bother.

"I think I had best be honest with you both. I made up that tale about a rendezvous earlier, because I did not know who I was dealing with and was anxious not to give anything away to a potential foe."

This announcement clearly kindled his hosts' interest and they paused in their bickering and stared at him intently, awaiting further revelations. The big man took a swig from his wooden goblet before continuing. He had their undivided attention, now.

"Although a Lumbeygan by birth, I have lived most of my adult life in the fair valley of Grath, far to the South in the land of Deliria. I was the blacksmith and weapon maker at the pleasant little village of Nurk. Several weeks since, a band of marauders fell upon us, burned the village and slaughtered the inhabitants. There were just two survivors of the butchery, a young lad of sixteen summers, only son of the village chieftain, and yours truly. After he had buried the dead, young Gorm swore an oath to avenge his family and friends and set off alone in pursuit of the marauders. He faces almost certain death, unless I can catch up with him before he enters the Darklands and catches up with them. Hence my need of a steed possessed of both speed and stamina."

Lon was the first to speak.

"You said you had lived many years in Nurk, so you must have known everyone who lived there. When Malroth and his men sacked the settlement and murdered the villagers, only you and the boy survived the horrors of the raid, yet you did not offer to accompany him when he set off in pursuit of the marauders?"

Blunt flushed puce at the directness of her question.

"I am not proud of my decision at the time, but guilt subsequently got the better of me and here I am, desperate to make amends for my negligence before it is too late."

A terrible coldness crept in to Broos' tone as he addressed the blacksmith, and there was an accompanying icyness to his stare that sent a shiver down the big Lumbeygan's spine.

"Negligence? You call playing dead when your friends are being butchered all around you negligence? Cowardice, more like. Shame on you, Blunt! You let a mere boy venture alone on a quest that spells certain death for him?"

Even as Blunt rose to his own defence, exclaiming:

"Gorm is no child! He has the weight and stature of a grown man, and I have seen none finer with bow or sword in all my years", Lon was calming her rising husband with a hand pressed firmly against his chest.

"Hush, Broos; it takes a big man, a courageous man, to admit to his fear and overcome it. Our guest seeks to make amends before it is too late, so he needs to sleep, now. He has an early start and a hard ride on the morrow…and a noble task to fulfill."

Blunt stared at her in surprise.

"Lon, we have yet to agree with you the price Broos and I discussed earlier for your horse."

Lon glanced towards the mezzanine for a moment before matching the blacksmith's cautious gaze.

"I have a young son, Blunt, remember? Your young friend has no mother or father now…just you. The horse is yours. If you are successful in your quest and return here I will accept him back from you, but I will take no payment for him.."

"What!" exclaimed Broos, who had mentally already spent the money the sale of the horse would have raised.

"And if I'm not?" enquired Blunt, ignoring his host's outburst in the certainty that it was the wife who ruled the roost in this particular coop.

Lon considered the question carefully.

"Malroth will not be an easy man to kill. He is a monster, cruel, powerful, violent, and without a shred of mercy or compassion to his spirit. If you do not return, we shall pray your souls enter Gonoreya swiftly and with honour."

CHAPTER 13

"Huhh munnies thut muk?"
Norvul screwed up his face fearfully as he struggled to decipher the essence of Malroth's query. Elbows tucked in to his sides, hands upturned, Malroth mimed a gesture of encouragement with a repeated up and down motion of his forearms.
"C'mn mun, c'mn, huh munnie?"
A hand shot up from behind Norvul's right shoulder and a surprisingly high-pitched voice squeaked:
"Six!"
"Sux! Gud."
The swollen faced Malroth glared at his second in command.
"Sih, wuss sumple. Efun thut twut buhund yuh knu thuh unswur."
Norvul made a mental note to kill Moik, his own second in command, at the earliest opportunity…unless the creepily sadistic twerp proved able to provide him with a comprehensive list of interpretations of Malroth's most common pronunciations, in which case he would kill the irritating little weasel only after he had taken possession of the list. He turned to whisper a suitably worded suggestion to Moik to keep his mouth shut until spoken to, and noticed an irregular movement behind the shorter man's right shoulder.
Norvul loved killing, preferably armed men against whom he could display his undeniable speed and skill with a variety of weapons, thus enhancing his reputation as a formidable warrior. Malroth, in complete contrast, employed sheer brute strength and almost demented ferocity in a fight, but preferred to kill unarmed individuals, slowly. His victims could be of any age or sex, but the variety of creepily inventive tortures at which he excelled invariably produced the same end result. On this particular day however, his own, personal torture had forced him to resort to a more prosaic form of execution of his prisoners. He had insisted that Norvul have them lashed inverted and spreadeagled to a wooden frame before having the soles of their feet tickled with feathers, so that they were still laughing hysterically as their living entrails were torn out and their throats severed with a blunt blade.
 Norvul stared at the row of bloody, upside down bodies behind his

second in command and realised that one of them was still twitching involuntarily, despite the gaping wounds in his abdomen, chest and throat, the pooling gore and heaped intestines on the ground below him, and the feather still wedged between two of the toes on his right foot. Glancing at the other inverted flesh and wood obscenities, it struck him suddenly, like a thunderbolt. Six! There were six of them.

He swiveled his feet neatly in the dust to realign himself and caught Malroth's own gaze as his leader's eyes reopened after yet another violent spasm in his bulging jaw.

"We're going to need another raid soon, Lord. Those *six* pathetic excuses for men were the last of the expendable prisoners."

The smugness in his tone at his sudden grasp of the situation was so intense it was practically visible to the naked eye as an entity in its own right. Malroth recognized it immediately and squashed it flat.

"Rudd! Luk thus? Wunnker!"

Rising from the rickety, lop-sided wooden stool a since deceased minion had dropped on its side as he attempted to set it down beneath his leader's descending posterior, Malroth stormed off in the direction of his yurt, and even from a distance could be heard to mutter:

"Yuh jus cn't gut the fukkn stuff, this duys."

CHAPTER 14

Blunt swung the heavy, leather saddlebags Lon had laden with victuals for his journey over the horse's broad back, but the great beast barely twitched a muscle. White as the thigh of a temple maiden, it was the most beautiful horse Blunt had ever seen, and quite unlike any of the sturdy ponies or farm nags he had ridden over the years. Bred exclusively for transporting a lightly clad and armed warrior in to battle at breakneck speed, the animal was huge by Delirian and Lumbeygan standards, at least seventeen hands high, and the blacksmith suspected its ancestry was of pure Anthraksian stock. The horse turned its head slightly and regarded the big man with an intelligent gaze, as the blacksmith bade his farewells to Broos and Lon.

Blunt was careful not to catch the woman's eye directly, nor the man's for that matter, for he did not trust himself not to give anything away. Lon had come to his bed in the night, seeking (so she had informed the startled blacksmith) to calm his nerves with the reassurance that it might be the last chance he ever had to lay with a woman. Reassuring the suggestion had most definitely not been, but she had proved an enthusiastic and surprisingly inventive lover, and if it should subsequently prove to be his last such encounter, then at least it had been a prolonged and most pleasurable one. As she had lain naked beside him his exploring fingertips had traced the relief map of stretch marks across her belly, reminding him of other nights, other women, tiny verdant islands in a vast ocean of loneliness, and he had wondered if he would ever find true love and contentment. Given the task he had set himself for the morrow, that possibility had seemed more unlikely than ever.

As Blunt heaved his considerable bulk awkwardly in to the saddle and Broos bent in to tighten the strap behind the top of the beast's forelegs, his host whispered:

"Terrific shag, isn't she?"

"Eh?"

Blunt practically tumbled out of the saddle again and had to grip the horse's mane fiercely for support. The horse snorted indignantly and shook its head in disapproval of this uncouth

treatment. Broos glanced up at the blacksmith and patted his thigh in an effort to reassure him.
"It's okay, my friend, I know all about last night. Lon and I decided it was the right thing to do, seeing as you are determined to ride to your doom."
Not knowing quite how to respond, Blunt shrugged his big shoulders as he blushed his confusion.
"Er, I'd prefer to think of it as my fate, if you don't mind. Doom smacks of something more unpleasantly terminal. Anyway, I suppose it's better to do the right thing late, rather than never to do it at all."
Broos nodded his head at the wisdom of this statement.
"Very true…and if I gave you a bit of a hard time over it last night, then I apologise. It's easy to be wise long after an event, especially for someone who was not there to witness the event in the first place. Your young friend is obviously headstrong and not willing to listen to reason."
Blunt accepted his new friend's proffered hand and shook it warmly.
"There is no need for an apology, Broos. You spoke the truth as you saw it, and I daresay there are a great many more who would view the situation just as you did."
Broos smiled up at the blacksmith, towering above him astride his magnificent mount.
"Then let's just say we have both learned a valuable lesson about ourselves and leave it at that, eh?"
"Agreed."
The horse whinnined and shook its head. Blunt could feel its powerful muscles flexing beneath the insides of his thighs; it was eager to be off.
"Grun be with you and your young Delirian friend, Blunt." Lon called to him, and blew him a kiss that caused the blacksmith to blush even more furiously. He glanced up at the light intensifying irresistibly above the trees, as the last vestiges of night slipped away in search of other lands to darken.
"The dawn arrives apace and I must be on my way. Farewell, my newfound friends. I shall miss your company and the warmth of your hospitality." he informed them truthfully, but omitted to

mention that he would miss the warmth between Lon's thighs even more. From this moment on, he suspected, his life was likely to become a lot less comfortable and, perhaps, all too short.

Lon waved briefly and wondered if she would ever see horse or rider again. For a big man Blunt had proved surprisingly energetic in the hay (literally), and she knew she would always remember him with great fondness.

"And treat my beautiful horse with respect. He is not easily mastered by strang…"

Before Lon could complete the sentence Blunt had dug his heels in to the animal's great flanks and, with a speed that would have astonished the most accomplished of horsemen (in whose august company the blacksmith was never likely to figure), the horse bolted across the clearing, through the open gaps in the earthworks surrounding the settlement and headed for a nearby stream at terrifying speed. Blunt, hanging on to the reins for dear life, screamed:

"Whoooooaaaahh! Stooooppp!"

The horse took these instructions literally, skidding to such an abrupt halt that the occupant of its saddle, his feet still flapping uselessly the wrong side of the stirrups, was catapulted at an astonishing velocity in to the water, creating a shockwave that traveled some considerable distance downstream, like a miniature tidal bore in reverse. Released of its considerable burden, the horse celebrated its newly acquired freedom by rearing on its hind legs, whinnying loudly and thrashing the air with its raised hoofs, before hurdling the stream and galloping across the meadow towards the distant horizon.

CHAPTER 15

As the sun climbed higher in the sky (that being the custom in the plain of Haemorrhoyde) the young Delirian sought shade beneath the shelter of a large boulder, moving frequently to remain within its shade as the solar orb circled him like a remorseless hunter. When the sun finally tired of the deadly game and dipped below the western horizon, dragging the intense heat of the day in its wake, Gorm crawled out from beneath the life-preserving overhang and pulled himself stiffly to his feet. He stared up at the star filled heavens in awe; they looked so close he felt moved to reach up with a fingertip, half expecting to touch them or see the firmament ripple beneath his probing digit. The lack of celestial response brought him back to earth with the metaphorical jolt of sudden insight in to his current predicament.

"Is this it, Great Grun? Am I to survive being devoured by demons, only to die thus, alone, of hunger and thirst in this barren wilderness?"

The lad was startled by a loud snort close at hand and spun around, reaching instinctively for his sword, for he knew the night brought prowling predators from their lair's in search of easy prey. To his undisguised astonishment, not ten paces away stood the biggest and most beautiful horse he had ever seen, saddled, provisioned bags athwart its broad and muscular back, and clearly ready to ride for one bold enough to take up the challenge. White as the deep, virgin snow that fell in the valley of Grath come winter, the animal regarded him with large, intelligent eyes. In reciprocation the youth studied the horse intently; it bore no tribal ownership brand that he could see, and little resemblance to the short legged, sturdy ponies to which he was accustomed. This was a thoroughbred animal, elegant, graceful, built for speed rather than toil on the land…a gift from the Gods, perhaps.

"Well, my fine friend, after my recent experience, you are certainly not what I expected to see, but a welcome vision nonetheless. I am Gorm of Grath. Step forward and introduce yourself…unless you be another demon?"

The horse whinnied gently, tossed its head a couple of times and walked slowly towards him, lowering its muzzle in to his outstretched, right palm.

Gorm rubbed beneath its chin for a moment, then lifted his hand and stroked the front of the animal's head from ears to nostrils, feeling the heat of its breath on his palm.

"No demon…and no name, huh? Then I had best give you one, if we are to spend some time together."

He walked slowly around the great animal, running a hand along the ridge of its back and patting its flanks as he studied its form. Everything about the creature from its muzzle to its magnificent tail was as perfect as he was ever likely to see in such a creature.

"Truly, I have never seen a horse such as you, my friend. Elegant, graceful, powerful and bred for thrilling speed…I think I shall name you…Concorde, though I have not the slightest idea why. The name just came to me and it seems to fit. Do you agree?"

The horse whinnied again and nodded its head, scraping at the ground with a hoof as it did so, as if anxious to be on the move.

"Keen to go, eh? Me too." Said Gorm.

"I have an appointment with Destiny and don't wish to be late. I think maybe you can help me keep it."

He patted the horse again to calm it for a moment longer before leading the animal gently to a nearby rock. To his surprise it made not the slightest effort to resist him. It was as though they had travelled together many times before and had become accustomed to one another.

"Stand steady now, Concorde. I am going to stand on this rock and climb on to your back. It will put less of a strain on you than if I just pull myself up."

As Gorm clambered on to the rock, he leaned forward and whispered in Concorde's ear:

"I think it only fair to warn you that I am following some very bad men who will not take kindly to our arrival."

The horse's ear twitched once, but other than that the youth could detect no reaction to the information at all.

"So, there will undoubtedly be dangers ahead for both of us, but with your help I shall catch those evil men and avenge my family and friends."

The horse stood perfectly still, but turned its head to look at him as he clambered on to the rock and eased one leg over its broad back. Gorm had ridden ponies before with his father, but seemed to be seated twice as high now as he had been then. The horse snorted and steadied itself briefly, adjusting to his weight, and he could feel great muscles twitch beneath his legs as it prepared itself to move.

"Ready?" he enquired, filled with an inexplicable sense of delicious anticipation. The horse nodded and scraped the ground with a hoof again, as if raring to go.

"Come on then, Concorde, let's fly!"

CHAPTER 16

Malroth the Malevolent was not a happy man, even at the best of times, and although a successful raid on a rich settlement could certainly be counted amongst the best, chronic toothache, accompanied by a suppurating abscess of mountainous proportions, could not.

"Lurd! Uh nid Lurd!" he snarled, glaring at the swarthy, long-haired, garlic-breathed warrior who had been attempting to wrench the offending tooth from his mouth with a length of gut. Smiling an inane, lopsided smile by way of apology, Norvul, his psychopathic second-in-command, loosed his grip on the other end of the gut and turned to the men watching inquisitively from a safe distance.

"Fetch Lard!" he snapped at them, the livid scar across his right cheek twitching uncontrollably. Almost falling over themselves in their eagerness to obey the command, three of the newest, youngest recruits to Malroth's ever-growing band of ruthless, but predominantly dim-witted marauders scurried off in search of Lard. They found him, snoring loudly, beside an empty flagon in which a colony of fire ants was now taking a more than passing interest.

"Lard!" yelled Ranuk, the boldest of the youths, kicking the sleeper in his substantial gut. Lard smiled lasciviously in his sleep.

"Thassit, my beauty. Now, smear `em with honey and I'll lick it off."

Grinning wickedly as he watched the great, discoloured tongue slide over the blubbery lips, the messenger who had kicked him reached down to the bottle, scooped up a fistful of irritated ants and slipped them in to Lard's pants, then stepped back, quickly. The three young men did not have very long to wait.

"Aaaiiirrrgghhhhhaaaa! Me balls!" screamed Lard, struggling to his feet and tearing off his pants to scratch furiously at his reddening scrotum.

"You bastards," he snarled at his escort, who were doubled up with laughter.

"I'll skin you all alive for this!"

"Malroth wants you...now." said the first of the three to recover his composure. Lard turned his pants inside out and thrashed them on the ground several times, before pulling them back on.

"Bloody fools. Why couldn't you just say so?"

Still hot and swollen with rage, indignation and ant venom, Lard minced past the sniggering young men, the coarse seams of his leggings chaffing his already abused testicles and the insides of his thighs. The sight of him approaching very nearly caused Malroth to forget about his toothache, but it wasn't quite that funny.

"Uh've thuh duvul uvv uh tuth pun, Lurd. Yuh're thuh busturd wuth ull thuh bruns; wut muhst ah duh tuh reluv ut?"

"Have you tried thinking about something else? I always find that thinking about naked women with big ti..."

"Dun't nud tuh duh thut. Uh'v gut uh larve wun buk thur un thuh yurt."

"Oh. Well, how about chewing a couple of cloves; that usually hel...?"

"Dunn thut."

"Torturing a captive is always good for a laugh."

"Bin thur...und buhsuds, uh thunk wiv run ut'v thum."

"Hmmm, tricky one this, then. I take it you have tried to pull the bugger?"

"Duh uh luk thuck?"

Lard decided to sidestep that one, on the grounds that the truth might result in his being tied between two stretched saplings and afforded a split personality. He scratched his head for a moment, but brightened as a spark of genius illuminated the cavernous space between his ears, albeit briefly.

"Please, come with me, Great One; we're going to climb to the top of yon cliff. You three, fetch one hundred and fifty feet of strongest gut and the heaviest two-handed battleaxe you can find."

The three young men glanced at Malroth, apprehensively.

"Juss duh wut hih sus!" snapped their leader, who was now in so much pain he would have dived naked in to a bed of nettles if he thought it would help.

Twenty minutes later, Lard, Malroth and an extremely nervous Norvul (who had no head nor stomach for heights) stood at the edge of the cliff top, surrounded by all but the outlying members of the watch. One end of the length of gut was tied to the offending tooth and the other to the haft of a mighty, double bladed axe that Malroth was now cradling in his arms, like a baby. Aided liberally by several flagons of home brewed, psychosis inducing mead, the malevolent one had been psyching himself up for this for at least fifteen minutes and knew that it was now or never.

"Ulruht!" he announced to the gathered throng of bemused cutthroats who, bereft of an interpreter well versed in the language of oral agony, were quietly placing bets on what their leader was actually saying to them. The other popular bet was whether or not Lard's scheme would work and, if it did not, the likelihood of the fat fool's remaining attached to his limbs and extremities until nightfall, beyond which all bets were off.

"Stund buck, cus ah umm ging tuh duh thuss."

So saying, Malroth took a couple of very deep breaths, held the axe out at arm's length over the precipice…and released it.

CHAPTER 17

Blunt could see her lips moving, but could make no sense of the content of her animated speech, filtered as it was through lugholes full of freezing water. He slapped at each of his ears in turn with the flat of the relevant palm, evacuating the liquid by tilting his head first one way, then the other.

"What's that you say, Lon?"

The iron skillet struck him on the left side of the head with such force the reverberation travelled all the way back up the handle to her fingers, causing her to drop the improvised chastiser of men abruptly. The crunching sound as six pounds of roughly cast iron crushed several of the metatarsals of Blunt's booted left foot could be heard from the ramparts. It inspired Broos, who was standing nearby, to wince and employ what was quite possibly the understatement of the year:

"Ooohh, that's got to hurt."

Blunt's response was altogether more eloquent.

"Aaaarrrggghhhhhhh! Me fucking foot!" he screamed.

"That was my left foot! You've broken my poor left foot, woman! And my poor, flattened ear throbs like a Nymph's nipples."

"And you'd know all about them, I suppose?" was Lon's snarling retort.

"You got no more nor less than you deserved, Blacksmith. Have you any idea how much that horse cost me?"

Broos, who had absolutely no idea how much it had cost his wife either and had never dared to ask, looked at her with renewed interest. Sensing his eyes upon her, Lon lowered her tone significantly and became almost sheepish, confusing the blacksmith even more.

"It cost me more than any woman should ever have to pay for anything," She announced in a voice little above a whisper, "but from the moment I first saw the creature I knew I had to have it…and the horse's previous owner knew it too and took full advantage of my weakness, many times over."

She bit back a sob and stared at the ground in shame.
The blacksmith's anger subsided as understanding dawned.

Suddenly enraged on her behalf instead of his own, Blunt demanded to know:

"And what was the name of the foul and despicable wretch who took advantage of your desire to own the creature by bespoiling you?"

After a moment's hesitation (or it could have been three; I wasn't keeping count), she glanced awkwardly at her husband to see if he was still attempting to eavesdrop, before meeting the blacksmith's stare.

"Malroth." She whispered.

CHAPTER 18

Malroth sat on the stump of a severed tree outside his yurt, holding a cushion soaked in water from the lake to his throbbing jaw. The pain had been washing over him in waves since dawn, interspersed with tides of nausea. His current lay still lay on her belly in the yurt, while an older female camp follower applied soothing goose fat liberally to her tender bottom.

The tortured leader of men of a not very nice disposition glanced up at the sound of horses hooves and spied Norvul and three more riders approaching him slowly through the mist enveloping the camp. A wan light filtered through the nearby trees at the base of the cliff and divided in to spectral shafts as it pierced the topmost branches, throwing the mounted men in to eerie relief.

"Wul, uny sihn'f th' burstrd?"

"He wants to know if we found any sign of Lard." whispered Arak, the rider to his right, scarcely moving his lips.

Norvul shook his head, nervously.

"No, my lord."

Malroth was perplexed by this news, the excruciating pain he was experiencing once more clouding his faculties.

"Bud shurly th' mun I chrgd with strngng 'im up cun rumumbur whur they dud ut."

Turning in his saddle as though he was checking the trail behind them, Arak provided the puzzled Scroffulan with another whispered translation.

Norvul cleared his throat. He was anxious not to enrage his leader yet again, but could see no way to avoid reminding him of the uncomfortable truth.

"If you recall, my lord, when you demanded to see Lard again and I pointed out that the men you had ordered to take him away from the camp somewhere and string him up by the ankles for the buzzards to gorge themselves upon his fat, living carcase confirmed that they had obeyed your command, you flew in to a justifiable rage and had them both executed before I could quiz them as to just where they had carried out your order."

Malroth regarded him balefully.

"Suh yur sayin' iss mah fult?"

"No! No, far from it. If anything the fault is...is...somebody else's."

Norvul thought quickly, as if his life depended upon the result of his ruminations which, judging by Malroth's unconvinced expression, it most certainly did.

"Actually...no, it was *my* fault...for not thinking to interrogate them *before* you had them put to death."

Norvul and his companions arrived before the huge man on the stump and dismounted. Malroth dismissed the other two with an impatient wave of his hand, leaving his second-in-command feeling more exposed than ever.

" Of course" Norvul added dangerously, in his own defence, "I hadn't expected the sentence to be carried out quite so swiftly. And may I just add," he added, equally swiftly, "the speed of your reaction was most commendable and quite astonishing to behold. Those double-sided battleaxes are pretty damned heavy."

"Cud th' crup, Nrvl. Eithur yuh fund hm or ah'll huv yur hud un uh spuk befur durk."

Norvul regarded his terrifying leader with a mixture of fear and loathing in roughly equal measure. Deprived of his translator, he hadn't a clue what dreadful fate he had just been threatened with, but was under absolutely no illusion about its violent and permanent nature. Words like 'clemency', 'leniency' and 'painlessly' simply did not figure anywhere in Malroth's limited, but graphic vocabulary.

"Then we'll search again, Lord...but I will need to take more men if we're to find him; the forest is vast, as you well know. And I have already dispatched another party to locate Jennah the Witch, who is renowned for the efficacy of her medicinal potions, just in case we are unable to locate Lard, inconceivable as that seems given the big oaf's prodigious proportions."

"Jus duh ut!" snapped Malroth, easing himself up from the stump.

"Uh need Lurd!"

CHAPTER 19

Shrouded by a vast forest of towering trees that dissipated or absorbed natural light, reducing the ground beneath the whispering canopy to a state of perpetual gloom during the hours of daylight and an almost impenetrable obscurity by night, the Darklands presented a forbidding prospect to all but the most intrepid of travelers. From his position astride a magnificent white horse, just below the skyline of the low escarpment that rolled down to the first rank of trees stretching the entire length of his visible horizon, an intrepid traveler studied the shadowy interior minutely for signs of movement, but could spy nothing save for the occasional, almost imperceptible sway of topmost branches, as the light breeze blowing down off the higher ground sought to find a way through the natural barrier. Leaning forward, Gorm patted the horse's flank, reassuringly.

"This is no time for speed, my friend. We dare not fly like the wind if even the wind struggles to find a way through."

The animal nodded its great head several times, as if in agreement with this statement. After a moment's hesitation, the young Delirian threw his leg across Concorde's back and slid easily to the ground. The horse turned its head to regard him, quizzically.

"I'll present less of a target if I walk beside you." Gorm explained, and laughed at himself.

"Ha ha. I'm talking to a horse! Perhaps I'm losing my mind, but you give me that knowing look and it seems you understand what I'm saying or are aware of what I'm thinking. My father used to tell me a great warhorse can sense your intention in battle and act without the necessity of command at crucial moments, but I used to think he was crazy when he said such things. Now...well, I am not so sure."

The young Delirian was evidently not the sharpest blade in the scabbard, Concorde had long since decided, but he could not help liking the youth. Humouring him now, he scraped at the ground with a hoof as if impatient to be off once more.

"You're right yet again, my friend. This is no time to loiter in idle gossip."

Gorm patted the animal's flank one more time, slipped the bow from his shoulder, flipped the toggled lid from the tubular, leather arrow case on his back, took out an arrow and fitted the notched end behind the fledging to the string of the weapon. Holding the bow at its centre and with the poised arrow secured between the index and middle finger of his left hand, he gripped the reins with his right hand and led his mount down the escarpment towards the trees. As the pair crossed the last few yards of open space the light was already fading, but the young warrior decided to press on, anxious to continue narrowing the distance between himself and his quarry.

After the firm, packed earth of the open slope the forest floor came as something of a surprise to both youth and beast. A dense carpet of moss, into which Nature had haphazardly woven the interleaved fallen branches and twigs of Grun alone knew how many centuries, undulated underfoot like a living entity. Toadstools, delicious crouch mushrooms (so called on account of the fact that you had to crouch to find them, hidden amongst the fallen leaves) and other fungi sprouted in profusion amongst the decay, but other than these there was precious little sign of life, save for within the occasional natural glade, where an ancient tree may have uprooted and fallen, taking others with it. In these isolated enclaves that had inadvertently opened up a route through the canopy from whence light could enter, grass and wild flowers grew and pools of water had formed, like oases amidst the dark desert of otherwise unremitting gloom.

As young warrior and mighty steed picked their way cautiously amongst the trees, Gorm became increasingly aware that the silence of the forest was a lie, as minute, almost imperceptible sounds insinuated themselves in to the nervy fabric of his consciousness with viral stealth. After a time his neck began to ache from swivelling his head this way and that with a frequency that Concorde was beginning to find irritating. The youth was unable to decide if his imagination was playing tricks upon him, but as they advanced deeper in to the forest he felt sure they were being followed and four great, misshapen shadows appeared to be creeping silently through the trees, two to each side of them, just at the extremities of his vision.

After a time Gorm drew back the drawstring of his bow and held the arrow in readiness, making great play of the exercise to warn whatever was stalking them that he was armed and potentially lethal. Concorde whinnied and shook his head, sadly. Who did the youth think he was kidding? Given the amount of pull required to draw the bow, he was unlikely to be able to hold the pose for more than thirty seconds at most, despite his obvious strength. Within moments the same thought had occurred to Gorm, whose arms had begun to burn with the physical strain of maintaining his readiness to unleash the arrow. With a sigh he relaxed his arms, replaced the arrow in the case on his back, slung the bow over his left shoulder and drew his sword from its leather scabbard. Concorde uttered what sounded to the youth suspiciously like a laugh. He was about to take issue with the great beast when something cold, moist and fleshy grabbed his face.

Flailing his arms wildly, Gorm stifled a scream lest he give away their position. Concorde did likewise as he swerved to avoid being skewered by the young Delirian's sword. As his initial panic subsided, Gorm realised that what he had taken to be an enormous spider dangling from a branch on a thick strand of web was actually a large, human hand, suspended on a leather thong. He was about to heave a huge sigh of relief when yet another anomaly distracted his attention. In a glade just ahead of them and illumined by a beam of moonlight stood an unnaturally tall and undoubtedly feminine figure, clad entirely in black. Against the raven dark material of her dress and high necked cloak, over which a lengthy fall of velvety black hair cascaded, the white of her hands and face stood out like inversions of slivers of jet on a patch of undisturbed snow. She wore an intricately fashioned necklace of platinum about her neck from which a huge, lozenge shaped crystal hung down between her hidden breasts. When she spoke, her voice had a honeyed warmth in complete contrast to her intimidating appearance.

Gorm's massive young shoulders slackened in dismay.

"Aww, no…not again."

The vestiges of a smile twitched at the corners of the woman's mouth.

"Fear not, Gorm of Deliria, for Balustraad cannot harm you, now."

Still clutching his sword, the young warrior studied the woman intently. She was terrifyingly beautiful. And how come she too knew his name, he wondered? Everyone he met on this odyssey seemed to know of it, despite the fact that he was travelling through lands entirely unfamiliar to him? And who was this Balustraad the mysterious woman in black seemed to think might have meant him harm?
"Balustraad?"
"A great sorceror, once upon a time, but he aspired to higher things…darker things, powers best left to the entities the gods chose to invest them with. He attempted to climb beyond the heights to which humanity may aspire, but in so doing forfeited his life. It is his hand you encountered just now, dangling from yonder branch."
Turning slightly, so that he could still keep one eye on the woman while snatching a glance at the obscene thing tethered to the thong, he said, more out of bravado than any real conviction:
"It matters not to me. I did not know the man; it is just a thong at twilight. A dangle-hand. On the rare occasions when a man of our village was caught in the act of theft, he would forfeit a hand and it would be suspended thus as a warning to others…but you say theft was not his crime?"
"I do not recall saying so, but yes, a theft of sorts was at the heart of his…misdemeanour. Like so many before him he coveted the great sword, *Skullsplitter*."
"Gorm turned back to face the woman, intrigued now by her talk of a mystical weapon.
"Skullsplitter?"
"No, *Skullsplitter*. Never forget the italics and bold type."
"Ah."
The lad nodded to indicate that he understood the significance, though in fact he was merely humouring her. He knew as much about italics and bold type as he did about women's undergarments. In other words, bugger all.
"*Skullsplitter*…is that how you say it?"
"Yes, Gorm, a fabulous, magical sword of great power and inestimable value. Nobody knows its origin, not even I, although popular belief has it that it was forged by the Gods, but whatever

the truth of the matter the rumours of its existence have circulated ever since humans first discovered the Forest of Improbable Fate. Many adventurers have sought it, a handful have discovered and tried to possess it, but misfortune has befallen each of them."
"Misfortune?"
"Each time the sword is discovered anew, it is always embedded to the hilt in its previous victim, and he who discovers and seeks to possess it becomes the next. It is also said that the sword is protected by four fearsome guardians, which may also help to explain why no living man has yet succeeded in possessing it."
Gorm thought immediately of the four huge, dark shapes he was convinced he had seen stalking him through the forest.
 "And will anyone ever succeed in possessing this wondrous sword, do you think?"
"Each man who seeks to own it must retrieve it from its previous victim and hope to survive the encounter, but 'tis said the sword waits for he or she destined to become its one, true master or mistress."
Gorm considered this startling information.
"Then a man would have to be a fool to try."
"Or be the Chosen One, perhaps?"
The young Delirian considered this suggestion, too; it was an intriguing one, to be sure.
"And how would a bo...man know if he had been chosen…just out of curiosity, you understand?"
"Some believe it, some suspect it, but it is often the way with such enchantments that the least likely candidate proves ultimately to be ***the One***."
More italics and bold type; the lad shrugged his shoulders.
"Well, it is certainly an interesting tale…"
He cocked his head to one side and regarded the woman intently.
"…but I do not understand why are you telling ***me***? I am not yet quite a man, although when I have fulfilled my vow of…"
Gorm paused. He knew nothing of this woman and the tale she had been relating to him might be a complete fiction. He had been duped far too easily by Bahber and was not about to fall for such a ruse again.

"But who are you, anyway? I am learning swiftly that the people I meet are not always who they claim to be."
"I am the Thongstress."
Gorm's expression, as was so often the case, registered intense puzzlement.
"You are a singer of songs?"
The woman heaved a great sigh of frustration and traced a broad arc through the air from left to right with a hand as pale as milk, freezing youth and steed in an hypnotic trance. Satisfied she was not about to be interrupted with any more inane questions, she glanced up from the page at the author.
"Bard, I suspect this jest shall wear a trifle thin afore long."
"He said it, not me."
"Pah! Do not place the blame upon the boy; it ill becomes you."
"Okay, if pressed I might admit to a certain limited liability, but the ball is most definitely in your court. He asked *you* a question, after all."
"A rhetorical one. Still, I shall give you both the benefit of the doubt...on this occasion."
"Glad to hear it. I'm not supposed to get involved, you know; it's strictly against the rules."
The Thongstress traced a reverse arc with her other hand and Gorm and Concorde shook their heads simultaneously, as if surfacing from a shared dream.
"It is my given role to abide here within this glade and offer fair warning to all who approach…"
"Fair warning of what?" Gorm interrupted her.
 "That a search for **Skullsplitter** may result in their own, severed hand being suspended ignominiously from a branch. So beware, young Gorm, for many such thongs ring this and other glades throughout the Forest Of Improbable Fate."
The young Delirian swallowed, nervously.
"A sad task indeed, mistress. And do you recall all of their tales? Do you know the fate of the owners of each hand?"
"Oh yes, for we have branches throughout the forest," she said, through gritted teeth, "and they are all recorded in…the great thongbook."
'Was that absolutely necessary?' she muttered under her breath.

The author stifled a grin and admitted:
'Sorry, couldn't resist it.'
Gorm lowered the sword Blunt had fashioned for him and approached the Thongstress, leading Concorde gently by the reins.
"Then your work is done this day mistress, for my name shall never number in the thongbook. I hold here a thuperb…sorry, superb weapon, fashioned and honed for me by the finest armourer in Deliria. What need have I of yet another sword?"
Once again the ghost of a smile materialised momentarily about the woman's lips.
"Only you may answer that question, Gorm."
And with that the Thongstress dissolved in to the moonbeam with such startling rapidity Gorm was immediately left wondering if he had not somehow dreamed the whole incident. He glanced at Concorde.
"I didn't imagine what just happened…did I?"
The horse shook its head emphatically, its white mane tossing as though it was auditioning for an advertisement for an exotic shampoo in another age.
"No, I thought not. Well, mind that big head of yours when we reach the opposite side of the glade. I don't want either of us being spooked by dangling digits again."
Sheathing his sword and releasing the reins for a moment, Gorm refilled his water pouches from a nearby pool while his mount munched contentedly on the profusion of small flowers and lush grass that grew around its bank. Finally, sated, the pair resumed their trek in to the heart of the Darklands, thankfully ignorant of the encounter awaiting them deeper within the Forest of Improbable Fate.

CHAPTER 20

"Hmmm, could do with a little more paprika…and possibly a dash of saliva of purple spotted salamander, just to liven it up a touch?"

Jennah licked her lips, put the ladle to one side and drank an entire flagon of water, lest she felt compelled to molest the next man to cross her threshold. Dabbing her lips dry with a wad of cotton retrieved from one of her rolled up sleeves, she wandered off to the shelved wall of her hexagonal, thatched hut in search of the missing ingredients. Love potions were invariably a hit and miss affair and this latest one was no exception. Handsome, lovesick swains and besotted beauties were simple enough to satisfy, as they unwittingly did the bulk of the work themselves and the potion merely had to taste pleasantly medicinal to convince them of its potency. Clients challenged in the 'features perfectly acceptable in polite society' department were altogether more problematic however, and she had encountered few men more challenged than Grunk.

The travelling codpiece salesman (popular solely on account of his prodigiously padded wares) had something of the imagined appearance of a union betwixt a warthog and a sloth, his nostrils dribbled copiously at the first hint of Spring and his table manners would shame a hyena. Unfortunately, the subject of his unrequited longings was Mara, the sexy mead maid from the Queen's Legs tavern, whose obscenely muscled conquests were legendary and whose potential suitors numbered in the dozens of a Saturday night. Thus was a potion of truly prodigious power required on this occasion. Jennah hummed quietly to herself as her fingertips brushed across the surface of the stoppered jars and flagons ranged along the tiered shelves, as though they could read the labels.

"Ah, here we are."

She pulled two small, earthenware jars to her chest and hurried back to the large copper pot suspended above the glowing embers in the hollowed out granite furnace at the centre of the room, three quarters of which was surrounded by a low, wooden work bench. In the rafters above the furnace, dozens of sheaves of assorted herbs, together with a side of pork and several haunches of lamb, hung inverted, drying in the smoke as it made its way towards the hole in the apex. Removing the stopper from the jar of Paprika, Jennah was about to shake some of the contents in to the pot when she was startled by a loud crash from somewhere behind her. Spinning around, she was just in time to see several fierce-looking, heavily armed men of the enormous variety struggle in to her hut past the now only partially hinged door.

The leading man approached her, sword in hand, eyes swivelling nervously about the room, as though he expected to be attacked from some unexpected quarter at any moment. Apparently satisfied that any such assault was unlikely after all, he turned his attention to the woman, who was not at all what he had been expecting. Not yet many years more than twenty, halfway between five and six feet in height, well proportioned and full breasted, she was possessed of very pleasing features, with a firm chin, bow shaped lips, slightly flushed cheeks, a fine, straight nose, challenging, grey-green eyes, and a high forehead partially obscured by a somewhat wild, but not entirely unkempt mane of straw coloured hair that fell almost to her waist. Her expression as she regarded him intently spoke of a cool intelligence to which he was entirely unaccustomed, and went some way towards distracting him from her rather obvious allure.

Pleasantly surprised but not about to reveal it, the lead intruder, whose name was Ozzmun, pressed the tip of his sword in to the cleft between the woman's breasts, which were fully covered by a thick, dark blue woollen dress that descended almost to her leather-slippered feet, and was gathered in at her waist by a pale blue, tasselled cord. She wore a leather thong about her neck, suspended from which was a small, beautifully carved representation of a timber wolf.

"You the witch?" he demanded to know.

The woman displayed not the slightest indication that she was afraid of him, much to his annoyance. Nor did she appear unduly perturbed by the proximity of the tip of his sword to her heart.

"And which witch would that be?" she asked him.

"Eh?"

"Well, if you don't know which witch is which, how do you know which witch you want?"

The man shrugged his broad shoulders, somewhat perplexed by this entire business. Killing people was easy. You didn't have to ask stupid questions or fathom the riddles embedded in their answers. In battle you killed the other buggers before they killed you. On a raid you just killed anyone who got in your way, or chased the runners down and killed them just for fun. But these other tasks he was sometimes required to perform were just a pain in the arse.

"Dunno. Malroth just said: 'Fetch Jennah the Witch'. You Jennah?"

"Indeed I am Jennah the **Herbalist**, but who is this Malroth of whom you speak?"

The man and his companions raised their eyebrows in unrehearsed harmony.

"You've never heard of Malroth the Malevolent?"

"Would I have asked you who he is if I had?"

Jennah was all too familiar with Malroth's reputation, but was not about to do this ignorant, uncouth character any favours. The ignorant, uncouth Ozzmun had to admit to himself the woman had a valid point.

"He is the most feared brigand in the four kingdoms."

"His wrath is terrible. His word is law." The four men intoned. Clearly, unlike the business with the purely coincidental eyebrow extravaganza, this brief litany had been oft rehearsed.

"Truly? Then I had best accompany you four gentlemen post haste. Shall I be required to fetch any of my accoutrements hither…or thither?" she added, as an afterthought.

"You what?"

Jennah heaved a sigh of resignation.

"Do I need to bring anything with me?"

The intruder's blank expression spoke volumes (Volume One being: Empty Cranial Cavities).

"Alright, let's try another question. Why did this Malroth of whom you speak so reverentially summon me to his presence?"

Ozzmun's brow furrowed with the complexity of interpreting her response.

"Oh. He's got a real bastard of a toothache."

"And he said he's got an Abbess on his jaw." Piped up the third intruder.

Jennah hid a smile.

"Then I shall require oil of cloves, a pinch of cinnamon, a spoonful of frogspawn, the ground up legs of a dung beetle and a clutch of fresh nettles. You will find the latter growing in profusion just outside my humble abode, if one of you fine gentlemen would be so kind as to go and fetch some for me. You, perhaps?" she said, looking directly at the third man, who actually did bear an uncanny resemblance to the young Orson Welles.

"Sorry? What did you want me to do?"

"Fetch me a bunch of fresh nettles, my dear."

He nodded.

"Ah. Right."

"The other ingredients I shall fetch from my stock, over there on the shelves." Jennah informed the others, indicating the assorted vessels with a slight inclination of her head. Ozzmun glanced at the shelf in search of possible weapons, only to be disappointed. If he had been forced to kill the woman in self-defence, it would have made his onerous task a whole lot easier. Reluctantly, he lowered his sword, allowing her to move without becoming impaled upon it. As she made her way across the room the other occupants were jolted by a loud scream from somewhere just outside the hut.

"Owwwwww, fuckkkking Haletosysss!"

"Ah, your friend has discovered the nettles, I think."

As an afterthought, she enquired, addressing herself to Ozzmun:

"Young man, this thought has been occupying my mind for some minutes now and I must know the answer. Given the natural proclivities of your ilk, do you all intend to ravish me?"

Although Ozzmun had clearly not been expecting the question, he had to admit to himself that the opportunity had not gone unrecognised, but as the act had not been specified or sanctioned by Malroth he had deemed it wise to subdue his natural inclination in that direction.

"No. Why?"

"If you had, I should have liked to have made the bed and removed my undergarments aforehand. If the deed had been inevitable, I might as well have made myself comfortable and protected my clothing as best I could."

The intruder regarded her with new respect. She was a pragmatic sort and he liked that. Witch she might be, but she was still a woman, after all, and a damned attractive one to boot...and boot her comely arse he would if she didn't hurry up. As he observed the fluid motion of her hips as she busied herself amongst the ingredients lining her shelves, he decided that if Malroth had no more use for her than to cure his affliction, then he might press his suit (which he'd been saving for just such an occasion). At nearly twenty-five years of age he was not getting any younger and settling down with a capable house wife might not be such a bad idea. He determined to give the notion further consideration, if the opportunity presented itself.

"Not necessary, but you'd best bring a warm cloak. Malroth's camp is several days ride and we'll have to sleep under the stars."

"Ooohh, how romantic. How about a packed lunch?"

He gave her a sharp, sideways glance as he turned to leave.

"We will hunt deer or elk before entering the forest."

If she was jesting with him she certainly gave no indication of it. She was a tough one, of that there was no doubt, but she would break just as easily as all the rest. A few sound beatings and floggings, a few nights incarcerated in the scold's pit without food or water and she would become completely subservient. He smiled her a humourless smile.

"Romantic? Stranger things have happened. Perhaps it will prove to be so. Now make haste woman, for Malroth is not a man to be kept waiting."

Jennah maintained her expressionless composure, but read the story behind his eyes. She had read it many times before in men just like him; it was the way of the world in which she lived, but that did not mean she had to agree or conform to it. When the moment came he would perish, just like the others, and she would continue to wait for the man she believed existed for her, somewhere in the wide world; a quiet, capable man, slow to rouse, reluctant to fight, but a man of courage and honour, nonetheless. A man worthy of her love.

Once Ozzmun was seated comfortably astride his mount,

Ocks, the strongest of the other intruders, flung Jennah unceremoniously across the animal's (the horse's, not Ozzmun's) back, where her shapely, upturned rump was held in position by the pommel of the saddle, while her head and shoulders dangled across one heaving flank and her legs and feet across the other. The little party set off for the Forest of Improbable Fate just as soon as the others had saddled up, and Ozzmun amused himself by gripping the herbalist's buttocks hard whenever she began to slide head or feet first from her inverted position, and just as frequently when she did not. Devoid of other options for the present, Jennah bore this boorish behaviour with remarkable stoicism, biding her time until she could make good her escape and plot her revenge. Tough, battle-hardened and in complete control of the situation as he was, Ozzmun still found her occasional, surreptitious sniggering more than a little disturbing.

CHAPTER 21

Gorm paused and placed a cautionary palm against Concorde's flank, encouraging the animal to do likewise. A veil of thick cloud had been drawn across the scarcely visible night sky some time since, effectively obscuring the moon and reducing visibility within the forest to virtually nil. Nevertheless, something he could not see had alerted the lad to the presence of danger, some prickling sixth sense inherited from his ancestors (or it could have been the frequent snapping underfoot of nearby twigs). The horse turned its head to look at him now, equally aware of something amiss in their immediate vicinity, but uncertain as to what the youth's response to danger might be. Like every horse, Concorde's natural inclination at such times was to take flight, but he knew that to do so now, here in this cavern-like darkness amidst the millions of trees would be suicidal. Instead, he waited for his young companion to reach a decision. He did not have long to wait, for Gorm was already slotting the notched tip of an arrow to the string of his bow once more.

"We must tread stealthily now Concorde, for danger may manifest itself at any moment; its aura lingers on the air like a foul stench. Stay alert, my friend."

Together, Gorm and Concorde advanced, step by cautious step, every sense prickling until the young Delirian's right foot struck a solid, but yielding obstacle that rolled away from the impact before returning to its original position against his stationary footwear.

"Ye Gods!" hissed Gorm, stepping back in alarm.

"That was no aura. That was indeed a truly foul stench, and I suspect we have just located its source."

Backing up slightly and encouraging the horse to accompany him, Gorm stood perfectly still, bow at full stretch, listening intently for any indication that they were not alone. The acute silence remained undisturbed however and the lad finally laid his bow and arrow carefully at his feet before rummaging in his bag for the flints and a fistful of the straw he used to light his campfires. Crouching down he created a tiny pyramid of straw before feeling on the ground around him in the darkness for small, dry twigs that he then arranged around the miniature pyre.

Satisfied with the result, he knapped one flint against the other at the base of the construction, watching intently for the resulting sparks to catch in the straw. Kneeling forward and cupping his hands around the tiny pyre he blew in to it until little tongues of flame began to snatch at the twigs and the dry timber caught alight. As the burning construction began to collapse the youngster fed it with slightly larger twigs. Finally, certain the blaze could survive for several minutes without his assistance, he looked up and caught his breath.

Not more than a dozen paces from where Gorm was kneeling, the decaying corpse of an enormous, once muscular man lay spreadeagled across a large, low, almost egg-shaped rock. The empty eye sockets and opened chest cavity suggested scavengers had visited the body more than once, and the flickering of the flames imbued the rotting limbs with an eerie suggestion of twitching movement. Yet none of this appeared to bother the normally superstitious youth, seduced as he was by the great, gleaming sword rising bloodily from between the ribs. The polished pommel, gleaming ivory hilt with its embedded precious stones, grip and cross-guard were clearly visible, as were several inches of the burnished, double-edged, steel blade on which one end of an elaborate inscription could be discerned. All of which suggested to the astonished Gorm that not only had the rest of the blade penetrated the man's chest, but that a considerable portion of it must now be embedded in the rock beneath him.

"*Skullsplitter*!"

Gorm's excitement at their discovery of the legendary sword was obvious, but Concorde remained unimpressed. The horse was more concerned with the disturbing stench of rotting flesh in his nostrils and the uneasy feeling that, despite the deceased state of the partially devoured human pinned to the rock, he and his enthusiastic young companion were no longer alone in this particularly spooky spot.

CHAPTER 22

"Gee up! Gee up, you feckless nag!"

Blunt twitched the reins irritably and flicked at the pony's ambling rump with his hazel switch, but to no avail. The surly brute paid little heed to the blacksmith's exhortations and was, presumably, accustomed to this sort of treatment as an occupational hazard. As a result, it paused to graze whenever the inclination took it, which appeared to its inexperienced driver to be every fifty yards or so. Blunt slumped back on to the driver's seat of the little cart in defeat. Had this been a contemporary tale, he mused, he would simply have pulled out his cell phone and summoned assistance (or a taxi), but sword and sorcery yarns of a fantastical nature are the very antithesis of such things. Heaving a great sigh that spoke volumes for the innate fatalism of his race, he flung his switch into the undergrowth the animal had just paused to sample, tethered the reins to a bent nail protruding conveniently from the seat, clambered in to the back of the cart, lay down and went to sleep.

Blunt was woken by a sensation akin to being tossed in a sheet (don't even go there), as had oft been his misfortune in his youth, when the leaner boys of his village had made fun of his not inconsiderable girth by repeatedly flinging him in to the air above a bed of young cacti. At the height of the seventh toss, the pranksters being exhausted and incapable of performing an eighth, the sheet had invariably been whipped away. The only difference on this present occasion was that the cacti appeared to have been substituted by splintered boards. Baffled, the blacksmith gripped either side of the bucking, jolting cart and hauled himself in to a sitting position, revealing his predicament with a clarity that momentarily dumbfounded the big man.

Although reluctant to scream: "Whooooooa!" in view of the historical context of his last such exclamation, Blunt's apparently suicidal pony's headlong downhill gallop over an undulating, rocky slope towards a looming precipice convinced the big man that it was definitely worth another shot.

"Whooooa, ponyyyy! Whhoooooaaahhrrggghhhh!"

Executing his first (and probably last) ever triple somersault, as the cart collided with the rock the pony had just cleared with a pre-Olympic, equine vault of grace, majesty and not a little luck, Blunt witnessed the animal veer away from the abyss at the final moment. Lacking the pony's quadrapedal dexterity, the disintegrating cart, wheels still spinning at incredible speed, had plunged over the edge, to be followed almost immediately by its former occupant.

"Shhhiiiittttttttt!" screamed Blunt, arms flailing like the sails of a windmill, hands grasping hopelessly at thin air as it rushed past him in an effort to re-seal the atmosphere he was burrowing through like a plunging meteorite. As he tumbled over and over his whole life flashed before him, and he was disturbed to discover that it consisted of little but work, food, ale and big-breasted women. Was this it, he wondered, a trifle belatedly? Was Grun to afford him no final opportunity to make his mark upon the world, other than the substantial one he was about to make upon its surface when he collided with it, any moment now? Apparently not, the blacksmith concluded an infinitesimal fraction of a second later, as his headlong plunge was brought to an abrupt, if somewhat perplexing end.

Blunt decided there was now no longer any doubt about it, death definitely did hurt, quite a lot. But, there again, not nearly so much as he had been expecting. He continued to stare up at the empty sky for several minutes, surprised that it did not appear to be any different. Eighty feet above him the grass at the edge of the precipice over which he had fallen waved gently in a breeze wafting playfully across the landscape. Beneath him, an all too brief and somewhat odd sound of escaping gas that had nothing to do with his gaseous nether region, and a lumpy, but surprisingly soft, moist surface. Was he really dead, he wondered? Was it possible that he had survived that terrible fall and, if so, how? Rolling over on to his side, he drew up one leg, hauled himself to his knees and glanced back over his shoulder.

The four man hunting party, whom Blunt recognized immediately as having numbered amongst Malroth's murderous marauders, had been in the process of skinning the elk they had tracked and killed, when their own deaths had descended from the skies in the form of a partially disassembled, but still exceedingly heavy cart. Constructed, prior to impact, from aged oak, and featuring two sturdy shafts and a pair of enormous, solid wooden wheels, it had fallen on the marauders like a judgement from above. Outrageously fortunate Blunt had landed on the elk.

"Truly," he chuckled, "Grun does work in mysterious ways. He put the cart before the horse!"

"Mmmmmnnn…mmmmmnnnnnnn!"

Still kneeling on the deceased elk, Blunt ducked and weaved his head and shoulders and swatted the air instinctively as he sought to locate the mosquito that appeared to have singled out the only surviving member of the bizarre tableau positioned by Fate at the base of the cliff.

"Nnnnnnnuhhh! Nnnnnnnnnuhhh!"

The blacksmith paused and glanced around him, bewildered. Since when did mosquitoes acquire a two-tone drone?

"Uuuuuuuhhh!"

At the third sweep of his immediate surroundings the baffled Blunt paused, and his gaze homed in on a wriggling movement in the shade at the foot of a nearby tree. Sliding down from his deflated host, he approached the writhing thing with great caution until the dust thrown up by the motion settled as the creature lay still. Pausing to stoop beneath the leaf laden outermost branches of the tree, he was astonished to behold an attractive and admirably proportioned woman lying on her back beneath them, bound hand and foot, gagged with a strip of folded leather and secured by her outstretched wrists to the trunk of the tree. She watched him warily as he knelt beside her and carefully removed the gag, then sat back on his haunches as she gulped in a lungful of sweet air.

"Mistress, I take it those mangled ruffians over there were the perpetrators of this ungallant act?"

The woman nodded her confirmation as her breathing began to settle to a more normal pattern, much to the blacksmith's relief. The heaving of her fine, woollen clad bosom had been a cause of some concern, not least because of the secondary effect upon his libido.

Blunt smiled grimly as he cut through her bonds with his dagger.

"Then I believe I may have inadvertently meted out a form of poetic justice, for they have all been carted off to Haletosys." he chuckled.

"Oh, very witty. And *I* believe *you* may also be the luckiest man alive. You just fell nigh on one hundred feet and survived without a scratch. Truly, you must be favoured by the Gods." She replied, rubbing furiously at her wrists and ankles to revive the circulation.

"This is true. They do say Grun favours the bold."

"So, it was always your intention to rescue this damsel in distress?"

Blunt shook his head.

"Sadly, I can make no such claim. I had not the slightest idea you were here. Had I known, I would undoubtedly have sought to rescue you from those thugs, though I know not how I would have gone about it, given the unfavourable odds and my marked inexperience in such matters. The truth, however, is more prosaic; I had fallen asleep in my cart and my stupid pony took it in to its head to sample the tender grasses at the verge of yon cliff top."

Jennah regarded him in silence for a moment. Yes, he was certainly overweight, she noted, his bulging gut a testimony to all things edible or quaffable, and his receding hairline made him look a good deal older than he probably was, but he had a generally pleasing countenance, powerful biceps and wonderfully expressive brown eyes.

"You could have lied and said you flew to my rescue intentionally."

"That is so, but we both know it would have been an untruth."

A strange sensation fluttered suddenly in the woman's breast, like a caged bird set free from its incarceration.

"Then you *are* courageous and a man of honour, sir."

The blacksmith appeared genuinely taken aback.

"I am?"

"Indeed…and I would know the name of my bold rescuer…if that is not too bold a request on such a slim acquaintance?"

Blunt got to his feet and helped the herbalist to hers, steadying her by placing one hand gently beneath her left elbow, before affecting a courteous bow.

"My name is Blunt and I am a blacksmith and armourer by trade." He volunteered, smiling happily now.

"Blacksmith is a worthy trade, as for the other, I shall reserve judgement until we are better acquainted. And I am Jennah, a herbalist and mixer of medicines and potions, though many refer to me as a witch."

"Not I, Jennah." He assured her.

It was Jennah's turn to smile and of a sudden it seemed to Blunt he had just witnessed the sun, unfettered by stain of cloud, rise above an idyllic landscape on a perfect, Spring morning.

"So, what brings a Lumbeygan blacksmith to the verge of the Darklands?"

"Another rescue, would you believe? Not of a maiden, I hasten to add. A warlike youth with whom I am acquainted has sworn bloody vengeance for the murder of his entire family by Malroth and his marauders, four of whom have just suffered such a fate from a most unexpected quarter. The lad is but sixteen summers in age, yet he set out in lone pursuit, determined to hunt down and slaughter the miscreants, just as they slaughtered all the inhabitants of his village, save for his young self and yours truly."

Jennah considered this information carefully before making any comment.

"So, unable to talk the boy out of his foolhardy quest and not being of a combative nature yourself, you declined to accompany him on what seemed to you like a suicidal venture…yet you changed your mind. Why?"

Blunt thought equally hard about his response to her question. Finally, with a shrug of his big shoulders, he said:

"There comes a time in the life of even the most timid of men when he must stand up and be counted. I hid away for most of my adult life amongst one of the most warlike tribes in the four kingdoms, because I believed that it was actually the safest place to be. The day the marauders came I fought side by side with my friends, but they were prepared to fight to the death and I saw no purpose in that. When it became clear that all was lost and none would be spared, I feigned death and listened to the carnage continue around me. Gorm, the chieftain's son, had been ordered to hide out in the woods until it was over, and despite his disgust at his father's command he obeyed it like a dutiful son."

"And now he burns with shame for his own survival and seeks

to put an end to his life by waging war against insuperable odds?"

Blunt nodded.

"Something like that. He's a Delirian; it's what they do."

He glanced across at the crushed and broken bodies of Ozzmun and his companions.

"But at least the odds are a little shorter now, eh?"

Jennah held out a hand to him and he accepted it, holding on for just a moment or two more than was necessary before kissing it, much to her delight.

"Do you think there is any possibility your young friend is still alive?"

"Unlikely as the possibility seems, I certainly wouldn't bet against it. His father survived many seemingly impossible scrapes before his luck finally ran out."

"Then we have work to do. You and I both have a score to settle with Malroth, and a young wolf to save from himself."

Blunt regarded the woman with something akin to awe as he placed a large hand tentatively upon her shoulder.

"Jennah, you should go home; this is not your war."

"Oh, but it is, Blunt. Those extremely dead, brutal men over there and the truly evil one who sent them made it so. Now come along, we have to collect up their weapons."

"And carry them how? It may have escaped your notice, but my cart has been reduced to significantly more than its original component parts. There is also the unsavoury problem of the copious blood stains and squished cranial matter to be considered."

Hands on hips, Jennah shook her head, ruefully.

"Courageous you may be, master blacksmith, but observant you most definitely are not. Then again, when was any man ever observant; you all struggle to find the most obvious things, even when they are right under your nose?"

"I am as observant as the next man." Declared Blunt, his tone all outraged indignation.

"My point exactly. Grunk couldn't find the hairs in his own nostrils!"

"I thought he was the average man."

"Same difference."

Hands on hips now, to signify his indignation at this

unwarranted slur upon his sex, Blunt demanded to know:
"So what, pray, are you implying is eluding me?"
"Our late but not lamented friends' four ponies."
"Ponies? What…where…?"
"Standing there patiently beneath the shade of that adjacent tree." She replied, pointing with outstretched arm.

Whipping around to peer beneath the shade of a large beech, not thirty paces away, the blacksmith was astonished to note the animals in question all present and correctly saddled.

"Well fuck me!" he exclaimed, forgetting himself momentarily. He put a hand to his mouth in dismay, but the expletive was out.

"A trifle presumptuous, Blunt." Jennah teased him.
"We've only just met."

CHAPTER 23

An open leather satchel lay on the ground at the base of the rock supporting the mutilated corpse. A mallet, three chisels, a metal straight edge and a large, half eaten pasty lay haphazardly around one end of the rock, as though they had all slid suddenly from the top of it. The slightly inclined slab of rock itself was so low at its near end that the leather boot shod feet of the corpse rested on the ground, which was how Gorm had almost tripped over one of them in the dark. Avoiding any further contact with the dead man, he picked up the mallet and balanced it on the palm of his left hand, head down, haft upright.

"Well proportioned. A good weight. You know…knew…your tools, my deceased friend."

The young Delirian raised his eyes with some reluctance to stare at the ruptured body, but his gaze was drawn inexorably to the sword. He shook his head to clear his mind of the seductive voice that seemed to be whispering to him:

"*Take hold of me…release me. Do it now, for it is thy destiny, Gorm of Deliria*."

Instead of responding to the appeal, though he was sorely tempted, Gorm addressed the weapon's lifeless host, in the hope that the sound of his own voice might dispel the disembodied whisper.

"So, you were a stone mason? Was the sword already embedded in the rock when you found it? Were you planning to chip it free, rather than pull it? Did you think that would enable you to avoid the fate you failed to avoid?"

Silence. The corpse was giving nothing away and the bemused youngster concluded that he was just going to have to work it all out for himself.

"If that was so, how did it get to be where it is now, hmm?" Gorm continued to muse aloud.

"Did some monstrous creature snatch you up and impale you bodily on the hilt? Such a possibility seems most unlikely, but so does the only other remotely plausible scenario. Who in Grun's name would have the strength to gut you with the blade before continuing to plunge it deep in to this lump of solid rock, eh?"

The sharp nudge between the shoulder blades caused the startled young Delirian to drop the hammer on to the end of his right foot.

"Owwwwww...fu...!"

He hopped around on his other foot to confront the horse and the expletive perished on his lips. A very alarmed looking Concorde stood just behind him, making wild eyed gestures with his magnificent head towards the direction from which he and his erstwhile rider had but recently arrived. Narrowing his eyelids, Gorm squinted beyond the feeble light provided by the guttering torch he had perched on the rock between the mason's legs before the fire had gone out. No more than thirty feet away from them, forty at most, although it was difficult to judge in the meagre illumination, a scarcely definable mass of intense darkness appeared to be congealing within the darkness itself, as it assumed a form that suggested his last question was about to be answered in most unwelcome fashion. Yet Gorm might still have suspected he was imagining this process, had it not been for the simultaneous materialisation of a pair of huge, yellow eyes with small, dark pupils that now stared back at him with frightening intensity. That stare suggested malice of a pure and unadulterated nature that did not bode well for the youngster. The fact that its perpetrator appeared to be at least eight feet in height did little for his confidence, either.

"Shit!"

Grabbing his bow and slotting the arrow to the string, the young Delirian was already taking aim when yet another sharp nudge between the shoulder blades caused him to let fly prematurely (a common occurrence with lads of his age). The arrow clattered harmlessly in to the trees several yards from its intended target. He spun around angrily to see the horse gesturing frantically once more, but this time in the opposite direction. Another yellow-eyed element of the darkness was spawning amongst the trees just beyond the rock. With a sick feeling in his stomach Gorm recalled the words of the Thongstress:

'Each time the sword is discovered anew, it is always embedded in its previous victim; it is also said to be protected by four fearsome guardians.'

Fishing out another arrow and fitting it to his bow with fumbling fingers, Gorm turned slowly through three hundred and sixty degrees and counted the apparitions. Sure enough, there were four of the enormous creatures and whereas before they had appeared to be loitering at the extreme edge of his night vision with limited, if undoubtedly malicious intent, they were now lumbering towards him with an abundance of it. Taking swift aim, he loosed the arrow and heard it thud in to the chest of the nearest monster at a velocity that would, at that distance, have surely killed any man alive. The "Urrghh!" the creature uttered before snapping the end off the missile and flinging it aside was more an expression of mild irritation than pain, and the young Delirian knew instantly that expending any more of his valuable, but currently useless arrows was going to prove a complete waste of time. He glanced at Concorde in desperation and the great animal returned his gaze as if to say: "The situation looks dire, old friend, but do not fear for I am with you," before galloping off through the forest at a speed that seemed certain to lead to a bone crunching collision with a tree trunk at any moment.

"Oh, that's just great!" the lad exclaimed in despair and cast around for some means of defending himself. In a rare moment of inspiration, he grasped the torch and touched the meagre flame to the mason's tattered clothing before frantically heaping what dry tinder he could find on to the resultant blaze. Aided by its own remaining layers of subcutaneous fat the corpse was soon burning healthily, filling the air with the sweet, nauseating stench of roasting human flesh.

"You may have suffered an ignominious death, my friend, but you're going out in a blaze of glory." Muttered Gorm, grimly as he drew his sword and turned to face his nearest attacker.

If the youngster had hoped the creatures would prove as fearful of fire as every other animal he had ever encountered, he was in for a disappointment of serious proportions. The flames served merely to accentuate the enormity of his nemeses as they continued to advance on him with what he could now see clearly was intent of the predatory variety. Gorm concentrated his attention on the nearest monster, which stood easily eight or more feet tall on its prodigious hind legs and elongated, clawed feet. The snarling beast's torso was slightly forward leaning, enhancing its aggressive intent, and balanced by a thick, bushy tail that appeared to act purely as a counterweight to the massive frame. A black, sinewy body composed almost entirely of dense muscle was covered in dark, shaggy hair that had the appearance of thick fur. Its powerful, jointed forelegs had something of the look of muscular arms and ended in huge, five-taloned, hand-like claws, but it was the head that troubled Gorm the most. There was a very faint, but unmistakeable trace of the human in the massive skull, but with a more protruding jaw filled with an indecent number of enormous, flesh tearing teeth set off by huge fangs in both the upper and lower jaws and topped by canine looking nostrils. The menacing, merciless eyes were forward facing and the erect ears tapered to a point. The youth had never seen a werewolf before, although he had often been regaled with tales of their existence, but was almost certain he was in the very unwelcome presence of several of them now, and the overall effect of their demeanour was suggestive to Gorm of his imminent demise in a singularly unpleasant manner.

"Thongstresssss!" he screamed in desperation and immediately recalled something else the woman had said:
'Some believe it, some suspect it, but it is often the way with such enchantments that the least likely candidate proves ultimately to be *the One*.'
Could it possibly be that he, sixteen years old Gorm of Deliria from the sacked village of Nurk in the valley of Grath, was *the One*? Was that why Grun had led him to this desolate place? Surely not…and yet, he reasoned, what other purpose could there be in his stumbling upon the mason? If ever someone's fate was set in stone, then surely this was it?
With the nearest monster scarcely more than a spear's length away the young Delirian dropped his own sword, leapt on to the rock behind what was left of the mason's head, thrust his hands in to the flames and grasped the hilt of the mighty *Skullsplitter*, to the accompaniment of enraged roars from the startled guardians and a whispered "*Yessssss*! ringing in his ears". The effect of his two-handed grip on the sword was instantaneous. An immense surge of energy pulsed up through his arms with the speed and ferocity of a forest fire and Gorm sensed rather than heard the grating of steel

on stone as he heaved on the weapon with all the strength he could muster. As the magical sword slid effortlessly from its grisly berth it seemed to burn, its polished surfaces reflecting the flames and illuminating the scene like a mighty flare. Nonplussed by this extraordinary display, the four guardians eased themselves almost fully erect around the foot of the rock upon which the youngster stood and howled their frustration, before a coarse, grinding sound emanated from the ground beneath them and raced up through their great bodies with paralysing speed, transforming their living flesh to inanimate stone in the blink of an eye (actually, it could have been several blinks, but you get the picture).

Gorm stood transfixed, scarcely able to believe either what he had just witnessed or what he had accomplished. He stared at the mighty weapon in his hands in wonder; it seemed to him to have no more weight than a hazel switch, yet he knew for certain that its weight was considerable. He also knew his hands should have been burned beyond recovery by the flaming mason, yet they were unmarked and the blaze he had started had extinguished miraculously without his even noticing. Suddenly aware of another presence in his immediate vicinity, he looked up expecting to see a repentant Concorde and was thus more than a little surprised to find himself accompanied by the Thongstress, standing motionless between two of the petrified werewolves.

"Just as I suspected, you are indeed *the One*, young Gorm of Deliria, and my task here is fulfilled, at last. But be warned, the sword **Skullsplitter** is a weapon of immense power and unfathomable magical properties. Use it wisely. Never draw before your opponent, never draw in rage, never use it in anger, for its power is intended for a singular purpose known only to the Gods and should not be corrupted by base human emotions. You are its keeper now and may be tested ere long, for the Gods will want to know they have chosen wisely."

Gorm nodded in assent.

"The Gods may ask of me what they will, and you may be assured I shall not fail them, but I still have my own quest to fulfill."

"That is as it should be, and so I take my leave of you, Gorm of Deliria, for you are no longer a boy, but a man, bound by an unknown fate to the tempered steel of mighty Grun." confirmed the pale, but ethereally beautiful woman in black."

"Farewell." Said Gorm the man, as the Thongstress was swallowed by the darkness from which she had issued, leaving him alone with nought but the petrified guardians for company. He picked up the torch and blew gently on its glowing end, sending a shower of sparks like tiny fireflies in to the atmosphere, before holding it aloft to illuminate the glade. To the young warrior's dismay, Concorde was still conspicuous by his absence.

"Hmph, some friend you turned out to be." he muttered, before collecting up his other sword, bow and arrows and setting off deeper in to the Forest of Improbable Fate.

CHAPTER 24

Blunt and Jennah sat astride their motionless mounts, the remaining ponies tethered behind them laden with an assortment of weapons, armour and supplies. Man and woman stared apprehensively in to the virtually impenetrable gloom of the forest, fifty yards ahead of where they had halted. It was not the intimidating nature of the landscape they were approaching that had persuaded them to pause however, but the sudden cessation of alarming crashing sounds and high-pitched, animal shrieks emanating from thence. After a minute or so of edgy silence they exchanged glances, their expressions registering mutual apprehension, before the sounds from within the forest not only resumed suddenly, but approached apace. Finally, to the couple's undisguised astonishment, the ghostly blur careering through the trees towards the edge of the forest finally resolved itself in to the shape of a magnificent white horse. Initially unaware of their presence, Concorde burst in to the welcoming embrace of the early dawn light, only to come to a skidding halt as he caught sight of the unexpected cavalcade for the first time.

"I recognise that surly brute!" Blunt exclaimed, as he recalled his recent ignominious dunking.

"He's the stroppy bugger that flung me in the river."

Jennah was unable to resist a smile at the blacksmith's indignant tone. For his part, Concorde had recognised Blunt too and had never been so pleased to see a seriously overweight human before, despite the possibility that the great lump might now choose to swap mounts. Picking his steps with care, the horse advanced to within a half dozen paces of the little party and volunteered the equine equivalent of a bashful grin.

"You appear to think I have a short memory, Mr Horse." Said Blunt, his voice all prickly disapproval.

Realising there was nothing further to be gained by hamming it up, Concorde whinnied in alarm and commenced tossing his head in the direction of the forest, before turning to face the trees and glancing back over his left shoulder at the two humans in pointed fashion. Blunt heaved a sigh of exasperation.

"What on earth is the stupid brute doing now?"

Jennah, who (despite the blacksmith's primary calling) was far more attuned to the nuances of horsey communication, studied the animal intently.

"He's trying to tell us something, Blunt. I think he wants us to follow him." she said, and wondered why her pronouncement sounded so familiar.

"Ha! I've already followed one stupid horse over a cliff and I'm in no great hurry to repeat the experience."

Jennah tilted her head from side to side a couple of times.

"Understandable, under the circumstances, despite the notable absence of any cliffs hereabouts, but he appears to me to be an intelligent beast..."

"Intelligent!"

"Yes, and perhaps it might just have something to do with your young friend, Gorm."

At the mention of Gorm's name Concorde pricked up his ears and neighed and dragged at the ground with one hoof. This combination of actions did not go unnoticed by the herbalist or the blacksmith. Blunt urged his pony forward with a clicking of his tongue and an increase in pressure on its flanks from his knees. Feeling somewhat foolish, but eager to appear to know what he was doing for Jennah's benefit, he addressed the white stallion:

"Is this true, horse? Do you know something of the whereabouts of my young friend, Gorm?"

Concorde nodded his noble head emphatically, several times.

Hiding his astonishment as best he could, which was not very well, Blunt beckoned to Jennah to follow him with an over arm motion that would not have disgraced John Wayne in his heyday, although he did resist the temptation to call out:

"For...ward...hoooooo!"

Instead, in a turn of phrase more befitting the situation, he declared:

"Then let us make haste, valiant creature, for there may be precious little time left to lose."

"If you insist," Jennah replied, "but I'd prefer not to be called 'a creature'...not even a valiant one."

"I was talking to th..." Blunt began, but was stopped abruptly by Jennah's inability to stifle her laughter.

CHAPTER 25

Midnight in the Forest of Improbable Fate and a lone figure stood at the centre of a clearing defined by the length of the fallen trees that had created it. Clasping the sword **Skullsplitter** in a firm, two-handed grip, Gorm lunged and parried, thrust and cut, chopped, diced and skewered his imagined opponent, while serpent like tendrils of mist entwined his legs as they wove through the silent forest. Above him, a full moon beamed its smirking approval of this danse macabre, burnishing the cold steel with an equally cold light befitting the witching hour. And far beyond the trees, at the root of a range of mountains, a giant of a man woke in his yurt in a cold sweat, tortured by the pain of a festering wound and terrible dreams of an approaching nemesis.

Meanwhile, back in the dark heart of the forest, a thud and an "Oooofff!" invoking crash, concealed within the darkness lurking just beyond the edge of the clearing, put Gorm on his guard. Head cocked slightly to one side, weapon raised in anticipation, he listened intently for the careless whisper that might just give away the position of approaching assassins. No such whisper was heard, but the lantern seen swinging wildly through the trees with a bizarre bobbing motion served the young Delirian's purpose equally well. Crash, bang, wallop!

"Ooofff…owwwww!"

Gorm watched, puzzled, as the light approached like a drunken corpse candle, colliding with as many trees as it avoided.

"Ohhh! I say, you chaps, do please be more careful. Deenah, are you alright back there, my darling?"

Of a sudden a second lantern appeared, some way behind the first and proceeding in more stately fashion.

"Yes, I'm fine, Father. Thank you." a youthful, feminine voice responded.

"Well, I wish I could say the same, my dear. I'm being tossed like a salad, here!"

On the still, chill night air of the forest the voices carried effortlessly.

"Then you should not have offered those ignoramuses so much money to get you there swiftly. My stout fellows are proceeding with far more care, because I promised them a sizeable bonus provided I arrive in one piece."

"You have your mother's forethought, my sweet. I only wish…"

The forward litter bearer stopped abruptly, to avoid colliding with another tree and adding yet another undesired trophy, in the form of a sizeable contusion, to his forehead. Given no advance warning, the rear bearer continued his forward motion, forcing the man at the front to his knees and flinging the corpulent, expensively attired occupant of the litter from his padded seat and through the curtain before him. His fall was broken by the kneeling bearer, who was immediately flattened into the mossy earth by the weight of flesh bearing down on him. Carried forward inexorably by the momentum of this sequence of events, the rear bearer crashed through the back of the disintegrating litter to complete the human sandwich.

Gorm's astonishment gave way to uncontrollable laughter as he observed this unexpected tableau unfold before him, but stopped almost as abruptly as the litter, when the vehicle following it arrived at the scene of the accident. The more cautious bearers set their carrying poles and burden down at the edge of the clearing and hurried to one side of the litter to hold back the heavy, gilded flaps of the brocade modesty curtain enclosing the travelling compartment. Despite the snuffling, grunting and cursing emanating from the sprawling heap of humanity beside which the second litter had paused, Gorm forced himself to maintain a straight face as he watched for the occupant to emerge.

The young woman who stepped carefully from the second, wheel-less carriage was, without the slightest shadow of a doubt on his part, the most beautiful member of the opposite sex the young Delirian warrior had ever seen. Approximately his own age and very nearly as tall, her long, red hair, astonishingly aquamarine eyes and perfectly exquisite features were beyond compare, in his humble estimation. As she adjusted her attire he noted she was clothed in finery and jewels that served only to accentuate her unparalleled beauty. Sheathing his newfound sword, he stepped down from the mist shrouded tree stump upon which he had been perched and strode across the clearing to offer his assistance. For her part, Deenah, whose initial preoccupation had been her father's welfare, looked up in surprise as she detected purposeful movement at the periphery of her vision and caught her breath as she executed a half turn. The tall, broad and incredibly handsome, but warlike looking young man with the thatch of fetchingly unkempt, sun-bleached hair approaching her was the physical fulfilment of every youthful fantasy she had ever explored.

Stepping over the girl's father and his bearers, Gorm bowed his head politely and enquired:

"My lady, I am Gorm of Deliria. May I be of any assistance to you?"

The young woman smiled shyly as she glanced up from beneath eyelids lowered modestly, as befitted her station as a practiced (and not always in front of a mirror) seductress.

"Thank you, kind sir, but I am in need of no assistance. My father, on the other hand, appears to be in dire need of your manly help…and I would be most grateful for it, on his behalf."

"Then it will be my very great pleasure to comply with your request." Replied gullible Gorm, gallantly.

Without further ado he flung the topmost bearer in to the undergrowth and, straining every youthful, but already seasoned muscle in his body, hauled the grunting merchant to his feet. Deenah watched without comment, fascinated by the way the young man's biceps bulged as he took the strain, which was not inconsiderable.

"As a rule I am light as a feather," the merchant explained, dusting himself down with freshly soiled hands that replaced more than they removed, besmirching his crumpled clothing, which was clearly of the most expensive, handmade variety, "but am weighed down by the enormous weight of responsibility for the safety of my daughter, you understand?"

"She is, indeed, a rare treasure, sir."

Mammot Tytewadd, the merchant of Vennys, caught the glance exchanged between the star-crossed youngsters; it was filled with mutual lust, longing and the newly experienced anguish of, as yet, unrequited love.

"She is, indeed." Mammot agreed.

"But not one in which you will be burying *your* sword." He added, pointedly.

"Eh?" said Gorm, as yet unrehearsed in the finer points of adult (a debatable point) innuendo.

"She is promised to another, boy!"

"Promised to another boy?"

The merchant raised his eyes to the midnight sky, clearly visible above the clearing.

"I take it you were last in line when they were handed out, eh?"

Unfamiliar with this expression also, Gorm continued to look bemused.

"He means that I am promised to Malroth of Eebollah, in return for impunity for our townspeople from rapacious attack by his fearsome marauders." Deenah explained.

"Oh."

Crestfallen at this latest cruel twist of fate, the young Delirian found himself at a loss for further words. At which awkward juncture capricious Fate took a hand, for the waning moon had suddenly infused the jewels embedded in the hilt of **Skullsplitter** with a cold fire that captured the merchant's greedy eye (the left one, as I recall).

"That is a remarkably fine looking weapon you have there at your side, young man."

Gorm glanced down at his newly acquired sword.

"Yes, it is." The youth concurred.

"May I see it?"

Deenah observed this exchange silently, but with growing interest, for she was accustomed to her father's acquisitiveness and suspected the imminent offer of some form of exchange.

"Of course." Said Gorm and extracted the sword from his scabbard, before resting its horizontal length on his upturned palms for inspection. Mammot studied the weapon carefully and at length before clearing his throat to enquire:

"Very nice, but I have seen better, of course. Is it for sale? I would pay a fair price for such a sword."

This statement was what was known in bartering circles as being somewhat economical with the truth, or as everyone else knew it, a downright lie.

Gorm shook his head.

"I very nearly paid for it with my life, so no amount of riches would persuade me to part with it."

The merchant glanced slyly from the youth to his daughter and back again. He wanted the weapon now, at any cost. He trusted Malroth would pay handsomely for such a gift, which just goes to prove how little he actually knew of his prospective son-in-law.

"Most commendable…however, I believe I can offer you a treasure upon which no price could possibly be placed, in exchange for such a trade."

Gorm studied the man, suspiciously.

"A treasure of no value? Of what use would that be?"

Mammot sighed, heavily. This was proving much more difficult than he had anticipated.

"A treasure **beyond** value. The maidenhead of my daughter!"

Twin gasps of astonishment and disbelief rang around the little clearing.

"Father!"

"Your own daughter?"

"I heard she lost that years ago." one of the bearers muttered under his breath.

His companion blushed furiously, but said nothing. In the gloom at the edge of the clearing his guilt went unrecorded.

Mammot shrugged his shoulders in a feeble and far from convincing attempt at sheepishness.

"'Twill be lost soon enough, for Malroth's camp is but a stone's throw from here."

"It will…it is?"

"Certainly, no more than a mile or two at most…and definitely not more than ten or twelve. Deenah is promised to the lord of the Darklands and that is a bargain I dare not break, but I have seen the way you two young sweethearts gaze longingly at one another. We may yet be several days trek from the marauder's secret camp, so what harm can it do, hmm? One night…possibly several nights… of connubial bliss with the girl of your dreams, in exchange for your sword."

Gorm and Deenah glared at the merchant in mutual disgust until their own eyes met once more, and the prospect of their proposed, but all too brief union superseded all other emotions.

"We may spend an entire night together, uninterrupted?"
The merchant nodded.
"Possibly several nights?"
"The moon wanes swiftly now. I will have our bearers make camp here and the pair of you can spend the entire day and following passage of the moon in sweet embrace...or whatever other activity may take your fancy. I will have these incompetent oafs build you a shelter for your privacy. All I ask in exchange is your sword, young sir. If you feel naked without it, I will have one of my men give you his perfectly adequate weapon. I can vouch for the fact that it has never been used in anger." he added, glowering momentarily in the direction of the youngest bearer.

Gorm shook his head.

"I already have another superb sword, forged by the finest blacksmith in Deliria...though it is still not so fine as this one."

He stared again at Deenah, whose bosom was heaving in most appealing fashion at the prospect of their imminent union. Another part of his own anatomy was likewise enthused.

"Then we have a deal?" Mammot urged.

Gorm hesitated for just a moment, but the temptation proved too great a prize for his currently under achieving loins to resist.

"We have a deal, merchant...if...and only if...your beautiful daughter desires the binding nature of the contract, too."

Deenah was practically swooning with excitement at the prospect now and clasped her hands to her heaving breasts in anticipation of Gorm doing likewise ere long.

"Truly, *nothing* would give me greater pleasure, Gorm of Deliria."

"Then, I believe this is yours." Said Gorm, gripping **Skullsplitter** in his right hand and holding it at arm's length.

As the merchant reached hungrily for the weapon a great boom of thunder rumbled across the treetops far above the scene, and a lightning bolt came scorching through the canopy to strike the blade, as the seven humans clustered in the glade looked on aghast. Momentarily blinded by the intensity of the light it was a moment or two before they realised the violent hissing was not the aftermath of the strike, but the result of the transfiguration it had wrought.

The girl shrieked, the merchant screamed, the bearers exclaimed: "Goodness me!" or words to that effect, but Gorm stood open-mouthed and rooted to the spot as he stared in disbelief at the stretched jaws and glistening fangs of the huge, crimson snake he was holding in his right hand, just behind its head. Still hissing, the creature fixed him with its orange eyes as its sinewy body wrapped itself thrice around his arm and began to crush.

Finally moved to speech, Gorm yelped:

"Holy shiiitttttt!"

He gripped the creature's twitching tail with his left hand and struggled to unwrap the crushing coils without success, staggering across the clearing uttering oaths and curses aplenty, before losing his balance and toppling on to the campfire.

"Sorcery! Witchcraft! We are doomed!" screamed the merchant, clambering in to Deenah's litter.

"Daddy, don't leave me." Deenah squealed, before being yanked off her feet by his podgy hand protruding from the brocade and dragging his prized bargaining chip in after him.

"Come back you spineless worms and I'll quadruple your wages." He yelled after the fleeing bearers, who paused at this prospect, but made no immediate move to return. Something dropped through a hole in the canvas roof of the litter, straight in to the lap of the quivering girl seated most uncomfortably upon her father's podgy knees. Cue more shrieking and screaming as the pair identified a severed and mouldering human hand.

"Alright, alright, I'll increase them tenfold. Lord Malroth will just have to come to us."

No sooner had the newly enriched (if the IOU's were to be believed) bearers galloped off in to the forest with the bulging litter than the snake resumed its more customary form. Gorm, miraculously unharmed by his second descent of the night in to the flames, sat on the ground and stared at the magical weapon in disbelief.

"Surely you could have waited one hour to do that?"

On this occasion the seductive, whispering voice in his head was conspicuous by its absence.

"I shall take your continued silence as a 'no', then?"

Gripping the mighty weapon with both hands, he shoved the tip of the blade in to the earth and used it to push himself to his knees.

"So, it would seem you and I are now bound together, **Skullsplitter,** though whether by Fate or the whim of the Gods I cannot say for certain. But if, as the Thongstress suspected, it is what great Grun has decreed, then so be it." he muttered disconsolately. Scrambling to his feet (no mean achievement when hampered by a throbbing erection) he picked up the remarkable sword, wiped clean its blade, kissed it reverently and slipped it back in to his scabbard, before patting the hilt with renewed respect.

"And now, my magical, murderous friend, I believe you and I have an appointment with destiny."

CHAPTER 26

A minimal amount of early daylight had begun to force its way through a rare thinning of the canopy, revealing a macabre scene to the astonished Blunt, Jennah and Concorde. Four huge, grotesque stone statues stood at the four points of the compass that had not yet been invented (although, true to form, Fyl the Ferryman was rumoured to be working on something along those very lines), surrounding a low, fire-blackened rock upon which lay an upturned, badly scorched human skeleton. The white horse trotted around this scene several times, whinnying in troubled fashion as it struggled unsuccessfully to fathom what had occurred there in its absence. Blunt and Jennah looked on, baffled by the animal's behaviour. After a moment, Blunt dismounted and strode over to the rock, one hand on the hilt of his sword, ears attuned for the slightest sound out of place, although nothing in his experience to date had prepared him for these present circumstances. He studied the human remains intently before turning to Jennah and announcing with undisguised relief:

"It's not him."

For her part, the herbalist had become preoccupied with an examination of one of the petrified werewolves.

"What's that you say, Blunt?" she asked, running her right hand slowly over the surprisingly warm stone, almost as if she was caressing it. Without quite knowing why, she placed her left ear to the torso and stepped back suddenly in disbelief, convinced she had detected a heartbeat.

Blunt had already wandered away from the fire-blackened rock to pick up something lying in the mossy earth at the base of a nearby tree.

"That abomination on the rock is not Gorm, thank Grun…but the lad was here. This was one of his arrows, and I should know; I helped him make them."

He held up the partial length of feathered shaft.

"Then we cannot be far behind him, now." The woman observed, still staring intently at the nearest werewolf, half expecting to see it move or its petrified, shaggy pelt to ruffle beneath the caress of the faint breeze blowing across the clearing.

After a moment or two more she tore her gaze away and stared at the ground about her feet, fingering the wooden wolf figurine about her neck as she did so.

"See where the earth here has been trampled by hooves...his hooves, I am almost certain."

She indicated Concorde with an inclination of her head. As if in knowing response, the horse crossed the clearing to stand beside her and quite deliberately placed each one of his hooves in turn in to a series of corresponding prints, confirming the herbalist's conclusion beyond any doubt.

Blunt shrugged his shoulders, seemingly unimpressed by her deduction or what he took to be the horse's party piece.

"What of it?"

"Our big, white, four legged friend had not set hoof within the circumference of the statues since we arrived, yet as you can clearly see his feet match them perfectly...and they are all still fairly fresh."

"Which means?"

"He was here as recently as last night."

Concorde whinnied and nodded his head in agreement.

"I could have told you that; this rock is still warm, as are the remains of the unfortunate wretch stretched out upon it."

"So we know where your young friend was last night, but I can find no clue as to where he was going when he left this eerie, Grun forsaken place." Jennah admitted.

"I believe I know exactly where he is headed." The blacksmith announced, confidently.

Woman and horse regarded him with surprise.

"You do?"

Jennah crossed the narrow clearing to stand before him.

"How?"

Smiling so smugly Jennah was almost tempted to slap him, Blunt produced a rolled up parchment from within his jerkin and proceeded to unfurl it.

"My newfound friend Broos provided me with a map of the Darklands. We are now but three or four days ride, half a dozen at most, from the Mountains of Reffews and the site of Malroth's encampment at the far edge of the Forest of Improbable Fate, on the shores of Lake Vuronicuh. Where else would a youth bent on vengeance for the murder of his family be bound but the lair of the blackguards responsible?"

"Where else, indeed? And assuming you are correct, then we should tarry not a moment longer, Blunt. Given his youth and impetuousness, Gorm may well prove to be his own worst enemy in his understandable, but ill-conceived venture, and we have to face the fact that we may already be too late to save him from a truly appalling fate."

CHAPTER 27

Despite the vast area of densely forested earth the region covered, the Darklands was not composed entirely of trees. The mighty river Twai and several of its tributaries had their origin in a mountainous region of limestone at the heart of the landscape and through which they had carved plunging gorges and hollowed out a multitude of caverns and narrow, fertile flood plains. In the passages of the Moon between the dread ice of Autumn and the blessed melt of Spring these rare and invaluable tracts of naturally irrigated land were rich with an abundance of fresh game, fat fish and sweet pasture, which was no doubt why Malroth had chosen the most inaccessible of them for his permanent campsite.

At dusk on the nineteenth day since leaving the hot and uncomfortable wasteland of Haemorrhoyde, Gorm set about his nightly task of searching out a defensible haven, preferably a cave-bear free cave, from whence he could observe the approach of nocturnal predators of both the human and animal varieties. Stooping low to reduce his profile on the skyline he scrambled up a weathered outcrop of rock, from the top of which he was startled to hear a muttered voice not too far below him. The young Delirian dropped to his belly, lowered himself carefully down the opposing face of the rock and slithered forward through the tall ferns. Throughout this painstakingly cautious advance he was careful to keep his torso within the lengthening shadow of the rock, until he could peer down from an overhanging ledge towards the wooded banks of a meandering stream from whence the voice had appeared to emanate.

"Why do folk have to be so damned ungrateful, hmm? I mean, the idea was a good one...it could have worked...in fact, it bloody well would have worked, so why take it out on me?"

Lard threw his fat fingered hands towards his rippling reflection on the surface of the water below him in a gesture of despair.

"He asked me for ideas, so I gave him an idea...and it was a great idea...a brilliant idea!"

Gorm could make no sense of this one-sided conversation, but was content to listen as the fat man continued his litany of complaint:

"Was it my fault the fucking gut was six inches too long? Am I supposed to wander around this accursed countryside measuring every length of gut, rope and twine we're likely to acquire? Does he expect me to interrogate prisoners on the exact measurements of all the lengths of gut in their miserable villages? Get real, Mal!"

Gorm pulled himself even further forward in an attempt to see who the fat man was talking to, but could make out no other figures in the gathering gloom. He was anxious to know whether he had stumbled upon the entire raiding party, for he had certainly seen this bloated, brutal oaf amongst their number, hacking down fleeing women and children with a large, curved blade.

"Big baby that he is! It's only a rotten tooth, after all. Can you believe the injustice of it, thrown out for messing up on one, stinking, rotten tooth? It's just not fair!"

As Gorm listened to this petulant tirade, he began to divine some notion of what had taken place, and a very dangerous idea began to form in his head. This process took several minutes, during which the fat man continued to berate his reflective audience with the monstrous injustice meted out to him.

Ten minutes later Lard stopped himself in mid vocal flow as his ears detected the casual approach of a not very good whistler. It might be Malroth coming back to check up on him he thought, overlooking the fact that Malroth whistling through his abscessed jaw was about as likely as Norvul whistling a lullaby through his arse. Whoever it was, the corpulent raider was in no position to defend himself against them, and he held his breath, in the rather forlorn hope that they would not notice him as they followed the narrow path alongside the stream, above which he had been left dangling upside down. He did not have long to wait, and his relief as he caught sight of the youngster was not only disgustingly audible, but smelt pretty noxious, too.

Gorm stopped in his tracks as if startled and stared at the enormous bulk of Lard, as the evening breeze swung the hulking thug gently above the water. The man's soiled and sodden looking leggings gave an instantly identifiable clue to his reaction to the sound of an approaching stranger. Emboldened by the knowledge, Gorm pretended to be alert to the possibility of an ambush as his gaze panned the tree-lined banks of the stream with an exaggerated intensity

"Greetings, young man." the inverted cutthroat hailed him, as though he did not have a care in the world.

"You have nothing to fear, for we are alone in this blighted bower."

Without a word of reply, Gorm flipped the lid from the leather case at his shoulder, selected an arrow, slotted it to the drawstring of his bow and drew it back along the length of his outstretched arm in a single, fluid movement. The lad's astonishing speed and the wear on the laced, leather wrist guard suggested to Lard that this was not the first time the youth had performed such an action. Even when viewed upside down, the young archer's pose now struck him as positively life threatening.

"Wh...what are you doing, my young and impetuous friend?" enquired the killer of innocent women and children, anxiously.

"Don't worry, sir; it's just a precaution. The callous swine that suspended you thus may still be in hiding nearby. I must be ready to protect us, should they return."

Lard trumpeted his relief, causing several attendant hover-flies to expire abruptly.

"Beg pardon, squire, but hanging around like this all day has done sod all for me guts. Cut me down, there's a good lad."

Gorm lowered his bow for a moment, then raised it again, sighting along the shaft of the arrow, the head of which was now aimed squarely at Lard's heaving chest. The young Delirian was enjoying spinning out this charade; it was hardly adequate payback for the sacking of his village and the murder of his family and friends, but it was an entertaining start.

"A thought has just occurred to me. How do I know you did not deserve to be strung up like a fowl? You could be a thief, or a murderer, or a bent accountant, or an abuser of women and children…possibly of men and animals, too"

"Me? Ha! I'll admit I've pilfered a loaf or two in days gone by, and must confess to a liking for lasses with big titties and nipples like ripe raspberries, but I would no more harm one precious hair on thy head than beg thee to pierce my throat with thy murderous missile."

Then that is exactly how you shall die, fat man, Gorm thought to himself, as he smiled winningly at the unrepentant slayer of innocents.

"In that case, you must tell me how you came to be suspended thus," Gorm insisted, as he put away the arrow, shouldered the bow and pulled the dagger from his belt, "and I shall tell you about my journey home to my village, after three years apprenticed to the finest tooth-puller in Deliria."

Great, flabby arms now folded across his chest as he watched the lad crawl out along the bough towards his suspender's complicated knot, Lard regarded him with renewed interest.

"A tooth-puller's apprentice, you say?"

"Aye, and although I am just sixteen years of age, I am skilled enough now to take up my craft alone, which is why I am returning home; there is always work for a proficient puller of teeth."

"Indeed! Well, I have a tale that may interest you, my fine young friend, and the promise of great riches too, if you have a mind for such a thing."

Apparently, the fact that tooth-pullers assistants were not customarily armed to the teeth (at least, not with weapons of war) had been overlooked by the fat oaf.

"Riches, eh?" replied Gorm, watching in satisfaction as Lard, whose means of suspension he had just severed, plunged head first in to the deep pool below him at breakneck speed.

"I daresay I would be a fool if I had no mind for great riches."
"Bbbrrrbblbrrppppbblbblbblll!" exclaimed Lard, by way of reply.

CHAPTER 28

"Now what, for Grun's sake?"

The litter's forward motion had ceased, though not as abruptly as on the previous occasion, and the carriage was in the process of being lowered to the ground, to the accompaniment of much grunting and straining on the part of the overburdened bearers.

Mammot pushed his daughter's head (still attached to the rest of her, thankfully) through the curtains.

"Tell me what you see, daughter? Why have we stopped?"

"Give me a chance, Daddy! It's still jolly dark out here." Deenah's disembodied voice informed the merchant. One of the leading bearers unhitched the lantern from his litter-bearing pole, where it had been illuminating the ground immediately before them to aid their progress through the forest, and held it aloft.

"Good gracious!" Deenah exclaimed, as the wan light revealed a magnificent white steed upon which an attractive, but somewhat plainly dressed woman was seated, and a quartet of heavily laden ponies. The little caravan (longer than a Swift Elegance, shorter than an Eldis Buccaneer) had also paused, less than twenty paces from where the litter had been set down.

"Ill met by moonlight, eh lads?" a decidedly gruff, Lumbeygan accented male voice suggested, from somewhere behind and to the side of the litter. The cowering bearers, cowards to a man, made no reply.

Deenah's head swivelled around as though turning on a spit to regard the owner of the voice, and noted a large, middle aged and greying (where it still existed) haired man of not inconsiderable bulk sighting along a lethal looking arrow fitted to the string of a fully drawn bow. The arrow was pointing directly at the bearer with the lantern, whose knobbly knees were knocking in fright as a result.

"Who is it, my treasure? Who's there…and who's that knocking?" the invisible occupant of the litter demanded to know.

"Hush, Daddy. I think it's a dirty, robbing hood. He has a wicked looking, fully fletched arrow trained upon poor Sedwyn. 'Tis the bones in old Sed's knees you can hear. The unprincipled wretch with the instrument of sudden death is clearly bent upon highway robbery, sexual molestation and murder most foul…although not necessarily in that order."

Blunt looked perplexed as he relaxed his pull on the bowstring and lowered the arrow until it was pointing at the ground just ahead of his feet.

"Who…me?"

"Sir, do you deny that you intend to murder our humble bearers and have your wicked way with us maidens, and possibly also my Daddy, before stealing what little we have and making good your escape to some squalid lair, deep within this forbidding forest?"

Deenah had evidently assumed the mystery archer was attempting to pull off a double, possibly triple, sexual molestation and highway robbery single-handed, despite the rather obvious absence of a highway. It was now Blunt's turn to look astounded, but his astonishment soon gave way to outraged indignation.

"Certainly not, Miss! What kind of a monster do you take me for?"

"Well, you cannot blame me for my assumption sir, when I peer out of our humble transport and find you about to skewer us with a barrage of deadly missiles before ravishing us with your own arrow."

Blunt glanced pointedly at his single arrow and raised one eyebrow, but resisted the temptation to upbraid the undeniably attractive girl for her rampant exaggeration. Instead, he sought to reassure her with a simple explanation.

"Young mistress, I can assure you that I, too, do nought more sinister than journey through this accursed forest, in the welcome company of the fair maiden upon the white horse."

Jennah blushed happily at the 'fair maiden' and blew Blunt a kiss.

"We are but weary travellers, like your good selves. I caught sight of yon lantern some distance back and suspected mischievous vagabonds or cutthroats preparing to waylay us. Thinking to outwit them, I dismounted and tracked around behind the lamp to get in a clear shot before we should be overwhelmed."

"Ohhh, I seeee. That puts an entirely different perspective on matters, doesn't it, Daddy?" she answered, almost gaily.

Deenah's head disappeared momentarily and a brief, muttered conversation followed before the curtains parted once more to reveal not one head but two. The second, much larger and considerably less agreeable head addressed the blacksmith in condescending fashion.

"A seemingly satisfactory explanation, yet you choose a curious hour to be traversing the Forest of Improbable Fate sir, if I may be so bold...and with a vulnerable maiden for company, too." he added, leering lasciviously at Jennah.

Blunt took an instant dislike to the owner of the head, but kept his temper as he replied:

"I might say the same about you and your…daughter, is it?"

Mammot's hackles rose at the implication of impropriety. The fact that he had a particular fondness for young girls of less than half his age (of his daughter's age, in fact) was neither here nor there in this particular instance, so far as he was concerned.

"*We* have a perfectly legitimate reason for travelling the Darklands at this ungrunly hour. My fair daughter was to be betrothed to a local warlord on the morrow of the morrow, but we ran in to a spot of unseemly bother en route and elected to return home rather than submit to the terrors of darkest sorcery."

Blunt glanced at Jennah, who had not spoken throughout this exchange but spoke up now.

"I know something of sorcery, sir, having once been wed to an alchemist."

Blunt's eyebrows shot up in synchronized surprise at this revelation; it was the first he had heard of any such union.

"What exactly was the nature of the dark force you encountered?"

"*Once* wed?" Mammot enquired, suspiciously, ignoring the actual question to which she had sought an answer.

"Aye," Jennah nodded, her expression one of sorrowful reflection on her loss, "he was a good husband, but a poor alchemist. He quite literally blew himself to pieces when one of his infernal experiments backfired."

"He was attempting to transform base metal in to gold?"

Jennah shook her head.

115

"No, he had been trading in exotic spices from the East and it was his first attempt at a Chicken Vindaloo. It took me several days to remove all traces of him from the remains of his laboratory, and the smell of curry lingered on for weeks. Scrubbing hither and thither on my hands and knees for almost a month, I was. He was a very large man, you see…not unlike yourself, in fact."

"Hmph."

Even from the distance separating them Blunt could see the mischievous glint in her eye and sought vainly to suppress a grin. Fortunately for him, both Mammot and Deenah were looking straight at Jennah, whose sarcasm was disguised beneath a mask of painful regret so pitiful it would not have disgraced a suffering saint.

Deenah, anxious not to be left out of this most unusual exchange and equally anxious to change the morbid subject matter, sought to explain the events from which she and her father had been fleeing, just as fast as their overburdened bearers had been able to carry them.

"We encountered a bold and handsome young warrior, deeper in the forest to the East."

"North!" Her father corrected her. He had spent a fortune on Deenah's education and, to his continuing dismay, had yet to notice any return for his considerable outlay.

"Yes, to the northways…not that the direction matters. Anyhow, the young gentleman possessed an extraordinary, magical sword, but appeared to have no control over its monstrous power, for it transformed in to a great serpent and flung him in to the flames of his campfire, at which point we fled the scene before some even more terrible transformation could overtake the poor soul."

"Made a strategic withdrawal, in the face of such evil." Mammot corrected her, again.

"Pah, do you expect us to believe all that magical nonsense?" Blunt asked, ignoring her father's pathetic explanation of their cowardice, although he was concerned that they had evidently encountered Gorm and that his young friend might have come to some harm.

"It may not be nonsense, Blunt." Jennah advised her travelling companion as she rode over to him, leading his mount and the other ponies behind her.

"Warlocks and Werewolves are said to infest this region."

Blunt stared at her scornfully.

"Werewolves? You cannot be serious?"

"Really? And what do you suppose those enormous, petrified beasts we left behind in the clearing were, for Grun's sake?"

Jennah fingered the little, carved wolf dangling from the leather thong at her neck.

"It is why I wear this charm, to protect me from such creatures."

"Petrified beasts? Pah! They were nothing more than statues, woman."

Blunt was about to dispute further with her, but the woman had turned away from him to address the merchant once more. Mammot was otherwise engaged however, searching the darkness for the werewolves he was now convinced were about to leap upon him at any moment and tear him limb from succulent limb.

"Did you note an inscription upon the sword, sir…a name, perhaps?"

"Had something to do with skulls, I believe." replied Mammot, absently. In the flickering light from the lantern he had espied the reflection of a pair of eyes, just beyond the effective range of his night vision; they were staring straight at him.

"Werewolf!" he screamed, pointing with outstretched arm. Startled by his exclamation, the small Roe deer turned and scampered deeper in to the safety of the forest.

Jennah uttered a little gasp.

"The great sword, **Skullsplitter**! Then it does exist." She whispered to Blunt.

"You believe them?"

Blunt was incredulous.

"Yes, I do. And if Gorm has pulled the sword of the Gods and lives, then he is ***the One***."

"The one what?"

CHAPTER 29

Malroth was now in so much pain he was more than ready to eviscerate someone, very slowly, simply to see another unfortunate mortal suffering even more than he, although he suspected it would still be a close run thing.

"Nrvl!"

Despite Norvul's enviable lack of schooling, he was almost certain his increasingly inglorious leader's speech was devaluing in direct proportion to the increase in the extent of his suppurating abscess.

"Lord Malroth?"

"Wut kupt yuh, yuh iduhl tossah?"

"Er, I suspect there may be some rain before sunset, although it is pleasant enough at present."

For just a fraction of one second, Norvul thought his leader was about to burst in to tears.

"Guv mh fkn strunth!"

Malroth did not burst in to tears of frustration or anguish, although he was sorely tempted on both fronts. Instead, he buried his head in his hands and uttered a primal scream of animal pain so distressing Norvul very nearly felt sorry for him. Very nearly, but not quite. Sensing instinctively that he was somehow responsible for his deeply troubled leader's disturbing utterance, he took a step back. Finally, Malroth took a deep breath before looking up and fixing his second in command with a stare of such baleful menace Norvul very nearly wet his pants, and hated himself for his unaccustomed weakness. He feared no man on Earth, with the sole exception of Malroth, whose immense physical strength, violent temper and lack of patience, allied to a total disregard for other peoples' lives, pain or suffering, made him an individual to be feared by even the bravest and most skilful of warriors.

"Bgr thuh wuthuh, yu fkn murun! Wur us Uzzmn n thuh wutch? Thuh shud'v bin hur ba nah. Un wur us Deenahh, mah braad tuh bih? Shuh shud huv bin hur bah nah, tuuh."

Norvul's face lit up like a beacon as he realised that, contrary to all expectation, he had actually understood the question...or the first part of it, at least. The answer was somewhat problematic in that he didn't know what it was, forcing him to reply with the only element he did know to be truthful

"I have already sent men to look for them, Lord." he enthused, excitedly.

"They will be back before dark, I have no doubt." he added on a whim and immediately cursed himself for his stupidity. He had serious doubts about his pronouncement, but was playing for time now and living in hope.

"Thud buttur beh."

Norvul opened his mouth to respond with yet another flailing interpretation, but instantly thought better of it and restricted himself to a nod of affirmation, before sending the guard lounging idly outside Malroth's yurt to fetch a pound of butter beans.

Across the lake the early morning mist had begun to lift as a lazy sun forced itself above the tops of the trees and beamed happily upon the camp, which was dominated by the large, central yurt occupied by Malroth and whichever unfortunate woman happened to have inadvertently taken his fancy of late. Twenty-two more yurts of varying sizes, but all smaller than the leader's own immense affair, were dotted about the patch of ground rising gently from the lake shore, to form a rough semi-circle around the larger construction. A long, limestone bluff rose to a height of at least one hundred and forty feet behind the portable dwellings, and the broad, shallow river with its undulating bed of rocks and pebbles expanded to form a small lake that bounded the far side of the encampment, before making its exit via a series of cascades in to a winding gorge. On the far shore of the lake, beyond this easily defensible haven, lay a narrow area of open grassland some sixty yards in width at its broadest and rimmed by the edge of the great forest. The camp had become a more or less permanent fixture, and after three years during which no enemy had ever been foolhardy enough to attempt an assault, many of the occupants had become dangerously complacent.

In addition to the thirty or so men who did most of the looting, pillaging and ravishing, there were at least half as many more, less accomplished, armed defenders and lookouts, plus a lame but skilful older man who repaired weapons and fashioned horseshoes, two ever busy cooks whose culinary skills left a great deal to be desired but made up for it to some extent with the quantities they produced, and twenty or more women who made, washed and repaired clothing, helped with the cooking and had sex with the marauders, usually by choice though rarely with any great enthusiasm, given how many of them went down with the clap. There were no children because Malroth saw them as a weakness and had his men abandon any that had been born at the camp, at night at the edge of distant settlements (where they were usually eaten by bears, mountain lions or Kolyn the Cannibal), although of late he had begun to consider to whom he might one day pass all of this on.

Some mothers chose to crawl off into the forest and have their baby alone, there. Most of them died from hypothermia, attack by wolves or bears or lack of food and water. There was also a small stockade, erected around the mouth of a low, shallow, stinking cave, where prisoners were kept. Rich prisoners were retained for ransom, the poor for sport. Between raids, to keep the men sharp, the younger prisoners were released and then hunted by those due to go out on the next raid. Few older prisoners were ever brought back, but those that were could expect to be used as slaves until they were too old to fetch and carry, at which point they were used for target practice, or executed in a variety of inventive ways for Malroth's amusement or to vent his frequent and frequently irrational wrath.

On this particular morning, with many of the occupants of the camp just beginning to stir from a drunken slumber following the previous night's impromptu feast, the camp was suddenly roused by the sound of a warning horn being blown. Norvul stepped quickly outside Malroth's yurt and stared up at the craggy promontory to the South of the camp, to where the lookout who had sounded the alert was holding up two fingers; two men, approaching on foot. Had they been on horseback, the sign would have been two fingers from either hand, locked in a dovetail.

Norvul assumed the two men were the pair he had sent out at dawn to search for Ozzmunn and the others, but why were they returning so soon, if they had found no trace of the party sent to bring back the witch who mixed potions? And what had happened to the three men he had sent out again yesterday to search for

Lard? If they failed to return as well, then the next raid would have to be scaled down or leave fewer men to defend the camp. Either way, he did not relish the prospect of explaining the situation to Malroth. Men had had their tongues cut out for far less dispiriting news. The fact that their leader's dowry laden bride-to-be had yet to arrive either did not even bear contemplation.

CHAPTER THIRTY

"LaaaaaAaaaarrrrdddddd…aaaaarrrrrddddd…aaarrrdd…arrd…rd…d!"

The call echoed down the narrow gorge through which the river rushed and tumbled in its headlong descent to a deep pool it had scoured out over Grun alone knew how many millennia. The pool opened the waterway in to a broader, calmer run at the head of a small valley on either side of which irregular ranks of trees had, over several decades, advanced down the slope almost to the banks. Three heavily armed riders were descending the defile along a narrow track that followed the watercourse, but some thirty feet above it.

"Lard, you fat bucket of rotting guts, where are you? Malroth wants you back, although Grun alone knows why. He says all is forgiven." called the lead rider, leaning in to the cliff face to his left and trying not to look down to his right, where the foaming river crashed noisily over a cluster of lethal looking rocks.

A little over one hundred yards ahead of the party and some fifty feet above them, Blunt and Jennah observed the trio's cautious progress along the narrow, loose stoned and slippery track through the gorge.

"Nice of them to confirm their identity." The blacksmith whispered in to Jennah's right ear.

"Very. So, what do we do now?" she wanted to know.

Blunt considered the question carefully. They could simply remain hidden and let the marauders continue on their way, or they could attempt to lower the odds still further.

"Accidental it may have been, but falling on their comrades from a great height worked a treat last time. These three villains are in an even more vulnerable position and on this occasion it would be no accident, as I have no intention of pushing my luck by tumbling over another cliff. Nobody gets that lucky twice in one lifetime."

"I'm glad to hear you've ruled out that possibility, but how do you intend to stop them? Shout down: 'Gentlemen, can you all please sit still while I take aim.' They're not simply going to pause astride their horses while you attempt to pick them off with your arrows."

Ignoring her sarcasm, Blunt stretched out his left arm and pointed past her to a clutch of small boulders perched right at the edge of the cliff on which they were lying.

"All we need is a stout branch to lever that heap of rubble over the edge."

Jennah chewed at her lip for a moment as she flicked her gaze between the riders, river and rocks, considering the plausibility of his suggestion.

"Oh, is that all? It may have escaped your notice, but the nearest trees are way down there in the valley, unless…"

Blunt was intrigued. He had already learned to trust this remarkable woman's judgement.

"Unless what?"

"There is a stout lance amongst the weapons we collected, as I recall."

"By Grun, you're right! That should do the trick, provided it doesn't snap under the strain. And even if the rocks don't fling the buggers in to the river they should still smash away the ledge ahead of them. Whatever the result, the animals are going to be panicked and difficult to control. There's no room for them to turn around on that sliver of a path, so even if their riders do succeed in calming the beasts they'll still have to dismount and proceed to try and lead them backwards for more than a mile. Either way, they would play no further part in the defence of Malroth's camp."

"And if our timing of the avalanche is poor?"

Blunt shrugged his great shoulders. He had hoped she would not ask him that question.

"They'll assume it was a natural landslide…I expect."

"You expect? But if they don't assume it was a natural event…if they assume that someone up here was trying to kill them?"

Blunt smiled her a confident smile that belied his lack of confidence in his own suggestion. He knew she was right to feel apprehensive and sought to put both of their minds at rest.

"I have yet to meet the horse that can climb a sheer rock face, and men accustomed to fighting on horseback tend to feel at a distinct disadvantage fighting on foot against an enemy they cannot see. Don't worry, Jennah. We will be long gone before they find a way up here, even if they do survive. Now go and fetch me that lance while I choose a suitable fulcrum to aid me in prising our bombardment loose."

The boulders the blacksmith had selected for the task formed a rough pyramid with the largest one perched precariously on its narrow end atop a slightly inclined and surprisingly thin, flat slab, almost as though Nature had posed it thus in anticipation of a photo opportunity in aeons as yet undreamed of. Ignorant of the sculpture's future social media potential, Blunt accepted the lance from Jennah and slid the bronze head and a third of the shaft beneath the more eroded side of the rock and lodged the head in a cleft to test the stone's stability. To his surprise it did not even budge, the bulk of its mass concentrated down through the slender tip in to the rocks below, and the three riders were now no more than thirty yards away.

"Jennah!" he hissed.

"You'll have to give me a hand with this; the bastard…pardon my Delirian…won't move."

Jennah crept over and knelt beside the blacksmith.

"Okay, what do you want me to do?"

"I know it risks giving away our position, but you'll have to stand on the slab below, astride the shaft of the lance, and lean your back in to this stubborn brute; it's the only way we'll get it to move in time."

Jennah nodded and climbed on to the suggested slab without another word, before turning around to face him. Splaying her feet either side of the shaft of the weapon, she leaned her shoulders back against the perched boulder, arms at her sides, hands flat against the lower portion of the rock and stared at Blunt in anticipation.

"Say when."

"When it starts to…"

Blunt had intended to say: 'When it starts to move, jump clear and the removal of your weight and that of the boulder will release the tilted slab beneath you and start a chain reaction that will carry all of these stones in to the gorge.' but all Jennah heard was 'When'.

With a mighty backwards thrust she forced her entire weight in to the rock, which immediately leaned towards the gorge with a grinding sound as its narrow base spun out of perfect perpendicular balance, allowing the whole mass to topple almost soundlessly over the ledge, taking Jennah, who did not go soundlessly, with it. Blunt, who had been leaning all of his own considerable weight in to the wedged lance, discovered that with the sudden release of tension the shaft sprang upright from the end he was clutching, catapulting him across the narrow chasm and depositing him with a resounding thud in to the dust of the opposing cliff top. Startled by the inexplicable commotion, the bemused lead rider on the narrow ledge below looked up to be greeted by an all too brief glimpse of a screaming rock hurtling towards him at terminal velocity. A millisecond (possibly even a nanosecond) later he was dashed from his mount in to the raging torrent below.

His companions witnessed this extraordinary spectacle in stunned silence, following man, boulder and woman's descent into the river in disbelief. Had they been more alert to the ancient landmark's undignified removal, they might have paid more attention to the potential consequences, but so fascinated were they by the groaning woman now attempting to peel herself from the precariously lodged boulder, and the increasingly crimson colouration of the water issuing from beneath it (not to mention the panicked reactions of their companion's horse), they failed to notice the rest of the avalanche until it struck the track just yards ahead of their position. As the Wylie Coyote style fractures zigzagged back along the narrow ledge towards them to the accompaniment of a series of alarmingly loud reports, their ponies reared anxiously in anticipation of an early bath. With a final, almighty crack that rang the length of the gorge and back again, men, horses and a great many tons of dislodged rock thundered in to the river, creating a miniature tidal wave that washed the still confused and severely winded Jennah from her perilous perch.

"Shit!" exclaimed Blunt, watching in helpless horror from the edge of the opposite cliff.

"That's torn it."

CHAPTER 31

It took Gorm and his newfound traveling companion four more days to reach the clustered yurts of Malroth's camp, during which time the young warrior learned a great deal from Lard's boastful attempts to ingratiate himself. The raiding party was now made up of somewhere between thirty and forty men, but the hardcore of original fighters numbered between fifteen and twenty, the rest having joined them in ones and twos as they passed through the numerous kingdoms and principalities through which they had cut a bloody swathe. Despite the undignified and potentially terminal treatment that had been meted out to him, it had since become evident to Gorm that Lard was also anxious to ingratiate himself with Malroth again at the earliest opportunity, and the big oaf continued to sing his former leader's praises throughout their journey.

"Naturally, being a beneficent sort, Mal will reward you handsomely for your sterling efforts upon his noble gob, but by way of compensation for having pointed you in his direction, I have a smallish favour to ask?"

"Oh?" Gorm turned to look at the fat man labouring in his wake, as they struggled up a particularly steep, densely wooded hillside the youth knew to be a totally unnecessary ascent.

"Yes, perhaps you could put in a good word or two on my humble behalf?"

Gorm smiled.

"Of course. You have proved excellent and most interesting company Lard and it would be the least I could do, but I don't really see the need. After all, didn't you say that you and Malroth are the very best of friends…blood brothers, even?"

Lard positively dripped gratitude, laced liberally with sham insouciance.

"Ah, yes, I did say that, didn't I, my noble young friend…and spoke nothing more than the truth, naturally, but we didn't exactly part as chums when I took my leave of his band, and he may still hold a very slight grudge against me as a result...not that he's the type to hold a grudge, of course."

Just how slight Gorm was to discover that same afternoon,

when they finally met up with Malroth and his marauders on the shore of the currently placid waters of Lake Vuronicuh, deep within the heart of the Darklands, where the band maintained their pitched camp.

"Uh swaw thut if ah evah set ahhs on yuh ugly mug agun, ah wud kull yuh on the sput." mumbled Malroth through a mouth contorted and swollen by the now spectacularly gross abscess disfiguring his jaw.

Skipping lightly over this reminder of his imminent demise, Lard indicated the strapping lad beside him with an outstretched palm.

"This..." he paused momentarily, for dramatic effect, "...handsome youth I have brought hither for you is none other than Gorm, once apprenticed to the finest tooth-puller in all Deliria, but now a fully-fledged and vastly experienced extractor of molars and other assorted dental paraphernalia in his own right."

"Uz thus truh, buyh?"

"There is none finer in all Deliria, save for my former master, Yankyt Owtt." replied Gorm, without the slightest hint of the trepidation he now felt at the predicament he had got himself in to. Seeing his huge adversary at first hand had put an entirely different perspective on the possibility of killing the man with his bare hands...or anything else, for that matter. The prospect of having to also kill the evil looking band of armed to the teeth murderers protecting him was one to be set aside for the present, in favour of trying to stay alive long enough to come up with a workable plan. The fact that he had just spent weeks doing nothing but coming up with elaborate plans for their collective demise was no longer of any consequence, given the blatantly obvious fact that not one of his avenging schemes was likely to succeed.

"Und thus?" enquired Malroth, indicating the bulging abscess with the tip of a cautious index finger. Gorm knew instinctively from the man's expression that failure here was not an option, and that any pain over and above what the marauder was already experiencing would result in his own painful and untimely death. He tried to think back to what the village medicine woman might have used to cure such an affliction, but it was not easy. There was nothing wrong with his memory, but the thought of actually assisting in relieving the pain of his bitterest enemy was muddying his clarity of thought. A little lateral thinking soon put that right; he would simply kill the man somehow, as had been his intention all along, and suffer the consequences, which he could only hope (somewhat unrealistically, if we're to be truthful about this) would be swift and clean.

"It can be done," he said, "but I will need hot water, a sharp blade, clean rags, ginger root, juniper and nightshade berries…"

Malroth's face darkened, ominously.

"Nutshud iss uh poisson!"

Gorm stalled, his lack of understanding of the blending of all these ingredients, if indeed they should be blended, stranding him without a suitable reply.

"I agree, sir." Another voice intruded from somewhere amongst the gathered crowd of surly cutthroats.

"As the son of a medicine woman, I have some knowledge of these things, and our guest is right. The only way to fight the poison that afflicts your jaw is with another poison."

Startled by the intervention of his unknown saviour, Gorm glanced around in search of a face to put to the voice. His gaze settled at last on a strapping, dark haired, relatively clean-shaven lad no more than two or three years his senior, and with the briefest nod of gratitude for the additional thinking time, he accepted the lifeline and hauled himself to relative safety.

"Our friend over there speaks the truth. The poison in your jaw, Lord Malroth, is immune to the more common medicinal herbs, because it draws its power to inflict pain from your own great strength. To combat that power, we must pit it against a poison not of greater, but of equivalent power. Like two warriors, matched like for like in strength, wit and armour, they will wear each other down, without either one ever gaining the upper hand. When the abscess has been subdued thus, when it is at its weakest, then I shall pull your tooth, without pain or injury, and you will be well again."

"Uh wull?" mumbled Malroth, his voice tinged with doubt, but his expression one of desperate hope (or hopeful desperation, depending on how you look at it).

"Most assuredly."

"Thun luts duh it!"

"Very well," said Gorm, "but I shall need an assistant."

He pointed directly at the lad who had spoken up on his behalf (let's face it, he didn't have much option).

"He seems to know what he's talking about, even if he does look a bit dim. He'll do."

The tall youth was pushed to the front to stand beside young Gorm. As several members of the band were dispatched by Norvul to fetch the paraphernalia and ingredients Gorm had requested, the lad inclined his head towards Gorm and murmured in a low, but threatening tone:

"Any more cracks like that and your parents will be Gormless, not me."

"My parents are dead," hissed Gorm, "and you killed them!"

The other youth was taken aback by the vehemence of Gorm's accusation.

"You're crazy! I've never even met your parents." he hissed angrily, dropping his voice before anyone noticed their brief, verbal altercation. Gorm glanced up at him and the older youth shuddered in spite of himself. He did not like the look of the look he was getting; it was the kind of look a hungry lioness gives a hyena that is about to sneak off with one of her cubs.

"Hot water, a sharp blade, clean rags, ginger root, juniper and nightshade berries…anything else you're going to need?" Norvul enquired of them, breaking the spell locking their respective gazes.

"Yes," replied Gorm, "we must have absolute quiet…no interruptions. You had best clear this rabble from our midst."

He glanced slyly at Malroth.

"I doubt Lord Malroth would wish this delicate operation to provide entertainment for his men."

"Are you sure you know what you're doing?" whispered his young companion."

"No, but I assume you're going to put me right, son of a medicine woman."

The youth grinned sheepishly.

"I lied. She was a prostitute…and a bloody good one by all accounts, but I always felt medicine woman sounded more socially acceptable. She did know her arsenic from her elbow though. She was really in to all that mixing of potions malarkey."

"So she was kind of a medicine woman, after all?"

Ranuk shook his head.

"Nah, she used to poison her rich clients and rob them while they were spewing their guts up."

Gorm continued to smile in Malroth's direction as he commenced mixing the potion with the mortar and pestle that had been provided, but muttered out of the side of his mouth:

"Look, I don't know why you spoke up for me in the first place..."

"Stands to reason, surely. I thought if I could help you help Mal, it would put me in good favour with him and perhaps push me up through the ranks."

"I'm not going to help the bastard, I'm going to kill him, so if you're going to give me away, get it over with. If not, let me get on with what I have to do. That monster over there murdered everyone I have ever loved…all of them, and now he is going to pay the price…and that price is his own, worthless life."

The startled youth poured a little more water in to the pestle at Gorm's indication.

"Kill him and the rest of them will kill you, and it won't be swift and clean!" he hissed under his breath, as though he had been able to read Gorm's thoughts of a few moments ago.

"As long as I kill that murdering bastard first, I don't care what they do to me. He butchered my parents, my friends, my neighbours, hacked down fleeing women and children in cold blood, butchered babes in their cribs, even tortured family pets."

Ranuk's face darkened as he listened to this litany of horrors. He placed a hand on Gorm's shoulder and spoke earnestly.

"I was not a part of any of that, I promise you."

Gorm stared hard at him, looking for evidence of deceit, but could find none.

"Perhaps, but you *are* now a part of his bloody band of cutthroats and rapists."

"I was bored, Gorm. I'm eighteen years of age and I wanted action and adventure. When Malroth's men rode across the border in to Malherya looking for fighters to swell their number, I jumped at the chance to ride with a band of fearless mercenaries, which was how they portrayed themselves, but I have never drawn my sword against an unarmed man, let alone a defenceless woman or child. On that you have my word."

Gorm studied the youth's face intently and decided he was telling the truth.

"But you did take part in the raid on the village of Nurk...my village, less than six weeks ago."

The older lad shook his head.

"I joined up with them just two weeks since and have seen no action yet, but if, as you say, these murderous thugs are butchers of innocents and those unable to defend themselves, then I promise you I want no part of that. I seek to make a name for myself as a warrior in honourable conflict."

"Then you had best stay well away from me, or your first taste of battle is likely to be your last." Gorm warned him.

Ranuk leaned his head in closer and whispered:

"I have no quarrel with you, but I could be persuaded to support your quarrel with them."

The big youth straightened and stared intently at Gorm for a moment, then plucked up the dagger from beside the pestle, put it to his right wrist and cut slowly in to a vein until the blood welled to the surface and began to trickle across his skin. Satisfied, he handed the dagger to Gorm and held his own wrist upright.

"My name is Ranuk, and having no brother of my own, I seek a blood brother. One who is equal to myself in strength, courage and honour. One who will stand side by side with me in battle, back to back with me at the last. One who would shed his blood for me, give his life for me, just as I would for him."

Gorm smiled grimly, accepted the proffered dagger and cut in to his own wrist. As the blood welled up to the surface of his skin, he clasped Ranuk's arm and dragged it over the mixing bowl, so that their mingled life fluids dripped in to the contents of the vessel.

"Then we shall be blood brothers," he confirmed, "now and for all time!"

"Aye," replied Ranuk, "now and for all time, brother!"

CHAPTER 32

Jennah fluttered her watering eyes open and was confused to be presented with a blurred view of the world tilted at ninety degrees to the vertical, so that the hefty, wild looking, blood stained man wading waist deep through the water towards her, double-headed battleaxe held above his head with both hands, appeared to be impervious to the lure of gravity as he approached from a seemingly impossible to sustain angle, while the river flowed briskly past her from the general direction of what should have been the sky. She shook her head vigorously in an attempt to clear it and realized she was clinging to a more or less horizontal branch that her lengthwise weight had lowered almost to the surface of the water. Her pigtail was streaming away from her like a curious frond and every moment or two moving water splashed in to her mouth.

The transfixed herbalist continued to stare at the wading man, who had already halved the distance between them and was moving more easily as the decreasing water level of the shallows receded to the depth of his upper thighs. Her ancient instincts screamed at her to tear her gaze away and attempt to free herself, but she continued to watch in morbid fascination as her putative executioner lowered the axe to chest height and adjusted his grip, so that it was held out to his right side in preparation for a scything motion. The crystal droplets trickling in apparent slow motion along the slightly angled edge of his blade appeared to be presaging the forthcoming ebbing of her life's blood, but the enraged marauder was forced to pause for a moment as one of his companions drifted between them, face down in the water and clearly dead as a Foofoo (a distant relative of the Dodo and equally extinct).

What had happened to Blunt, she wondered as paralysis gave way to panic? Was he dead, too? If so, it appeared she was about to join him in the afterlife, for the mad axeman was on the move again and heading ever more menacingly in her direction. Rather than waste time and effort in screaming (although the temptation was considerable), she opted for the more practical course of attempting to free herself before her advancing nemesis could reach her. Wriggling furiously, she realized with a sinking heart that her dress had snagged more than one branch, and noticed too that the end of her pigtail had just become wedged in the fork of yet another branch, just below the surface of the water. To add to her terror, Jennah could also now hear the splashing made by the raider's legs above the other sounds of running water as they forged their way through the increasingly shallow river. She looked up again anxiously and was distraught to see that he had advanced to within no more than five yards of her and was raising the axe above his right shoulder once more, having realized that a downwards slash was likely to be far more productive in the decapitation stakes.

The marauder's expression mutated to a evil grin as he snarled:
"I'm going to ram your severed head on to a sharpened stake and leave it for the crows to pluck out your eyeballs, you evil, murdering bitch!"

Seeing no plausible alternative, Jennah gave up struggling to free herself in favour of the pathetic screaming she had previously eschewed, but this was not for fear of losing her head so much as the hot, animal breath suddenly circulating in her ear and the huge teeth grazing the skin on the nape of her neck as they clamped down on to the rear folds of her dress, dragging it tight against her throat. Suspecting a hungry mountain lion or cave bear, but unable to twist and confirm the identification for fear of being unable to avoid the battleaxe, she was yanked bodily from the branch, her dress tearing in several places as the descending blade kissed the spray of hair behind her ear and severed the very end of her pigtail, before thudding in to the branch in which it had become trapped.

"What the f...!"

The marauder's incomplete exclamation hung in the air, while his blood sprayed the herbalist from head to foot like paint flung from a brush, as the arrow that had severed his spinal chord and trachea punctured his throat from within. The projectile stopped abruptly, several inches clear of his Adam's apple, as the progress of the shaft was finally brought to a standstill by the muscle and sinew descending from the man's neck to his shoulders.

"Oh!" exclaimed Jennah, as she was lifted free of the undergrowth and lowered carefully on to the small beach of white shingle, still reeling from the unfolding sequence of events. She blinked her eyes in amazement at the second man wading across the river towards her, hunting bow balanced horizontally in his left hand and his chest still heaving from the exertion of having just employed the weapon.

"B...B...B...?"

"Of course it's me!" exclaimed Blunt.

"Who else were you expecting?"

Jennah grimaced and jerked a thumb over her shoulder, still not daring to risk a look behind her.

"Bear?"

The blackmsith laughed and shook his head.

"Horse. And nothing to do with me; it must have been all his own idea."

Turning over on to her hands and knees, the herbalist scrambled to her feet and stood staring in amazement at the enormous white horse, which rolled his head from side to side and bared his teeth in what could only be described as another cheesy grin. Jennah struggled to her feet, flung her arms around the animal's neck and planted a big kiss on his muzzle.

"You saved my life, mister horse. Thank you. I shall never forget your courage today."

Concorde whinnied happily, pushed his muzzle between the firm slopes of Jennah's sodden bosom and waggled it from side to side, causing her to giggle. Pushing herself away from the animal, she turned to Blunt as he stepped from the water's edge on to the shingle.

"Nor yours, blacksmith."

Blunt shrugged his shoulders as though it was nothing.

"Couldn't allow you to lose your head over another man. So, does my chivalry mean I qualify for a kiss, too?"

Jennah stood back and studied him in silence for a moment, before declaring.

"Oh, I think you qualify for a lot more than that, Blunt...but you may have to wait a little longer. We've encountered seven of Malroth's men in the last few days, so we cannot be far from his lair. If your young friend Gorm is still alive, we must make haste before the great sword of the Gods falls in to the hands of an unspeakably wicked man, who will not hesitate to abuse its power in the name of Evil."

Blunt considered this statement for a moment.

"I thought you said there could be only one who is capable of wielding the sword of the Gods?"

Jennah appeared not to have heard him as she regarded the remnants of her dress in dismay; they revealed far more of her womanly charms than she was accustomed to having on display. Blunt regarded the revelation of her womanly charms too, with something more akin to approval.

"I did," she muttered, attempting to pull the unnatural seams of her shredded garment together in a belated attempt to preserve a modicum of modesty, "but for every good in the world I believe there is a comparable evil...and, if that be the case, there may also be a Wicked One capable of wielding the sword...and I know of no man more wicked than Malroth."

CHAPTER 33

"It is ready, Lord Malroth." Gorm announced, carrying the bowl of liquid carefully across the clearing to where his intended victim sat nursing his ever increasing agony. Ranuk followed close behind, watchful for the least sign that their ruse had been rumbled. Despite his desperation, Malroth continued to eye them suspiciously, trusting neither youth. There was nothing unusual in this mistrust, however. The marauder did not trust anybody...ever...which was how he had managed to stay alive for thirty-nine years, while all of his siblings and many of his contemporaries had perished, frequently at his own hands and just as frequently at his command.

"Wut wus yuh tooh doon uver thur?"

Gorm knew their actions had been observed intently and had prepared himself for this very question.

"For the potion to be most effective, it has to be sealed with the spilling and mingling of youthful blood, sir. Not only will this aid your recovery, Lord Malroth, it will also rejuvenate your already extraordinary limbs and mind with some of our own youth and vigour."

From a study of his resultant expression, the idea evidently appealed to Malroth, despite his misgivings concerning the content of the bowl.

As an afterthought, Gorm added:

"This is, of course, a most powerful elixir and you may experience some initial discomfort as it battles with the evil distempers poisoning your blood, before it can administer its balm. Only once the medicinal effects have overcome those distempers can I pull the offending tooth from your head and release you from the grievous prison of your agony."

Gorm held out the mortar and Malroth accepted it from him with remarkably steady hands. Slowly he raised the bowl to his disfigured face, bent forward and sniffed at the contents, like a wolf sniffing at a marker left by a wolf from another pack. With his head still bowed over the bowl, the leader of the pack raised his eyes to meet Gorm's own.

"Nut un unplusunt ohdur, yung pullah uf tiith."

Gorm held the man's gaze steadily and prayed his surly bowels would not give him away.

"I am a great believer in sweetening the medicine, sir. Why make it more unpleasant than it need be?"

"Hhmmm."

Malroth sat up straight and lowered the bowl to his lap, watching the two youths standing before him for the slightest indication of disappointment, but neither of them gave themselves away. Both knew this game was being played for keeps. If either of them allowed their mask of indifference to slip for even one fraction of a second, the terrifying man before them would detect the weakness instantly.

"Luuurd!"

"Beg your pardon, sir?" said Gorm.

"He wants Lard." Norvul enlightened him. Even he had managed to interpret this particular demand.

"Laaaard!"

"Somebody call me?" enquired Lard, from what he hoped was going to continue to prove a safe distance.

"Lord Malroth wants you at his side, so get your big, fat, forever farting arse over here…now!"

Lard set down the bowl of heavily seasoned Calabar bean soup he had been wolfing down, pushed his way through the crowd and crossed the clearing to stand reluctantly before his master.

"You rang, sire?" he jested, nervously.

Malroth smiled, grimly.

"Um prumuting yuh."

"Really?"

Lard beamed at this unexpected turn of events. Fetching the young tooth-puller here had obviously been a masterstroke on his part.

"Yus…tuh mah uffishial tastuh."

He lifted the bowl from his lap and held it out for Lard to accept. Gorm and Ranuk snatched nervous glances at one another as the fat man blanched at the prospect of consuming their concoction.

"But I don't have toothache!"

"He has a point, sir." Gorm suggested, trying to sound

reasonable, but unconcerned.

"The quantity of nightshade I have used is equal to the distemper of your decaying tooth, but for a man unaffected by such a diseased jaw, the concoction could prove dangerous."

"Mmm, fatal, even." Ranuk added.

Gorm glared at him, but said nothing more.

Malroth smiled evilly, the action distorted by his misshapen features.

"Nurvul."

"My Lord?

His second in command stepped forward, ever eager to please, until the opportunity to rid himself of the savage moron without fear of failure or reprisal presented itself.

"Luuurd dssnt huv tuthuch." he pointing out, helpfully indicating his own jaw with an index finger, before aiming the digit at Lard's unblemished cheek.

"But sire…" Lard began to protest, but not swiftly enough. The sickening crunch as the hilt of Norvul's sword smashed in to his left cheek caused even Malroth, Gorm and Ranuk to wince.

"He does now." Norvul pointed out, obligingly.

"Uxullunt! Nah, yung tuth pullah, wuh will see if yuh poshun wurks."

CHAPTER 34

Blunt and Jennah lay in a shaded patch of long grass at the edge of the forest, studying the comings and goings at the camp across the water. The prolonged squinting against the sunlight reflecting off the mirror-like surface of Lake Vuronicuh had begun to strain their eyes. Finally, tiring of the effort, Blunt rolled on to his back and stared up through the last of the leafy canopy to where the sky performed its daily ritual of changing hues. Ignorant of their presence, an early bat signalled the approach of dusk as it skimmed between a cluster of bulrushes at the water's edge in search of juicy moths.

"Many years ago, as a fresh faced youth journeying from my native Lumbeygoe to Deliria in search of work, I met a brilliant young inventor. I had need to cross the notorious Black Swamp if I wanted to avoid a lengthy detour and the only safe way to cross it was by ferry. The chap who operated the ferry, a genial young fellow named Fyl, had a hutload of his own curious, but extraordinarily useful inventions of every description. If we ever get out of the Darklands alive, I may seek him out and enquire if he has come up with anything for increasing the distance a man can see, because this furtive spying is playing Haletosys with my eyesight."

Jennah rolled on top of him and kissed him, briefly.

"A fascinating little anecdote, my love, but not one of any great use to us at this precise moment."

"Very true, my sweet, but purely a diversion, I have to admit. For once I am at a loss for practical suggestions. We cannot cross the lake unseen, except perhaps at night, and even then it would be dangerous, given how far even the slightest sound travels upon open water of a placid evening such as this. Crossing the gorge downstream would be extremely hazardous and crossing upstream not much less so, because we would be in full view of the sentry up on that promontory, just as we would if we approached by that track the brigands appear to favour. And no doubt there are other sentries scattered about, but hidden from view. But whichever form of access we attempt, it has to be after dark or we will have no hope of success at all."

"Then we find ourselves in need of a miracle…or a diversion, at the very least."

Jennah mused aloud.

Blunt's face brightened immediately at the prospect of a possible solution to what had presented itself as a potentially insoluble problem.

"A diversion? What sort of a diversion did you have in mind?"

"I didn't, but now you come to mention it…"

Jennah puckered her lips, deep in thought, and rolled off the blacksmith and on to her back. Mistaking her expression for an invitation, Blunt rolled on top of her and began kissing her passionately, and was therefore most surprised when she pushed him away with some force (and given the size of him, it could not have been done otherwise).

"Blunt! Can't you think of anything else for once?"

"I have thought of everything else but that for years." He answered, churlishly, if not entirely truthfully.

"Ha! A likely story."

"But, I thought…"

"No, that's just it. You didn't think…or rather, you assumed, which is just as bad, if not worse. Like all men you had nought in mind but the satisfaction of those stupid knobbly bits in your pants."

Blunt decided not to dignify Jennah's unjust accusation with a reply and rolled away from her, surreptitiously tucking away his stupid knobbly bits as he did so. Just a few hours earlier he had saved her life for the second time in a matter of days and this was how she repaid him, with a completely unjustified tongue-lashing. The fact was, he decided morosely, he adored women but did not understand them; they were far too complicated for ordinary male mortals to fathom. He was on much safer ground with problem solving, no matter how complex the problem. Now if only he could come up with a solution to the burning issue of the moment.

The blacksmith sat upright so abruptly Jennah was half afraid she had been too harsh with him and he had determined to abandon her to the approaching night and its unseen, hungry denizens.

"Blunt…are you alright…my darling?"

"Alright? Yes, never better. You were absolutely right, y'know.

We need a diversion. A big one. A huge one, in fact. The biggest diversion ever created."

He chuckled to himself.

"A miraculous diversion!"

He had the look of revelation in his eyes and it worried the herbalist. Her former husband had exhibited precisely that look as he sought to create the perfect Vindaloo (and we all know how that ended).

"And just how do you propose the two of us achieve such a thing?"

Jennah was staring at him as though he had taken leave of his senses.

"We set fire to the Forest of Improbable Fate!"

She was right.

"Blunt, are you insane? It hasn't rained in weeks. If we set fire to the forest, there will be no controlling the conflagration. Have you ever seen a forest fire when it takes hold?"

The blacksmith considered her question for a moment or two.

"Er...no, can't say that I have."

"Well I have and it is absolutely terrifying. The flames can travel at ten times the speed of the fastest man (Hoosane Latch, a Lumbeygan court messenger) on Earth. Even if we did somehow manage to stay ahead of it and launch a boat or raft on to the lake, the flames would light us up like a beacon. We'd be sitting ducks for the marauders' crossbows."

"Oh, they'll light *you* up alright, but you won't be out on the lake and it won't be crossbows they'll have in mind."

"I won't? They won't?"

Blunt grinned fiendishly at her.

"No!"

He stared pointedly at the sizeable tears in her dress.

"You're already halfway there, so strip off the remainder of your clothes."

"What?"

"Take off your clothes...all of them...now! I want you naked as the day you were born."

Jennah glared at him, furious at his unseemly haste in spite of everything she had said to him just a few minutes ago.

"I see I was wrong about you. No, actually, I see that I was right about you before you convinced me that I was wrong about you. You're just another pathetic male, obsessed with rutting, like all the rest."

Blunt ignored the ice in her tone and the somewhat perplexing content of her speech as he informed her:

"I'm going to strip off all of my clothes too, crawl down to the water's edge and smother myself in mud…"

She stared at him aghast, convinced he was now describing some form of supposedly erotic Lumbeygan perversion.

"…then we'll hurry back together to where we tethered the horses, you beautiful, pale and naked, me ugly, naked and black as night. I suggest you unfurl your magnificent, long hair and pull it forward, divided over either shoulder; it will afford your breasts some protection from their lascivious gaze."

"Really? And what, pray, will protect that private place between my legs from such ogling?"

Blunt had thought of that, too.

"You will be seated upon the white horse. His great mane will protect your modesty. We will pack all of our clothing in to a saddlebag. I will help you on to the great, white beast and follow you on the little black pony, fetching the other ponies along with me. If all goes well we shall have need of them 'ere long."

Jennah stared at him, speechless for once. Clearly, he really had taken leave of his senses.

"Once you're a hundred paces ahead of me I'll start a fire, this side of that last clearing. There was a long, natural hollow there that should help to act as a firebreak and prevent the entire forest from burning to the ground. The breeze is blowing steadily towards the lake now so the flames are likely to follow us fairly swiftly, given what you just told me. We will stay within the cover of the trees until we reach the eastern end of the lake, from whence you will proceed across the river to the opposite bank once the trees are well ablaze, and I shall cross a little further upstream where the deeper darkness should remain immune to the light cast by the flames. A pale and beautiful, naked lady upon a great, white stallion will stand out so starkly against the flame-lit night they will not see me following some distance behind on a black pony.

They will only have eyes for you."

Jennah was still too stunned to disagree with him. Instead, she demanded to know:

"And what exactly do I do once I am accosted by those murderers over there? They're not exactly famed for their deferential treatment of women."

Clearly, Blunt had thought through this problem, too. True, not a great deal of thought had been involved, but he had not ignored the probability entirely.

"Identify yourself and demand to be taken straight to Malroth. We already know he has summoned you, so his men are going to be acquainted with the fact. They will not dare harm you while you are under his protection."

"It's being under Malroth I'm worried about."

Ignoring her rejoinder, the blacksmith proceeded to elaborate further.

"Tell him that when his men called at your abode you offered your services voluntarily, at which point they decided to join the search for that character Lard the three thugs in the gorge were seeking."

"And if Malroth proves not to be so gullible?"

"I will be hidden somewhere within the camp by then, if all goes well."

"If all goes...?"

"It will, it will, I promise you!" the blacksmith attempted to reassure her, hastily.

"I will tether the horses safely, find a place to conceal myself until the occupants of the camp are all abed, seek out Gorm and free him. Then we will find *Skullsplitter* and come for you. Surely if I rescue you a third time you must accept that I love you beyond all measure."

Jennah sighed, deeply.

"Oh, Blunt, I must confess I have known that all along...but you are an artisan, a fashioner of horseshoes, not a warrior. Can you really carry off a dangerous escapade like the one you are suggesting?"

Blunt took the herbalist's small hands in his own great paws.

"The three lives I treasure most in all the world are at stake here."

"Three lives could be burned at the stake here, if either of us gets this wrong."

"I know, Jennah...I know. Your most precious life, Gorm's barely commenced young life and my own sorry affair all hang in the balance, so I cannot afford to fail. Let us pray that mighty Grun and every other God you can think of are with us tonight. Now, get undressed woman and get down to business." he urged her, as he began to strip off his layers of clothing. Seeing no plausible alternative, Jennah did as she was bid, slipping off the remnants of her dress. Looking up as he dropped the last vestige of his own attire to the forest floor, Blunt sucked in his breath, drew in his stomach and wondered what on earth such a beautiful young woman saw in a overweight, timid, middle-aged man like him? He could hardly wait to disguise himself with the mud from the water's edge.

CHAPTER 35

Great tears were still rolling down Lard's blubbery, pink cheeks as he raised the bowl to his rapidly swelling lower lip with trembling hands.

"Jus uh sungl sup, suhr? He enquired hopefully of his watchful leader.

"Ur yuh tukn thuh pus?"

"Nuh Lurd, nuh! Us jus muh lup un tung us vuruh swulln n uh cnt tuk prupluh."

"Heh heh, nuh yuh naw hah ut fils, huh? C'mn, drnk uph."

Lard took a brief, tentative sip of the dark, noxious smelling liquid and, despite the intense pain of his bruised lip, cracked lower jaw and several empty tooth sockets, was astonished to discover that it did actually taste pleasantly medicinal. In fact, he decided, as he took a second, longer sip (known in some quarters as a sizeable swig), the legion of assorted pains besieging every bastion of his head did actually seem to be diminishing rather rapidly.

"Huh!" he exclaimed, attempting to smile as relief coursed through his system, like a powerful purgative. The attempt appeared to the onlookers to be a reasonable facsimile of a constipated man attempting to defecate in to a thimble, but the thumbs up as he removed one hand from the bowl was unmistakeable.

"Uts wurkun! Mah Gruhn, uts uctuwully wurkun ulreduh…ulthugh muh vuzhun us uh but wunky." He declared, as his pupils began to dilate, the throbbing carotid pulse in his neck went in to overdrive and he started to sway unsteadily.

"Wuts hupnin t'im?" Malroth demanded to know, although to most of the marauders, watching from a safe distance, the answer was patently obvious.

'He's dying', thought Gorm, echoing the thoughts of the crowd.

Judging from his darkening expression, Malroth had just arrived at a similar conclusion. The young Delirian fought down the panic threatening to engulf him and, in a tone as calm and reassuring as he was able to muster under the circumstances, pronounced:

"It is just the medicine taking effect and working it's powerful magic."

He snatched the bowl from Lard's slippery grasp, before the lurching brute could spill the remainder of the contents.

"What did you say?" Lard asked the fluorescent green, winged creature with the bulging eyes that had just removed the bowl from his hands. His pronunciation was perfectly clear and precise. The gathered crowd, led by Malroth and Norvul, gasped in astonishment.

"And what are you doing with my goblet, creature? I hadn't finished my drink!"

Without waiting for a reply, Lard sat down abruptly in the dust, forcing a small cloud of the stuff in all directions and flattening a yapping terrier that had picked up on the excitement of the crowd and taken to nipping at his heels.

"Mmm, t'was delicious…but I could do with a little nap, now."

And with that he slumped on to his back with yet another dust disturbing thud and was soon snoring loudly, but evidently still in robust health, broken jaw and missing molars not withstanding. There were claps, loud cheers and relieved laughter from the crowd as the little dog dug its way out from beneath him and waddled off in the direction of the yurts, whimpering.

While Malroth looked on inquisitively and Norvul inspected the great lump of sweaty human flesh at his feet for any adverse signs or reaction, prodding him sharply with the tip of his sword for good measure, Gorm whispered to Ranuk:

"How in Haletosys did that happen? He drank enough to kill a herd of buffalo!"

"I smelled calabar beans on his breath." Ranuk, advised him, as though this might actually mean something to his new friend.

"I guess he must have eaten some, recently." he added, stating the obvious.

"They're very difficult to get hold of, but my mother used to say they were an effective antidote to nightshade."

"I take it Malroth doesn't know that?"

Ranuk shook his head.

"Highly unlikely."

Gorm smiled, grimly.

"Then we are still in with a chance, my friend."

As if on cue Malroth looked up from his snoring taster at his two new medicine men.

"Vuruh umprussuve, Gurm uv Duluryah. Futch muh thuh buhl."

Gorm stepped forward with increasing confidence and knelt before Malroth, bowing his head deferentially before offering up the receptacle. Malroth the Malevolent accepted the vessel with both hands, raised it to his mouth and tilted its edge towards his lower lip. Gorm kept his head bowed lest his mortal enemy detect even a hint of his triumphant expression, but sadly that was not to last. As Malroth opened his mouth and began to tilt back his head, the evening sun, sitting low on the horizon, peered from behind a fiery cloud one last time and its lancing rays caught the multi-coloured jewels embedded in the hilt of the sword at Gorm's waist, setting them ablaze with incandescent light. Dazzled by the sudden brilliance, the startled marauder dropped the bowl, its contents spilling in to the dust as he glanced down to see what had blinded him momentarily. His gaze alighted on the glowing, gem-studded grip of Gorm's sword and a crazed look overtook him as he recognized the weapon he had coveted his entire adult life.

"Heh huz ut! Heh huz thuh surd, **Skuhllspluttah**! Seehz hum…seehz thum buth!"

Norvul, nonplussed, cast around frantically for his interpreter, but Malroth had already kicked the kneeling Gorm viciously in the side of the head, and as Ranuk rushed to the aid of his blood brother, he too was knocked to the ground by a series of brutal blows, before being pounced upon by a dozen or more armed men, two women with a thing for teenage boys and three large mongrels who assumed this was either a game or a free for all fight for valuable food. Thoroughly battered and pinned to the earth by numerous willing hands holding down their arms and legs, the two young warriors were rendered completely helpless.

Transfixed by the glowing hilt of the sword, but wary of the curse associated with the legendary weapon, Malroth demanded to know:

"Wur dud yuh gut thuh surd, buyh?"

"It is mine by right." Gorm snarled at him.

"I alone was able to draw **Skullsplitter** from the stonemason and live to tell the tale."

Ranuk regarded his new friend with something akin to awe; the legend of ***Skullsplitter*** was...well, legendary.

Malroth uttered a sardonic laugh that was immediately echoed by his men, who had had plenty of practice. He was about to approach and draw the sword from the impudent youth's scabbard when it occurred to him that the accursed thing might still bring down its terrible wrath upon anyone other than the boy who laid a hand upon it.

"Nrvl, futch muh thuh surd."

"Huh?"

Gorm unwittingly saved the second in command's hide, which just at that moment was in serious danger of being flayed from his flesh.

"Touch my sword, you foul fiend, and you will be cursed for all eternity."

"Possibly even longer." suggested the foul fiend, grinning evilly.

Unlike his leader, Norvul was not in the least bit suspicious when it came to portents, omens, ancient curses and other such pitiful fakery. Trampling over their outstretched legs in his boots, he reached down past the pinioned Ranuk and drew the sword from its sheath at the other youth's waist. To Gorm and his blood brother's collective dismay, absolutely nothing happened. Norvul simply stood there, inspecting the sword at length, sighting along its blade, drawing a fingertip along one edge and blood from said tip, balancing it upon the palm of one hand, swinging it in a series of thrusts and parries until...

"Whun yurve qut funushd...thuh surd, uff yuh plis."

The content of this request may have been entirely unintelligible to Norvul, but the tone in Malroth's voice most definitely was not; it said: 'Fetch that here right now mate or you are a dead man.'

Norvul stepped over the captives and handed him the sword, before indicating the two spreadeagled youths with an inclination of his head.

"And them?"

So fascinated was Malroth by the astonishing sword that he barely registered the question at a conscious level.

"Hmm? Uh, luk thum un thuh stuckadh. Uh wul dil wuth thum

un thuh murnun."

Norvul recalled suddenly why he had been unable to find his interpreter. He had slit Moik's throat and deposited his weighted body in the center of the lake, where it resurfaced from time to time in his nightmares, like a terrible portent of approaching end times and eternal darkness. He shuddered at the recollection of those nightmares, but pulled himself together, turned to face the crowd and called out:

"Where is Arak?"

A tall, rangy looking thug with a menacing scowl that could cause grown men to faint stepped forward from the crowd. He bore more than a passing resemblance to Lee Marvin.

"Here."

"Moik, my second in command, appears to have deserted me. I am appointing you his successor. Do you accept?"

Arak, who was well aware that failure to accept was not an option, was actually delighted with the promotion. He had been planning to kill the spineless Moik anyway, but saved the bother by the man's curious disappearance, although the vaguely corpse-shaped trail through the mud at the water's edge had been something of a giveaway, especially when considering its alignment to Norvul's yurt.

"I do."

"Excellent! Your first duty in your new role is to chain these two halfwits in the stockade and give them any rotting scraps the dogs have refused; it will be a fitting final meal."

Arak was relieved Gorm and Ranuk had been separated from the crowd; it would have proved much more difficult for him to pick out a pair of halfwits had they been standing amongst the rest of the marauders.

CHAPTER 36

From his lonely post of lookout on the limestone crag high above the camp, Aydun watched the diminutive figures below him return slowly to their yurts. A light breeze was blowing across the lake, but barely had the strength to ruffle the surface of the water. As the camp settled down to sleep, little save for the occasional whinnying of one of the horses, the screech of a distant owl or the splash as a fat fish leapt at its unsuspecting, insect prey, disturbed the calm of the night. Above him an entire universe had been unfurled for his sole delectation, so he settled his shoulders back in to a comfortable indentation in the elements smoothed rock that had probably topped the crag for centuries beyond recall (nobody having lived long enough to do so, bar the Old Man of the Mountains who, confident that carbon dating techniques had yet to be invented, let alone perfected, claimed to be more than four thousand years old) to inspect Grun's handiwork.

Night sentry on the crag was considered an onerous duty by many of the marauders, but Aydun rather liked it on evenings like this when all was calm and the air remained warm and fragrant with the scent of pine. The downside was that Malroth was given to making impromptu checks of the position, but since the business with his jaw he had delegated that responsibility to Norvul, whose dislike of heights meant that Aydun was unlikely to be disturbed and could afford to rest for a few minutes, now and again. He took one more, cursory glance around the scene below him, settled further back in to the warm embrace of the rock and closed his eyes.

Aydun was not entirely sure what had disturbed his sleep. The acrid tang of wood smoke often lingered for some time after the campfires had been doused, but the lurid light wavering and shifting beyond his closed eyelids did not correspond to any moonlight he could recall. Nor did the distant crackling and occasional sharp report resemble any of the night time woodland noises to which he was accustomed. The sentry's eyelids flickered open slowly as he struggled from the depths of sleep and continued to widen in horror as the blurred image before him slowly resolved itself in to a glimpse of the inferno of Haletosys. The entire Forest of Improbable Fate appeared to be ablaze. Huge tongues of flame, like solar flares, licked at the burnished underbelly of cloud that had followed the strengthening breeze, and mighty trees crashed burning to the ground, sending showers of hot sparks, embers and ash billowing across the lake towards the encampment.

"Holy mother of Grun!"

Aydun leapt to his feet and grabbed the great alarm horn from where it hung by a leather loop from a forked stake, hammered in to a small crack in the surface of the rock. Stepping right to the very edge of the ledge, he put the horn to his lips and was about to sound a warning blast when a movement way below him and to his right distracted his attention. Glancing down to the point at which the river fanned out to become the slender neck of Lake Vuronicuh, he was astounded to see a magnificent white horse picking its way carefully through the shallows towards the nearside bank and, seated upon its broad back, a very attractive woman, naked but for a garland of woodland flowers in her waist-length, straw-coloured hair, and slender bracelets of wafer thin, beaten gold curling about her limbs.

Aydun lowered the horn and rubbed at his eyes, but when he looked again, not only had the apparition not vanished, but the human element of it was looking directly at him and smiling and waving in what he would later describe to his best friend as a most inviting manner. He waved back, somewhat self-consciously, and almost dropped the horn, reminding him that he had yet to fulfill his duty. Without taking his eyes from the horse or (in particular) the nude woman, he returned the instrument to his lips and blew a series of long, lingering blasts, the first of which bore more than a passing resemblance to a strangled fart, on account of his distraction.

Some distance back along the river bank and well beyond the glow cast by the towering flames, Blunt smiled a smile of satisfaction as the sound of the horn reached him. The blacksmith loved it when a well laid plan came together, and this particular plan was proceeding like…well, whatever well laid plans proceeded like before the invention of clockwork (although it was more than likely Fyl the Ferryman was already working on something of a similar nature).

CHAPTER 37

Gorm fought his way to consciousness through layers of pain, applied liberally by a welter of boots, fists, clubs and teeth (not all of them canine). He parted bruised eyelids with an effort of will and watched a pair of cockroaches in silence for a moment as they scurried about just in front of his nose. His head felt as though it was being crushed in a vice, his chest burned with each inhalation of breath and his arms and legs felt like they had been ground beneath a millstone. But what of Ranuk, he wondered? Was his newfound friend still alive? After so many weeks alone, the thought that he might already have lost his only ally gave him a sick feeling in his bruised guts that served only to accentuate his abject misery. He had come so close to avenging his family, only to have his mortal enemy triumph right at the very moment of his own, imminent victory. How could Grun be so cruel, so insensitive to injustice?

A metallic sounding movement close at hand, followed by a long, loud, anguished groan, distracted the young Delirian from his self-pitying reflection. Struggling in to a semi upright position, supported by his forearms and elbows, he turned to look to his other side. Even in the unleavened gloom at the rear of the small cave he was just able to make out another human form beside him.

"Ranuk?"

"I think so. Most of me, anyway. That you, Gorm?"

"More or less. Mostly more, judging by the extent of the pain. How is your head?"

"Not nearly as sore as my bollocks."

Gorm attempted a grin, although the result bore more resemblance to an agonised grimace, given his split lips, swollen eyelids and heavily bruised features. Nevertheless, his eyes were beginning to adjust to the minimal light and he could see Ranuk's manacled hands exploring his sorely mistreated groin with great tenderness.

"Some bastard stamp on them?"

"I wish. One of those bloody dogs sank its teeth in to me! I was scared it was going to tear my cock right off and eat it." he explained, examining the offended appendage at length and with considerable care.

Gorm was forced to stifle his laughter to avoid attracting unwanted attention from the guards he assumed would be patrolling outside, but his own, manacled hands rattled with the effort. He stared down at them; there was just eight inches of heavy chain linking the two iron wrist cuffs. He peered down at his feet; they too were chained and manacled. Another length of chain linked the wrist and ankle chains, meaning he would be unable to stand fully upright, even if he did manage to get to his feet. The final security measure was yet another chain, one end of which was linked to the left ankle cuff and the other to an iron ring hammered in to the wall, six inches above the floor. Ranuk, he noted, was similarly secured.

"Where are we?" Ranuk wanted to know, as he too struggled in to a semi sitting position to the accompaniment of a series of agonised groans.

"You're the local here. I thought you would have known."

The young Maleryhan turned his head this way and that, squinting in to the gloom."

"I think it might be a cave."

Gorm laughed, in spite of his irritation.

"Of course its a cave, you pillock! The cave within the captive's stockade, unless I'm much mistaken."

Ranuk nodded.

"You could be right."

After a moment or two of reflection on their situation, he added:

"I seem to recall somebody saying something about killing us in the morning. I'm hoping I dreamed that."

"You didn't."

Gorm let the confirmation sink in before pointing out what he considered to be a glaringly obvious fact.

"I doubt Malroth intends it to be quick, either. We need to get out of here before they wake."

It was Ranuk's turn to laugh, though there was little mirth in his reaction, not least because of the fresh wave of pain it invoked. He raised his hands awkwardly and rattled his chains.

"Have you seen how they've trussed us? We're like a couple of campfire ready pheasants, Gorm."

"So, you're happy to sit here until they're ready to cook us, are you?"

"Unless you have a better idea. We may get a chance to overpower a couple of them and grab their weapons when they take these shackles off."

"You think? I do have a better idea, as it happens." Gorm informed him.

"We rip these chains out of the wall, for a start."

Ranuk studied the thick iron rings secured to the base of the cave wall.

"Call me pessimistic if you like, but I don't think those rings are just going to pop out?"

Gorm shot him his best 'Do I look that stupid?' look. Unfortunately, its impact was entirely lost in the gloom.

"Of course not. We'll have to persuade them."

"How? Tell them what a great service they'd be doing the good guys?"

Gorm pushed his friend, playfully.

"Don't be obtuse!"

"What's that mean?"

"Dunno, but my mother used to say it to my father a lot. Anyway, we shuffle over to the wall together and concentrate on one chain at a time. We'll start with yours. The rock is limestone so it's porous."

"It's what?"

"Porous. Means liquids just soaks in to it, I think. Anyway, they've left us a bowl of stagnant water each, so we wet the rock around the ring first, one bowl for each ring. If we can get the right angle on it we could piss on them, too...or I could, at least. I'm not sure your prick is up to anything more than looking pitiful right now." he chuckled, cruelly, before continuing with his suggestion.

"Once we've damped the rock around the rings we place our feet against the wall for leverage, grip the one chain with both hands, take the strain and start to pull slow and hard, to the left, to the right, up and then down…to the left, to the right, up and then down, and so on. Once we've freed your chain, we do the same with mine. Okay?"

Gorm was the younger of the two young men, but Ranuk now

regarded his blood brother with something akin to hero worship.

"Gorm, that is brilliant! It could actually work."

Gorm grinned a mouth full of remarkably white teeth at his friend, having licked off most of the blood in an attempt to rid himself of the metallic taste souring his mouth.

"It will work. It has to work, because I don't have a plan B."

Ranuk looked puzzled.

"What's one of them?"

"Dunno." Gorm admitted.

"But your mother used to say it to your father a lot?"

"No, it just seemed to suit the occasion, somehow. Now come on, let's get to work. It will be light in a few hours so we've no time to lose."

"Okay. Just one more thing."

Gorm waited, impatiently.

"What do we do once we're free of the rock?"

"Seriously?"

"Yeah."

"We sit here and wait for them to come and kill us."

Several seconds passed in awkward silence, before Ranuk punched the Delirian on his shoulder.

"Hey, you were just kidding, right?"

Gorm made a mental note to remind himself that if they ever got out of the Darklands alive, he would be doing all the thinking for both of them in the future.

CHAPTER 38

"Lord Malroth, the forest is ablaze!"

Like Aydun, Norvul's sleep had been disrupted by the towering inferno across the lake, as the great trees put on an unrivalled pyrotechnic display. He was sure he had not heard the alarm sound and suspected the sentry on the crag overlooking the entrance to the camp had been killed and that they were about to come under attack, assuming they were not already. As he had run around the yurts, yelling for people to get up and arm themselves, it had suddenly occurred to him that this was what it must feel like in the settlements they were about to fall upon when raiding. He had dismissed the thought immediately, recognizing it as an unfamiliar moment of weakness, and strode on towards Malroth's yurt.

Pushing his way through the heavy, weatherproof flap without advertising his presence in advance, Norvul paused momentarily at the sight of his leader. For the first time he could recall, Malroth was unaccompanied by one or more naked women. Instead, he lay in the center of his great, rectangular bed of cushions, pillows and rolls stuffed with down, all constrained within a stout wooden frame, curled up in a foetal position on his good side, arms wrapped around the hilt of the sword of the Gods.

When Malroth did not stir, Norvul risked shaking him out of his slumber.

"Lord Malroth, there has been no warning signal, but the great forest is ablaze. We may be under attack."

Malroth opened his eyes and stared stupidly at his second in command, while the information Norvul had just imparted wormed its way swiftly in to some instinctive corner of the big man's brain.

"Whut?"

Before Norvul could reply the night air was rent by what sounded suspiciously like a strangled fart, followed almost immediately by several blasts on the warning horn up on the crag. Malroth leapt up as though he had been struck by lightning, gashing his left arm on the edge of the sword, which fell to the fleece rug beside the bed, staining it with drops of his blood. Another long blast sounded and both men rushed to the entrance flap, forcing their way outside against a panicked guard trying to force his way in to rouse his leader. Malroth stopped in his tracks at the extraordinary sight that met his eyes. The great, dark forest was burning for almost the entire length of the lake, vast flames and a huge cloud of smoke and glowing embers towering in to the night and reflected back from the enormous cloudbank, drifting north on a warm breeze superheated now by the flames. Burning streamers of scorched bark and hot, orange-rimmed ash were drifting down on to the shingle beach on the camp side shore of the lake.

Norvul, who had already seen more than enough, glanced at his bemused leader and decided to assume command of the situation before it spiraled out of control. He snatched a glance up at the crag where the horn had just ceased sounding and saw the sentry illuminated perfectly against the skyline. He was holding the index finger of one hand horizontally above the index finger of the other. A single rider? What did that mean, Norvul wondered? An emissary? A messenger? He would find out soon enough, no doubt. In the meantime, there was a settlement to be saved from a more imminent danger. He turned and addressed the anxious men and women who had clustered around them as they emerged from Malroth's yurt..

"Listen to me, all of you, we need a dozen large buckets. I want two lines of sixteen people each between the yurts and the lake, two teams of ten soaking the yurts. Take one side of the camp each. Six buckets in each line from the lake. Fill them and pass them along the line to the dousing teams as quickly as you can. I also want two runners for each dousing team, to return the buckets to the team leaders at the water's edge. If we do this now we can save our homes and chattels. I will appoint one leader for each of the four teams."

He pointed out those he had already chosen to lead and called out their names.

"The rest of you must all obey their orders without question, just as if I had given them myself. Anyone failing to do so will be executed by me, personally. I must also tell you now that a lone rider approaches. Lord Malroth and I will go to meet him, accompanied by four guards. Now hurry to your assigned posts and act swiftly; there is much at stake, here."

CHAPTER 39

It had taken Gorm and Ranuk almost forty, back breaking, chest bursting, arm wrenching, buttock clenching minutes to loosen the first ring sufficiently for them to pull it free from the rock. After ten minutes rest they began the whole process all over again, on Gorm's chain. To their dismay, the second ring was proving much more resistant to their efforts than the first and their tired and aching muscles were soon burning with the pain of effort. Ranuk released his grip on the chain and tapped Gorm on the shoulder with the bleeding tip of an index finger.

"Two minutes, brother. We cannot keep up this pace. We need to work for five minutes at a time, then rest for two or we will both be dead of exhaustion before they have a chance to kill us."

Gorm shook the sweat from his forehead to imply a negative response to this suggestion.

"I know well from working in the fields to harvest a crop before the rains that if we pause for too long our muscles will simply seize up and stop working altogether. Better to die like this, attempting to escape, than be carried from here to our deaths like two leaves of limp lettuce."

Ranuk was forced to agree, albeit reluctantly.

"I suppose so, but we don't have long; its growing light outside already, and it's looking like it's going to be a very wet day."

"Huh?"

Ranuk pointed towards the entrance of the cave.

"You remember the old tavern saying? Red sky in the morning, landlord's wife shagger's warning."

Gorm grinned ruefully at his friend.

"I haven't had the opportunity to spend much time in taverns, as yet."

Ranuk clapped him on the back, which was neither easy for him to do nor comfortable for Gorm to experience, given their manacled situation.

"Stick with me brother and we'll soon put that right…once we're out of this mess."

Gorm stared towards the entrance, still scarcely able to believe the night was already almost over.

"Ranuk, you great ox, that's not the dawn!"

"It's not?" said Ranuk, puzzled by his friend's inability to spot the glaringly obvious.

"No, they're not fiery clouds; it's a real fire…and judging by the size of those flames in the distance, I'd say the whole forest is ablaze. Come on, let's try this again. Nobody is going to be paying any attention to us for quite a while yet, unless I'm much mistaken."

Clearly, he was much mistaken. No sooner had the pair resumed their painful rotating motion than they ceased again, startled into inactivity by a series of small pebbles being tossed into the mouth of the cave.

"Gorm?"

Silence, as the pair held their breath in disbelief.

"Gorm, is that you I can hear in there?"

"It could be a trap." Ranuk whispered in to Gorm's adjacent right ear. His blood brother stared at him in disbelief.

"A trap? Ranuk, we're beaten black and blue, manacled hand and foot and chained to the wall in a cave in the prisoners' stockade."

Ranuk stared back at him, his expression one of perplexity.

"Not a trap, then?"

"Gorm, answer me, for Grun's sake!" the voice from without pleaded.

The truth was, Gorm had recognized the stage whispered voice immediately, but not allowed himself to believe what he was hearing, given that he had long ago despaired of ever hearing it again in this life.

"Blunt?"

CHAPTER 40

Malroth, Norvul and four brutish, armed to the teeth (one of them actually had armed teeth, having filed his incisors to needle points and sheathed them with tin) guards, sat astride their mounts across the track, waiting impatiently. They did not have to wait long, for out of the flame-leavened darkness and around the base of the limestone buttress that flanked one side of the entrance to the camp, the lone rider appeared. From their open-mouthed expressions it was clear the six men were nonplussed, and none of them was more plussed than Malroth, because of all the things he had been expecting (and his lurid nightmares of an approaching nemesis had taken many forms), a naked young lady upon a white horse had definitely not been one of them. Apparently unconcerned by her lack of attire in their presence, the brazen woman rode her magnificent charger to within ten paces of where the men sat and had the animal pause.

"Lord Malroth of Roobellur, I am Jennah, white witch of the westernmost wing of the Darklands. I believe you sent for me?"

Norvul spoke up before Malroth could get his jaw in to gear, not out of any sensitivity to his leader's affliction, but out of a desire to control the conversation. He believed that if he were unable to understand one half of any conversation that should take place between his leader and their unexpected and undeniably alluring visitor, it would put him at a serious disadvantage. For his part, Malroth now found speech so painful that anything within reason that enabled him to avoid having to indulge in it could be tolerated, for the time being at least.

"I dispatched four heavily armed men to fetch you on Lord Malroth's behalf, yet you arrive alone. How do you explain that, woman?"

Jennah regarded him coldly.

"I did not address myself to an underling, but since Lord Malroth did not interrupt you I must assume you speak with his blessing."

Malroth smiled at that, his face tilting lopsidedly as he struggled to avoid including the grotesque abscess in the motion. The expression afforded his once handsome features the appearance of a particularly unpleasant looking gargoyle.

"When *his* men arrived at my humble abode and acquainted me with his terrible affliction, I volunteered my medicinal services immediately, as any herbalist dedicated to the easing of physical suffering would. The leader of the band...I believe his name is Ozzmunn...then informed me that if I was prepared to make my own way here, he and the others would ride off to assist in the search for an individual named Lard, of whom I know nothing, but believe your leader is anxious to contact."

Malroth and Norvul glanced at one another and the former nodded his approval, while Jennah held her breath and tried to appear unconcerned at the outcome of this meeting.

"Then I thank you...on Lord Malroth's behalf...but would also ask a question of you." replied Norvul, so distracted by their unexpected guest's appearance he forgot that Ozzmunn had been dispatched to fetch her before the search for Lard had been instigated.

"Ask away, sir, and if it is within my power to answer I shall do so, happily."

"This encampment and its occupants have acquired a certain...ah, shall we say...reputation, of which you must be aware. Why then do you arrive here naked as a newborn babe?"

Jennah had already prepared herself for this pretty obvious question as she crossed the river.

"Many of my clients have informed me that anyone foolish enough to arrive unannounced at your camp is summarily executed, for fear they may be a spy or armed assassin. I have been invited hither by Lord Malroth, but arrive unaccompanied out of necessity. Under the circumstances, I decided arriving naked would not only prove I was neither armed nor dangerous, but also pique your interest long enough to keep me alive to offer this explanation."

"Hmmm."

Norvul was forced to admit to himself that her explanation did make a lot of sense.

"And having explained your nakedness, do you now intend to dress? My men can be...unpredictable, where naked women are concerned."

"*Your* men?" echoed Jennah, glancing inquisitively at Malroth, who was not slow to pick up on her emphasis. When she returned her gaze to Norvul, he was glaring at her, angrily.

"Well, be that as it may, I am as you are all aware a witch and must observe certain rituals when the preparation of powerful magical potions is planned. I must remain naked, but untouched by other human flesh, for the mixing of the elixir that will surely cure your Lord's affliction. This process must be completed before the light of dawn disturbs the natural elements I have fetched hither in my saddlebag. However, I also carry a great, scarlet cloak within said bag, with which I will cover my nakedness so as not to inflame the unbridled passions of your men. Such a cloak is permitted when performing mystical rites of this nature."

Jennah was making most of this up as she went along, and hoped the knowledge of her nakedness beneath the soon to be worn cloak would continue to provide a distraction until Blunt had succeeded in establishing the whereabouts of Gorm and the sword of the Gods. She glanced up at the sky to where a bloody looking Moon could be glimpsed occasionally between the scudding clouds, which had begun to break up as the strength of the breeze intensified. The blacksmith still had a couple of hours before daylight in which to locate the boy. She hoped it would prove enough.

"Very well," Norvul replied, "but although it is clear you conceal no weapon about your person, how do we know you do not conceal such a thing in one of your saddlebags?"

"A valid point. Please, feel free to search them."

Norvul was sorely tempted to perform the task himself, but did not wish to appear weak or excitable before Malroth or the men accompanying them. Instead, he flapped the back of his right hand against the left arm of the nearest guard.

"You heard her. Go and search the saddlebags, carefully."

The delighted guard needed no second bidding. The bags hung either side of Concorde's great rump, immediately behind Jennah, and the fumbling marauder was soon investigating them at an unnaturally leisurely pace, as he continued to snatch surreptitious glances at her unnervingly close bare shoulders, back and bottom. In no time at all it became clear to Norvul, Malroth and the insanely jealous trio of remaining guards that the searcher was conducting his investigations blind, so fascinated was he with the smooth curve of her back, swell of her hips and roundness of her pink buttocks, where the pressure from the horse's spine had increased the blood flow.

"Get on with it man!" Norvul yelled at him, and the irritation in his tone finally overcame the man's lust. After a ridiculously brief fumble in the last of the bags, he called out.

"Nothing, sir. She poses no threat."

Norvul was not so sure about that, but kept his counsel for the moment and gave her the benefit of the doubt; that benefit could be rescinded in an instant, should it become necessary to do so.

The guard hurried back and resumed his place in the line, but leaned in to the man to his right and whispered rather louder than he had intended:

"Couldn't get a good look at her tits, but she's got a really nice arse."

Norvul instantly drew a mailed glove from where it had been tucked with its inverted twin over the top edge of his belt. Without a word, he swiped the man hard across the back of his hairless, heavily tattooed head with the handywear, drawing blood.

"Owww!"

Ignoring his exclamation of pain, Malroth's second in command addressed himself to Jennah once more.

"My apologies for the insensitivity of this cretinous oaf, but it is so difficult to find warriors who know how to treat a woman, nowadays."

"Apparently."

"I do have one more question for you." He added, unexpectedly.

"Which is?" Jennah replied, wishing she had been afforded more time to come up with a plausible answer to whatever the question would prove to be. She held her breath, trying to appear unconcerned.

Norvul glanced back over his shoulder to where the forest blaze was fast running out of combustible material as it neared the far shore of the lake.

"What do you know of yon inferno?"

Jennah heaved a tiny sigh of relief and shrugged her shoulders, knowing full well the action would provoke the movement of her breasts beneath her long tresses, and hopefully provide a distraction from any weakness in her reply.

"Nothing, sir, although I suspect it may have resulted from a hunter's carelessly doused campfire. It would not be the first time such a thing has happened and I daresay it will not be the last."

The guards muttered and nodded their heads in agreement and her reply seemed to satisfy their leaders.

"I daresay." Norvul conceded, his gaze still fixed hungrily upon the swellings beneath the curtains of hair draped demurely over her chest. He turned to the guards to his right.

"You men return to the camp and see what help you can give to the water fetching parties."

Turning again, he craned his head forward slightly to address the two men to Malroth's left.

"And you two can resume your positions on guard outside Lord Malroth's yurt, immediately."

The men hurried off to take up their former positions as Norvul returned his attention to Jennah. From the haste with which his commands had been obeyed and the fact that Malroth had been content to let him give them, she was under no illusion that the second in command was not a man to be trifled with.

"And *you* will accompany us to the Lord's yurt and commence the practice of your witchery, but be warned, woman, I shall be watching everything you do with the utmost care. **Everything**. And should I detect anything amiss…anything at all…even the slightest thing, I shall kill you without hesitation. No warning whatsoever…just a swift and violent death. Understood?"

Jennah smiled at him, but her smile held about as much warmth as an iceberg (the floating ice mountain, not the lettuce).

"I would expect nothing less of you, sir. After all, as Lord Malroth's faithful servant it is your sworn duty to protect him, is it not?"

She knew it was unwise to bait this dangerous thug, but could not resist the temptation to prick his pomposity. For his part, Malroth was unable to resist the painful temptation to smile once more at her impudence. She was a comely wench, he had decided, and would provide great sport and an interesting diversion once the waning of the Moon had released her from the necessity of temporary celibacy. Acutely conscious of their stares, Jennah retrieved the scarlet woolen cloak from her saddlebag and lifted it over her shoulders, but the action did nothing to lessen the intensity of either man's gaze. Gripping the stitched seams of the garment, she pulled it across her chest and snapped shut the bronze clasp at her throat, before urging Concorde towards the two men waiting impatiently for her to join them. As horse and rider drew level Malroth and Norvul turned their own mounts around and took up position, one on either side of the white horse, and escorted the scarlet woman in to their camp.

CHAPTER 41

Just as he had suspected he would, Blunt remained unseen in the darkness some one hundred or more paces behind Jennah, so distracted had the sentry been by her impressive steed and even more impressive nudity. When she finally paused ahead of him at the bend in the track where it rounded the limestone buttress beneath the crag, he dismounted and tethered the ponies to a sapling in a small copse at the base of the rock. Another, slightly lower outcrop, some sixty yards beyond the eastern end of the crag, ensured that the animals would remain invisible from the lookout post. The blacksmith remained there listening for several minutes until Jennah's conversation with the welcoming party ceased and she moved towards them and out of his sight. He prayed to the Gods to keep her safe, pulled on his clothes and buckled his sword belt, shouldered his satchel of tools, slung the quiver and bow over his other shoulder and began to climb the cliff.

Far above Blunt on the topmost crag, Aydun was temporarily out of breath and feeling somewhat light-headed, having sounded the horn for several more minutes, in the vain hope that this would make up for the fact that the alarm had proved a somewhat belated one. He was undecided on whether to remain up here on duty and well out of Norvul's current reach, or risk descending to the settlement and joining one of the watering parties, for despite their best efforts three of the yurts closest to the shore of the lake were currently alight and several more in imminent danger of joining them. In the event he opted for the latter course of action, gathered up his water pouch, shield and spear and began making his way down the well-worn path to the camp, blissfully unaware of the lethal arrow now trained (in the rather obvious absence of a laser targeting spot) on the general whereabouts, give or take an internal organ, of his heart.

Sixty yards away on the lower crag, Blunt relaxed his pull on the bow, returned the arrow to its case and exhaled, quietly. He was relieved he had not had to kill the sentry in cold blood. Taking a man's life when he was attempting to take yours was a necessary, but still deeply regrettable business. Taking a man's life when he was completely unaware of what you were about to do and consequently incapable of attempting to defend himself was an entirely different matter, and one which Blunt had struggled to come to terms with throughout his laboured ascent of the cliff. The sentry had therefore done them both a massive favour by electing to return to the camp; he had inadvertently saved his own life and salved Blunt's troubled conscience in to the bargain.

By the time Gorm and Ranuk had begun to attack the second iron ring there were no more than eighty or ninety trees still burning, and a light rain had begun to fall, producing clouds of smoke and steam that drifted silently across the lake towards the settlement like a dense sea fog, mysterious and somehow menacing. It was just as this fortuitous issue of a preternatural shroud was draped over the camp that Blunt chose his moment. Having followed Aydun down the path at a safe distance and hidden himself behind a cluster of long ago dislodged rocks, he doubled back and untethered the impatient Concorde and the raiders' ponies.

Blunt patted the flank of the great, white horse.

"I know we have not always seen eye to eye, my friend, but I need you to do something for me now. These lesser beasts are herd animals and will follow you. Lead them quietly across the river and in to the forest, then wait for us there."

Concorde nodded his great head and snorted, before leading his newly acquired herd quietly away from the camp, towards the river. Satisfied that the marauders would not be pursuing anyone on horseback, Lard sprinted for the stockade, having deduced that the internment pen would be the most likely place to find his young friend, in the unlikely event that he was still alive.

On hearing the young Delirian's whispered voice from somewhere within the cave, the blacksmith's relief mingled with joy and astonishment in equal measure. Despite his original certainty that the youngster was perfectly capable of looking after himself, the big man had endured six long weeks in which that certainty had been eroded to the point where it had become nought but a filament, strong but fragile as a strand of spider's web. There were tears in his eyes as he crept up to the stout timbers barring entry to or exit from the mouth of the cave and whispered:

"Don't make any more noise. I'm going to sever the lock on this gate while those buggers are still shouting insults at each other. I shall have you out of there in the blinking of an eye."

Gorm and Ranuk grinned at one another, their relief an almost palpable thing.

"Thank Grun, but we have another problem. We are manacled and chained to the wall of the cave."

"We?"

"I am imprisoned here with my blood brother, Ranuk. He saved my life, Blunt."

Blunt nodded in grim appreciation of the debt.

"Then I must save his life, too."

The young warriors listened intently to the noises of rummaging amongst an assortment of tools, followed by a brief silence, which was in turn followed by a sharp, metallic sound, as of a chain being parted forcibly. Within seconds the cave entrance darkened momentarily as the somewhat diminished (to Gorm's considerable surprise) bulk of Blunt blocked out the dying light from the distant blaze. The young Delirian introduced Ranuk and the blacksmith to one another by name, delighted at the unanticipated prospect of two friends, two allies, and the equally welcome prospect of survival. The blacksmith hugged the Delirian briefly and shook Ranuk warmly by the hands, but wasted no more time in following the remaining chain to the wall, where he snapped the link with a large pair of stout metal cutters. The short chains linking their wrists and ankles were dealt with next, but the thick iron bracelets posed a more intransigent problem. Blunt studied them intently for a moment before pronouncing:

"You will have to put up with these for now. I may need the use of an anvil if I am to avoid removing your hands and feet in the process of freeing you. The clasps are of a fiendish design and cannot be easily unpicked. The task would not be impossible, if we had the luxury of time…"

Gorm struggled awkwardly to his feet as his circulation returned. Ranuk did likewise.

"Time is something we don't have, Blunt. Malroth has the sword of the Gods, the mighty *Skullsplitter*."

"We suspected as much. And not only that, Gorm. The monster

also has my woman, Jennah. She is with him at this very moment, buying us valuable minutes, but I fear for her life."

"Your woman?" Gorm grinned at him.

"You kept that quiet, you dirty old rascal."

"It's a long story. I'll tell it to you if we ever get out of this place."

"If we ever get out of this place." Ranuk repeated.

"Sounds like something a minstrel would sing."

Ignoring him, Blunt unbuckled the sword from his waist and handed it to Gorm.

"Here, you'll probably make better use of this than I."

Gorm glanced at the belt in surprise.

"You've pulled it in a couple of notches. What's happening to your belly, Blunt?"

The blacksmith grinned sourly at him.

"You wouldn't believe the amount of exercise I've had in the last few weeks."

He fished about in his satchel for a moment as Gorm buckled on the sword.

"And for you, Ranuk."

He passed the Malheryan a small hand axe.

"It looks a bit puny in your great paw, I'll agree," he admitted, ruefully, "but I suspect it is no less lethal than a sword when used with violent intent."

Ranuk tossed the tool in the air a couple of times.

"Nice balance, easy to grip; it'll do. I can fell a few foul fellows with this."

Blunt slipped the bow from his shoulder and drew an arrow from the case, before glancing at Gorm and Ranuk. They reminded him of two young cave lions, poised and eager to take part in their first hunt…their first kill. He shuddered involuntarily; there was something chilling in their anticipation, a sense of relish for what was to come. And he had no doubt that what was to come would involve an excessive amount of blood letting. He just hoped it would not prove to be their blood.

"Malroth's yurt is at the very centre of the camp. You cannot miss it, for it is at least three times the size of every other dwelling in the settlement. He is there now, together with my Jennah and his second in command, a big, ugly brute whose name I do not know."

"Oh, we know him well enough." Ranuk assured the blacksmith.

"His name is Norvul and he will not forget Ranuk in a hurry, I promise you. That man will not die a natural death. Nor will he die a swift one, but my grinning face will be the last thing he ever sees in this world." the young man boasted, although he was not nearly so confident of the outcome as his declaration suggested. He had never seen Norvul in action, but he had spoken to plenty of the marauders who had.

Blunt shuddered again. Beside him, Gorm patted the blade of his drawn sword and kissed it, for luck. Ranuk ran a fingertip along the blade of the axe, feeling the tiny nicks in the metal where it had come in to violent contact with something hard and resisting. It was still good enough to cleave a skull or two, he decided, before being distracted by Blunt's continuing assessment of their forthcoming task.

"There are two heavily armed sentries outside the yurt. We must first silence them, if we are to gain access. The swifter and quieter their demise, the more chance we have of taking Norvul and Malroth by surprise."

"Then they are already dead men." Gorm said quietly.

"Blunt, when we enter the yurt, your priority will be Jennah. Do you think she can wield a weapon?"

"She is deadly with a bow, Gorm, the finest archer I have ever seen. She has not quite the full strength of a man to draw a great war bow to its full potential, but when using a hunting bow to shoot at anything up to a distance of sixty or seventy paces she is deadly, even when her quarry is moving at speed. She has fed us with the weapon these past days and has yet to miss a target at the first attempt."

Gorm nodded, clearly impressed. Blunt was a superb archer and if he had been impressed by the woman's skill then she must be phenomenally accurate.

"Good, then you must arm yourself from one of the dead guards and give her your weapon. Ranuk and I will depend on the two of you to defend our backs and hold off the marauders long enough for us to kill Malroth and Norvul. They will fight to the death

because we will give them no other option. Understood?"
Blunt clasped his young friend by the wrist.
"We will not fail you, though we both die in the attempt."
"Let us just hope Grun is with us and it doesn't come to that. Are both of you ready?"
"Aye!" they answered him, simultaneously.
"Then let's do this!"

CHAPTER 42

No sooner had the trio of Malroth, Norvul and Jennah stepped beneath the entrance flap of the huge yurt than the woman became businesslike and professional, taking command of the situation before either of the men could commence issuing her with orders. It was her intention to drive a metaphorical wedge between them at the earliest possible opportunity. Divide and conquer was a policy not limited to generals and Jennah had sensed the unspoken tension between the two of them, even from her recent position astride Concorde. Since then it had become increasingly obvious to her that Norvul hated being subservient to Malroth, believed he was more intelligent and was confident *he* had the respect of most if not all of the men.
Malroth, on the other hand, was physically more powerful, more unpredictably sadistic and always led from the front, which was why he believed *he* had the respect of *his* men. Of late however, the status quo had been disturbed, because Malroth had reluctantly been forced to empower his second in command to a previously unthinkable degree, on account of his own increasing debility. The notion that this woman possessed the power to restore the equilibrium by ridding him of his crippling affliction was making her more attractive and interesting to him by the moment. Had such a substance been available at the time, he would have been putty in her hands, despite his customary misgivings.

"Lord Malroth, sit here beside the table, if you please."

As Malroth eased his bulk on to a heap of cushions, she lifted the heavy saddlebags from her shoulder and placed them carefully on the floor beside the low table, enabling her to snatch brief, surreptitious glances about the interior of the yurt as she moved around it. She was anxious to establish the whereabouts of anything that might enhance their chances of survival once Blunt arrived to attempt her rescue. To the left of the only entrance a long, triangular rack held six circular, wooden shields. To the near side of the large cot bed a powerful looking hunting bow and a bag of arrows leaned against the hide wall of the dwelling, together with an elaborate and expensive looking scabbarded sword, although Jennah was almost certain the latter weapon was not the fabled steel she had been hoping to set eyes upon. She could see nothing that might prove of any practical use to them in the shadowy area on the far side of the cot.

"Wul, ur yuh reddeh?" Malroth demanded to know, recapturing her attention.

"Almost, lord. Norvul, I need a bowl of boiling water and a double edged, sharp-bladed dagger."

Both men stared at her in surprise, and she noted Norvul's hand go to the hilt of his sword and grip it in readiness.

"I will need to cut my right palm and bleed myself in to the bowl. If you so much as suspect I am about to stab Lord Malroth to death, you have my witnessed permission to slit my throat on the spot. As soon as I have bled myself, I will hand you back the dagger…unless you wish me to stop now and leave?"

Malroth clutched at the hem of her cloak in desperation, inadvertently tugging the overlapping edges of the garment apart.

"Nuh!"

It was the first time he had spoken in front of her and for just a moment she was quite taken aback by just how much the abscess was affecting his speech. He was equally taken aback by the momentary glimpse of her left breast, as the static in her cloak dragged the tangle of protective hair aside, before falling back in to place.

"Nuh, wuh truss yuh umplusutleh, Junnuh…dunt wuh, Nrvl."

Norvul took a moment to gauge his reaction to this latest burst of gobbledygook.

"Lord." Was the best he could manage without incriminating himself.

"Yuh suh. Nah, plis prosud."

"Very well, if you're **both** sure."

"Uv curs wi ur." Malroth reassured her, smiling fit to burst, literally.

Damn! She understood every word he was saying, Norvul noted with dismay. His deep suspicion of Jennah mutated in that instant in to loathing, spiced liberally with hatred and, confusingly for him, lust. He put the latter down to his mind's eye vision of her sitting naked on the white horse, which he was having incredible difficulty in pushing right to the very back of his mind, where it

173

could no longer trouble him. As if sensing his thoughts, Jennah turned to look at him, feigning surprise at the manner in which her cloak parted briefly with the movement, providing him with yet another, momentary glimpse of her wonderful body.

"Are you still here? I thought I made it abundantly clear what I require to complete the preparation of the potion that will rid Lord Malroth of his abscess…unless, of course, you do not wish me to succeed? My Lord grows weaker and more dependent on you each hour the affliction lingers, does he not? If I fail, perhaps you think he will weaken to a point where he is no longer fit and able to command the marauders?"

Malroth, Norvul noted with a queasy feeling in the pit of his stomach, was taking a keen interest in this largely one-sided exchange. This fucking woman didn't need a weapon, he realized with a jolt; she was a weapon!

"Don't be preposterous wench! I was about to summon a guard to fetch them when you interrupted me."

"Then you had better get on with it." She advised him, turning away so as not to catch his eye. Malroth, on the other hand, continued to stare hard at his second in command. He had known for some time that Norvul was ambitious, but to have his treacherous nature exposed by this increasingly attractive woman, who was clearly a gifted psychic in to the bargain, had opened his eyes to the very real danger he was in from within his own camp. He would do well to watch Norvul very carefully from now on. He snared Jennah's visual attention with a conspiratorial wink and said, in a low voice.

"Muh surd lahs uvr thur un thuh rhug un thuh fur sud uf thuh bud. Puss ut tuh muh, wud yuh?"

Jennah froze momentarily at the mention of another sword, before stepping back from the table and glancing across to where the tip of a blade was now just visible beyond the edge of the bed. She had been in the process of laying out the contents of her saddlebags on the low table in front of her patient, hoping fervently that she had not overplayed her hand. Now her thoughts took a different turn as she wondered could the weapon in question actually be the great sword of the Gods?

"Of course, my Lord."

Brushing past Norvul, who still had not moved a muscle, she crossed to the bed and saw the legendary weapon for the first time in her life, though she had known of its existence since her childhood. *Skullsplitter*! She moved to the edge of the low cot, stooped and lifted the sword reverentially, holding it in both hands and was astonished at its huge weight. Surely only a giant of a man could wield such a thing, yet young Gorm had apparently pulled it from its sacred berth unaided. How could that be, she wondered? The only plausible answer was that Gorm had to be **the One**; there was no other explanation that made any sense.

Jennah returned to the table and handed the sword to Malroth who accepted it greedily, like a small child snatching at a sweetmeat.

"Truly, this is a very fine weapon, Lord Malroth. A noble weapon."

The implication was lost on Malroth, but not on Norvul. He knew at once from her reaction that she recognized *Skullsplitter* (the name inscribed on the blade was a bit of a giveaway) and was aware of the immense power locked within its burnished length. He had to find some way of getting it away from the man before she alerted him to its full potential, for although Malroth was keenly aware of the legend, Norvul was convinced the great ignoramus was still unaware of its true and possibly unlimited power. Once within his own grasp, who knew what he might achieve, and perhaps then Jennah's attitude to him would change, too? The realization that her attitude mattered to him both startled and troubled the second in command.

Malroth interrupted his reverie.

"Frk muh, Nrvl! Ur yuh rutted tuh thuh sput, mun?"

Norvul did not need an interpreter for that one; tone was everything with Malroth. He volunteered a feeble smile, as if to say: 'I don't know why we're putting up with this stupid bitch? Can't you see she's trying to come between us?'

But to Malroth the Malevolent the smile said: 'Okay, you got me. I'm guilty as sin.'

Realising there was nothing to be gained by pursuing the matter, for the present at least, Norvul headed for the exit flap that doubled as an entrance flap, to summon one of the two men on guard duty

outside the yurt to undertake the errand he was not about to demean himself by carrying out in person. Instead, he flung back the heavy flap and, after a startled pause so brief as to be hardly worth the name, yelled:
"Gua…"

CHAPTER 43

The dousing parties had now become fire-fighting gangs, as two more yurts had been set ablaze by a combination of smouldering debris raining down on the settlement from the burning forest across the lake, and flames leaping the gap between the yurts that were already alight and those nearby that were not. The sight gave Gorm and Blunt enormous satisfaction as they recalled the burning of their own settlement, just six weeks previously, by the very men now struggling to contain the destruction of their own homes. Ranuk found it difficult to share his friends' enthusiasm however, as the yurt he had shared with three other young raiders was one of those now reduced to a heap of glowing ash, together with his few worldly possessions, most of which consisted of pornographic engravings of Anthraksian warriors and scantily clad wood nymphs.

With the exception of Norvul, Malroth and his two guards, the entire population of the camp was now engaged in the containment efforts, enabling Gorm and his companions to sneak between the yurts behind Malroth's dwelling unseen, until they were no more than ten yards from the nervy sentries on duty outside. Clearly, the thought that their own homes might be amongst those on fire had not escaped the guards, whose desire to rush off and investigate was tempered solely by their fear of Malroth or Norvul discovering their dereliction of duty. They had witnessed the punishment for such dereliction at first hand on more than one occasion and were not overly keen on being slit open, dipped in honey and staked over a fire ants nest.

Crouched against the hide wall of the nearest dwelling, the two younger men weighed up their options while Blunt covered their backs with his bow and primed arrow. Squinting in to the flame engendered, pre-dawn light, Ranuk whispered:

"I know the man furthest from us better than the other. If I cut around behind this yurt and approach him from the far side of Malroth's dwelling, I can engage him in conversation and get the drop on him before he knows what's hit him."

Gorm nodded.

"Okay, but just hitting him will not be enough. You'll have to kill him. We can't risk either of them recovering swiftly and sounding the alarm."

Ranuk stared hard at his friend.

"And you complain *I'm* always stating the obvious. I wasn't planning on singing him to sleep with a lullaby. Just be ready to move as soon as I have his attention. You'll have to tackle the nearest guard while he's still distracted by my assault on his comrade."

"Don't worry about me. I know exactly what to do, but you'll have to keep the axe in your belt. The bastard's wearing a helmet, so embedding it in his skull's going to make too much noise."

Gorm reached down to his right boot and withdrew a small, razor sharp dagger kept there for just such an occasion as this. It had been his father's idea and he murmured a silent prayer of thanks to him now as he held the blade up for Ranuk's inspection.

The Maleryhan nodded his approval.

"Very nice, but I won't need a blade."

Behind them, the shivering Blunt, who had become increasingly uncomfortable as he listened to their chilling conversation, glanced back over his shoulder and enquired of Ranuk:

"You can kill a man you like so easily?"

Grim faced and tense, Ranuk replied:

"I said I know him, Blunt. I didn't say I like him. He's an evil-mouthed, violent bastard who brutalizes women and bullies other men."

"Even so…" Blunt was not entirely sure what he wanted to say and left the sentence unfinished. In the event he switched his attention to Gorm.

"And you, Gorm? You've never killed a man before…"

Gorm returned the blacksmith's questioning gaze evenly, but there was a frightening intensity there the older man had never seen in him before, although he recalled having seen it often enough in the boy's father. Perhaps that was it, Blunt mused; Gorm was no longer the boy he had known, but had become a man he had yet to get to know.

"What do you suggest then, Blunt? Do we lay down our weapons and surrender ourselves to torture and execution? Do we allow your woman to become Malroth's sex slave? Do we allow ***Skullsplitter*** to remain in his possession? Do we permit him to continue burning and looting and murdering folk the length and breadth of the land?"

Blunt sighed. He knew they were right, but that did not make the prospect of what they were about to do any less objectionable to him.

"No, of course not. So, let us be about this sorry business and have done with it."

Gorm gave him a cursory nod, turned and patted Ranuk on the shoulder.

"Go!"

Ranuk needed no second bidding. He clasped Gorm's forearm briefly, gave Blunt a curt nod and sprinted around the back of the yurt beside which they were crouched. Moments later he appeared beyond it, stooping low as he crossed the open ground to the rear of Malroth's yurt and disappeared behind that. He reappeared around the far side moments later, striding purposefully towards the furthest guard, as though he carried an important message for him. The man maintained his casual stance, arms folded, legs apart, watching Ranuk expectantly, but showing no inclination to reach for his weapon.

"Soryn, you ugly wart, I have news of your yurt."

"Does it fare well?"

At the sound of Ranuk's voice the other guard turned towards his companion, presumably out of a shared interest to know what was happening down by the lake.

"Nope, it's burned to a fucking crisp!"

Without a word to Blunt, Gorm was up immediately and padding swiftly across the clearing towards the nearest man's exposed back. He was still five yards from him as Ranuk drew within arm's length of his own target and threw a lightning fast punch with such ferocity it took even the Delirian by surprise. The Malheryan's fist rammed in to the man's throat with tremendous force, rendering him incapable not only of speech, but the elementary ability to breathe. Ranuk did not wait to study the result of his assault however, but closed instantly and headed-butted the guard on the bridge of his unprotected nose and brought his knee up with sickening force in to the man's groin, before pressing him to the floor from his shoulders.

Even as Ranuk was retracting his fist from that single, debilitating punch, Gorm had yanked back his own target's head by grasping a fistful of hair with his left hand, while simultaneously drawing the lethal edge of his dagger blade hard and deep across the man's throat with his right, even as the guard was reaching for the hilt of his sword. A split second later his own right knee was pressing firmly in to the crook of the guard's knee as he pushed forward firmly with his left hand, pressing the dying man gently to the floor in a dark pool of his own blood. Even in the act, Gorm was aware of a sickening crunch, as Ranuk twisted Soryn's head around and broke his neck. From his crouched position beside the smaller yurt, the watching Blunt could scarcely believe it was over so swiftly and with scarcely a sound. Truly, he thought, Gorm is his father's son.

The two young warriors stripped the guards of their weapons in silence, before Gorm beckoned with a hand for Blunt to join them. The big man removed the arrow from the chord and slipped it in to the bag with the others before hurrying across the clearing and placed a hand upon the Delirian's shoulder.

"Gorm, let me go in first." he whispered.

Gorm shook his head.

"Blunt, you told me once you were a creator, not a fighter. You've never done this kind of thing before." He reminded the blacksmith.

"Neither have you."

"This is true, but do you remember what else you told me that day? You said that I was born the son of a famous warrior and that warfare is in my blood, and you were right. I may know farming, my old friend, but I am not a farmer, I'm a fighter…a warrior, like my father before me. I realise that now."

Blunt glanced from Gorm to Ranuk and back again and nodded his head, his acceptance of the fact evident in his resigned expression.

"I know it, too."

He glanced down disconsolately at the fresh corpses at their feet.

"The evidence suggests unequivocally that both of you are. It seems the Fates have brought the two of you together for this moment...but the woman I love is inside this glorified tent. If she is already dead then I have nothing left to live for anyway, but your two lives are just beginning and I can buy you crucial time, whatever else may already have come to pass. Please, let me go in first."

Gorm looked across to Ranuk, who merely nodded his assent. "So be it."

He unbuckled the sword belt from his waist and handed it to his old friend.

"Here, go with your own sword for I no longer have need of it. This gentleman on the ground has very kindly volunteered to lend me his, indefinitely. Oh, and leave me the bow and arrows, too. Once inside the yurt you will have little time to draw back the chord and may well hit the wrong target. I will pass the weapon to your woman as soon as I get the chance. Draw your sword now and remember, we will be following right behind you, so don't swing too wildly or you'll risk dismembering your recently liberated friends in to the bargain."

Gorm was well aware his father had rated Blunt one of the finest swordsmen he had ever met, despite the big Lumbeygan's reluctance to do anything more with a blade then play-fight with the children and instruct the young men of the village in the use of the weapon. He just felt that now was a good time to shore up Blunt's resolve with a little dark humour. Blunt grinned back at him.

"Impudent youth. You're still not too old to go over my knee and have your hide tanned, y'know."

It was Ranuk's turn to grin.

"Just say the word Blunt and I'll hold him down for you. He's too cocky for his own good and needs his arse kicking once in a while, to bring him back down to earth."

Blunt looked from one to the other and smiled, sadly. He loved the one young man like his own son and was growing fond of the other already, despite their brief acquaintance. He shook each of them warmly by the hand, slipped the bow and case from his shoulder and passed them to Gorm, before easing himself upright and sliding his sword gently from its scabbard.

"Let's get this over wi…"

Before the blacksmith could complete his sentence the flap of the yurt was flung aside suddenly from within, and the three of them caught an all too brief glimpse of Norvul's scarred and angry features as he yelled:

"Gua…"

CHAPTER 44

In the instant before he snatched the flap back in to place across the opening and took a smart step back inside the yurt, reaching for the hilt of his sword as he did so, Norvul had glimpsed a huge, unfamiliar man, lethal weapon already in hand, silhouetted against the orange tinged light as the fiery night bled in to a pale, damp and listless dawn. The head of one of the sentries had lain at the man's feet in what he could only assume was a substantial pool of the sentry's own blood, and the inert, down-turned feet of the other sentry had also been visible, just behind him. Judging from the toes to the ground position of those feet, Norvul had been forced to assume the other sentry was also very dead.

"Assassin!" he exclaimed in a stage whisper, putting a silencing finger to his lips with his left index finger as he half turned to warn his leader. Malroth, who had been too busy caressing ***Skullsplitter*** to take any initial notice as Norvul summoned the guard, had seen nothing, but Jennah certainly had. Her sharp intake of breath did not go unnoticed by either of the other occupants of the dwelling, but they had no time to question her about it. Uttering a mighty roar of pent-up rage Blunt, who had recognized Norvul instantly as the animal who had charged around the village of Nurk with the severed head of the blacksmith's faithful hound Berk dangling from the pommel of his saddle, burst through the flap and in to the yurt. Though not now entirely the surprise he had hoped for, his entrance still proved something of a momentary show stopper, not least for himself as he caught sight of Jennah, still naked within her cloak, kneeling at the feet of Malroth the Malevolent as he sat cradling the sword of the Gods.

Norvul was the first to react, side stepping the blacksmith's downwards chop barely in time to avoid being halved like an apple. Instead of lunging with his own sword while still off balance, which might easily have dealt Blunt a mortal wound but left his own flank vulnerable while he sought to steady himself, he brought it flashing across his chest in a vicious, sideways swipe, giving the Lumbeygan, who had caught the glint of a rising blade from the corner of his eye, a chance to swerve out of the way. Denied the killer blow he had intended to inflict, Norvul was further dismayed to hear a sharp metallic clang as his blade sliced through the leather of Blunt's satchel to become entangled amongst the blacksmith's tools.

Realising instantly what had happened, Blunt moved with astonishing speed for such a large man, swinging his bulk back the other way and forcing a loud crack from Norvul's blade as it snapped under the strain. The livid raider staggered backwards with the release of tension and Blunt followed through with his own sword. Despite his disadvantage, Norvul parried the lunge skillfully with his half blade, but was too late to avoid the unexpected dagger in the other hand, as it added yet another scar to his already much lacerated features, before sliding off his left cheek bone and throwing the blacksmith off balance once more. Seizing this momentary advantage, Norvul brought his broken sword's hilt smashing in to the side of Blunt's jaw as the big man staggered past him, sending him crashing to the floor.

In the three or four seconds this furious encounter had lasted two more crucial events had taken place. Gorm and Ranuk had burst in to the yurt and Jennah, who had assumed Blunt was acting alone in his attempt to rescue her, had punched Malroth right in the abscess, eliciting an ear splitting scream of pain that caused even the would be combatants to pause in astonishment. Thinking quickly, Jennah seized the sword of the Gods from Malroth's momentarily paralysed embrace and, discovering it far too heavy for her to wield a killer blow, flung it two-handed to Gorm. As Ranuk engaged Norvul, who had been swift to retrieve Blunt's inadvertently discarded sword, Gorm felt the familiar surge of power pulse through his arm as he gripped **Skullsplitter** lightly and adopted a poised, fighting stance.

Despite being enraged by this unexpected turn of events, Malroth was nevertheless quick to recover his customary composure in a fight, identifying Jennah as both nothing more than a comely and intriguing distraction, and an unwitting pawn he could deploy to his tactical advantage. Scrambling to his feet and throwing an immensely muscular arm about her neck and pressing the point of his own dagger beneath it in to the hollow of her throat, he yelled:

"Guntulmunn, plis, sis thus unsimly bikurung!"

Norvul and Ranuk paused in their violent attempts to slaughter one another, Gorm stood up straight and rested the sword's blade in the crook of his arm and Blunt sat upright, grunted, shook his head and rubbed ruefully at his jaw.

Norvul glanced uneasily at Ranuk.

"What did he say?"

Ranuk shrugged his shoulders.

"Buggered if I know."

They both looked at Blunt.

"Search me. I don't speak Abscess."

"I believe Lord Malroth wishes to volunteer a suggestion." Gorm informed them all.

Malroth beamed lopsidedly.

"Urgh, ut lust, sumbuduh wuth uh sumbluns uf uh brun un ur mudst."

Ranuk and Norvul exchanged bemused glances.

Ignoring them, Malroth addressed himself specifically to Gorm this time, having recognized that despite his youth, this enterprising lad was clearly the leader of the little group of invaders of his yurt.

"Yuh ur uh vuruh untullugunt yung mun. Yuh cun undrstund wut um sayhung, fur uh sturt. Yur quck, buld und cluvur, nut luk thut twut uvr thur." He said, glaring at Norvul, who glared right back at him, without quite knowing what was being said or where the conversation was going, but somehow sensing it involved him and his status within the camp.

"Kull hum nah und hus puzushun uss muh sucund n cummund iss yurs."

Gorm smiled.

"Such loyalty to one's underlings is touching Mal, but my suggestion makes far more sense. We intend to kill both of you."

"Und wah wud yuh wunt tu duh thut?"

"Why? Why indeed." the youngster replied, his tone as cold and hard as the heart of a glacier.

"You may recall the pleasant little village of Nurk in the valley of Grath you visited recently."

"Kunt seh thut uh duh. Yu've syn wun vulluge, yu've syn um ull."

185

"What can I tell you, boy? We are a merry band and enjoy travel, we see a lot of pretty villages." Norvul added.

Gorm continued to watch Malroth carefully as he replied:

"I know. I've passed through the scorched remains of several of them on my own travels and have made a solemn vow to a great many of their ghosts."

And with that Gorm sheathed ***Skullsplitter***, slid the bow from his shoulder, fitted an arrow to the string and drew it back to its full, lethal potential.

'Hmm, it'll save me the job.' Thought Norvul, ever the pragmatist.

Malroth was both astonished and enraged.

"Ut meh huv escupped yur nutiss buyh, bud uh huv uh knuff ut thus schemun butch's thrut. Yur urrugh meh wul strakh muh, bud shih wul beh dud befur ut dus."

Terrified she may have been, but Jennah had retained the presence of mind to watch Gorm's eyes very carefully throughout this exchange and thought she had discerned there some inkling of his intent. She blinked her understanding and knew instantly that he had received the scarcely perceptible message.

"Oh, I have no intention of killing *you* with this arrow, Mal; it's for the woman. She is nothing to me and therefore expendable. Kill her quickly and mercifully now and I can then kill you at my leisure."

Blunt's shrill exclamation of: "Gorm…no!" helped convince Malroth, who was so astonished by the young Delirian's pronouncement he relaxed the pressure on his dagger momentarily. A moment Jennah seized with relish, jerking her head backwards in to the marauder's chin with such violent force it smashed the rotten tooth from his festering jaw, momentarily paralyzing him with the excruciating intensity of the pain and causing him to drop the weapon involuntarily.

"Eeeeiiiiaaaaarrrrrgggggghhhhhhhhhhh!" he screamed, in his most intelligible pronunciation in days. Norvul certainly understood it, wincing in reluctant sympathy.

Ducking under her giant captor's arm, the herbalist flung herself across the floor and in to the waiting arms of the astounded Blunt. In that same instant Gorm released the arrow and the impact as it struck Malroth in the left shoulder sent him staggering backwards against the wall of the yurt, although it had not inflicted a critical injury due to the reinforced and heavily padded protective leather vest he always wore beneath the linen of his shirt. Enraged, the giant marauder snapped the shaft of the arrow, grabbed his own, sheathed sword from where it lay against the wall of the yurt beside him and drew it, just as Gorm had hoped he would.

The lines of his face now set in to an impassive mask that registered no emotion, the young Delirian warrior calmly flung the bow aside, slipped the leather case from his shoulder and raised **Skullsplitter** to the horizontal, so that the weapon's tip was pointing directly at Malroth's heart. When he spoke, his tone was cool and calm, but edged with murderous steel and in his icy gaze there was not one iota of mercy.

"Malroth of Eebollah, you murdered my family, butchered my friends and neighbours, tortured my pet, burned my village, pissed in my well and stole the sword given to me by the gods, and now you are going to die by that same blade!"

CHAPTER 45

When Norvul's face had appeared briefly at the entrance to the yurt, Gorm and Ranuk had been forced to abandon their intention of hiding the bodies of the two sentries. Less than thirty seconds after they had followed Blunt inside, Disuhn, Norvul's yurt cleaner and some-time bed warmer hurried up through the settlement to inform her master that the dousing parties had succeeded in putting out the fires, but stopped abruptly some distance from the entrance flap as the rain soaked, gathering dawn revealed the two, pallid corpses. She was certain they were corpses, because one of them lay in enough congealing blood to fill a bucket, and the other's head had been twisted around so grotesquely it appeared to be facing in reverse. Like many of the women at the camp, Disuhn was a superstitious soul much given to morbid fatalism and considered the macabre scene before her to be a very bad omen, an assessment reinforced by the sounds of fierce fighting from within the yurt. Putting a hand to her mouth to stifle a gasp, she turned on her heel and scurried back towards the lake, delighted at the opportunity to be the sole bearer of very bad tidings.

Arak, Norvul's new second in command and an acquaintance since childhood, although never previously a trusted one, was sifting idly through the smoking embers of a yurt with his boot when he spied Disuhn rushing down the slope towards him. Something in her manner (her hysterical shrieking and wild gesticulations, possibly) put him on instant alert as she fell to her knees before him and threw her arms around his powerful thighs, fulfilling a secret ambition she had harboured for many months.

"Treachery, Master Arak…truly terrible trauma and treachery!"

Arak dragged her to her feet with some difficulty. She was in no great hurry to relax her grip on his legs and used his attempts to haul her upright to slide her hands up the back of his thighs and grip the firm flesh of his buttocks.

"Stop babbling, woman! What is this treachery of which you speak…and get your grubby hands off my arse?"

"They're dead, master!" she shrieked at the very top of her voice, which was more than high enough to be heard from some distance (possibly several miles) away.

"Dead, dead…both of the poor bastards is dead. Cut down in their bleedin' prime, poor lads."

By this time her Oscar worthy performance had attracted a considerable amount of attention from the other camp followers, who would have welcomed any distraction from the dispiriting, back-breaking task of combating the residue of flaming forest that had but recently threatened their existence.

Arak slapped the woman hard across the face, fulfilling a secret ambition *he* had harboured for many months, but accustomed to this treatment from Norvul on a regular basis she continued to babble hysterically.

"Death…death…doleful death and dire disaster! The end is surely nigh for Armageddon is upon us."

"Armageddon?"

"The end of all things, master Arak. I read about it in the Daily Runes and now it is coming to pass, it seems. First the terrible flames of Haletosys and now this accursed tragedy. Oh woe, woe, and thrice woe, for we are all about to die!"

Arak shook her roughly by the shoulders. From the rising murmur behind him he could tell her hysteria was beginning to infect the rest of the exhausted crowd and knew he had to get a grip on the situation immediately. Seizing the initiative as Disuhn paused for what appeared to the marauder to be an unnaturally rare breath, he unclamped her hands from his bum, spun her around and clamped one of his own, filthy, calloused hands over her equally filthy mouth, before whispering in to her ear:

"If you do not shut up and listen to me right now woman, I swear I will slit your miserable throat without another word."

Knowing him to be a man not given to idle threats, Disuhn drew another deep breath in through her nostrils and waited in trembling silence for his question.

"Now, slowly…calmly, without any screaming, gesticulations or inane babbling, turn around and tell me…who is it you think may be dead?"

"Both of the guards outside Lord Malroth's yurt!" She blurted out.

Arak glanced up through the drifting smoke, fluttering flakes of ash and persistent rain towards the entrance of the great yurt at the top of the slope. There was certainly nobody to be seen guarding it now, but nor was there any sign of a pair of corpses, although a slight hump in the earth halfway up the slope did hide the ground at the base of the entrance. He returned his gaze to the gibbering woman before him.

"You actually saw both of their bodies?"

"I did sir…I did, with my very own eyes."

"Well you'd hardly have seen them with anybody else's." he sneered, sarcastically. "And you're absolutely sure they are both dead? You actually checked to see whether they were breathing or had a pulse?"

The crowd craned forward, anxious to hear her response.

"Didn't need to, sir. One had his head facing back to front. Twisted right round to face his arse, it was! The other one's throat was slit from ear to ear and he was lying in enough of his own blood to fill a tub. I'm no expert in such matters as you know, but by my reckoning, that means they're both dead as butchered lambs."

There was a gasp of fear from the troubled crowd, as the insidious spectre of armed enemies already within their camp loomed large in their collective imagination. Was this an indication that the day of retribution they all secretly feared had finally arrived?

"And there was terrible sounds of fuckin' ferocious fighting coming from within Lord Malroth's yurt." She added, in a largely successful effort to further dramatise her role.

"I heard terrible, blood-curdling shrieks and dreadful screams rend the night."

Arak shoved her away from him in disgust.

"Good Grun woman, why didn't you just say so? We're wasting valuable time, here."

He whipped around to address the crowd, drawing his sword and brandishing it above his head in a belligerent manner befitting an incensed brigand.

"Listen to me, all of you."

Arak need not have worried. He had the surly gathering's undivided attention.

"Lord Malroth and Norvul are in great danger; there are

assassins in the camp...in the lord's yurt, even. I want every man and woman who can wield a weapon to follow me, right now. The intruders must pay with their miserable lives."

The crowd, tired, dejected and somewhat listless prior to Disuhn's revelations, suddenly realized they were very angry too and anxious for something or someone upon which to vent that anger. The mere suggestion that there were intruders in their midst posing yet another threat to their livelihood sent them racing off in every direction to gather the nearest available weapon, before surging up the slight, but increasingly slippery, humped slope behind Arak towards Malroth's yurt. As ever, Lard was well to the rear, a fact that had nothing to do with his obesity.

CHAPTER 46

"Aaaaarrrggghhhhhh!"

Distracted momentarily by the thud of the arrowhead smacking in to Malroth's shoulder, Ranuk had made the mistake of taking his eyes off his opponent just long enough for Norvul to sink his teeth in to the Malheryan's left ear lobe. Norvul's mistake was to leave them there a fraction of a second too long as Ranuk's right hand gripped the marauder's throat and commenced squeezing the life out of him. In swift, if somewhat breathless retaliation, Norvul grabbed Ranuk's testicles in a vice-like hold and attempted to counter-squeeze the life out of them. Grunting, groaning and wincing in discordant harmony, the two combatants crashed over the low table behind them, scattering the contents of Jennah's saddlebag and sending the blacksmith and herbalist diving out of the way lest they become embroiled in the melee.

Across the yurt Gorm and Malroth were eyeing each other edgily, each sizing up his opponent and looking for the opening that would offer a potentially lethal advantage. Suddenly throwing caution to the wind and thinking to use his greater strength and intimidating appearance, the marauder charged at Gorm with a ferocious yell he was more used to uttering from horseback. Anticipating either a forward lunge for his heart or a chest opening side swipe, Gorm was caught off guard as Malroth deliberately swung his sword well short of his young opponent's torso in a downwards power stroke, with the intention of bringing the confrontation to a swift and decisive conclusion by severing the Delirian's sword arm at the wrist. And so the tremendous blow would have done, had it not been for the thick, iron shackle still locked in place there. In the event, the blade glanced off the metal in a shower of sparks, throwing the startled marauder off balance and leaving him fatally exposed.

With his right arm still reverberating from the impact of the blow, Gorm grabbed ***Skullsplitter*** swiftly with his left hand and swung the blade out and upwards with eye-blurring speed, slicing cleanly through Malroth's neck on a slight diagonal from left to right and with so little resistance he initially thought he had somehow missed his mark. The action stunned everyone else in the yurt in to momentary immobility, as though time itself had stopped. Their shocked faces registered disbelief as Malroth dropped his sword and stood completely still, an equally disbelieving expression on his contorted face. For a moment or two the only indication Gorm's extraordinary weapon had indeed found its target was the thin red line at the marauder's throat, like a very fine, if somewhat skewiff crimson necklace. The big man's eyes swiveled first one way, then the other, but appeared to lack focus, and as the gore began to form rivulets at his throat, driven by the waning pressure from the valve pumping furiously in his chest, he rocked gently backwards and forwards on his heels three times until the angle became impossible to maintain and his severed head toppled forward from his shoulders, to be replaced almost immediately by a great spout of pristine blood.

Sensing his moment of destiny, Norvul recovered his composure fractionally quicker than Ranuk, grabbed the fallen sword and turned to deliver a deathblow to the young Malheryan, but failed to heed his own, earlier assessment of Jennah, who had reacted more quickly than any of them. The arrow from Gorm's discarded bow, released at virtually point blank range, struck the former second in command cleanly in the center of his forehead, the armoured tip piercing the frontal lobe of his brain and exiting the occipital lobe at the rear. Such was the impact at that distance it lifted the new (albeit incredibly briefly) commander of the marauders clean off his feet and flung him against the wall of the yurt.

"Nice arrers." Ranuk commented admiringly, all too well aware of just how close he had come to a violent end himself. Jennah dipped in a brief curtsy and realized from Gorm and Ranuk's expressions that her cloak had just come undone again.

"Nice..."

"Don't even think about it, Ranuk." Blunt advised him.

"I'd hate to have to kill you so soon after we became friends."

Jennah blushed with pleasure at how quickly the blacksmith had come to the defence of her modesty, or lack of it. Having marveled briefly at Jennah's breasts, Gorm resumed marveling at his extraordinary sword. Now he was no longer wielding the remarkable weapon in combat, he had become suddenly aware of just how heavy it was. Blunt noted his fascination; it echoed his own. As an expert in the manufacture of swords, he recognized the quite extraordinary...perhaps even superhuman...effort that had been expended in its manufacture. As far as Ranuk was concerned however, **Skullsplitter** was just another sword. As long as a weapon did what it had been designed to do, as long as it was reliable, he did not care too much what it looked like. A sword was a sword, whatever it had been named. Women, on the other hand...

The young Malheryan's ruminations on the fairer sex were cut brutally short by a shouted voice from without, startling them all in to a state of combative alertness once more.

"Lord Malroth...Norvul...are you and the witch still in there? Are you well?"

Gorm hissed at the blacksmith.

"Blunt, you're good at accents. Can you mimic Malroth's mumbling?"

Blunt glanced uneasily at the headless corpse with distaste. Jennah had thrown a cloth over the head, which had rolled across the floor to rest at her feet; its sightless stare had been giving her the creeps.

"I don't have an abscess!"

Ranuk recalled Lard's sudden assumption of Malroth's distorted speech after Norvul's intervention and stepped in obligingly with a wad of cloth, which he then proceeded to stuff in to the blacksmith's cheek before the big man realized what was happening.

"Try, Blunt. Our lives may depend on it."

Carefully skirting the object beneath the bloodstained cloth, Jennah tripped across to the entrance flap, lifted it just a fraction to enable her to peer out and caught her breath.

"It appears most of the occupants of the settlement are approaching, but still some distance down the slope as yet. The bad news is they're all armed and look in a very mean mood."

She turned to stare at Blunt.

"This young man is right, my love. You may be our only chance of survival. As things stand right now the odds are ten to one against us, at the very least."

Blunt crossed the yurt to stand beside her and cleared his throat.

Gorm and Ranuk joined them and the Malheryan whispered:

"I recognize the voice. His name is Arak and he's Norvul's new lieutenant. He's a capable leader of men by all accounts and a fearsome fighter."

At that precise moment the fearsome fighter called out, again.

"Lord Malroth, I have forty of your best men at my back."

He may have been a fearsome fighter, but Arak was either rubbish at arithmetic or a compulsive liar; he had thirty-one men at his back, and only twenty of those had ever done any serious fighting, if hacking down fleeing villagers could be considered as such. The women were an unknown quantity, although it amused him to think that he could unleash Disuhn on the intruders and simply aggravate them to death. Nevertheless, it was reassuring to know that the odds were still stacked heavily in his favour, for it was unlikely that more than ten armed men at most could be occupying the yurt, given the additional room taken up by Malroth, Norvul and the witch.

"Do you need our assistance, Lord?"

Blunt cleared his throat again before issuing what he hoped would prove a plausible reply.

"Thunk yuh Uruk, bud uh huv nuh nid. Thuh whut wutch iss pruvung uh luttl fruskyur thun uh hud ucspuctud."

His friends were still congratulating Blunt quietly on the success of his mimicry when a cross-bow bolt tore through the hide flap, narrowly missing taking out Jennah's right eye as it whistled between her and Gorm and lodged, quivering, in one of the wooden bracing struts on the far side of the yurt. Outside, Arak spoke again, his tone undeniably threatening this time.

"Whoever you are in there with my lords, I suggest you release them, come out now and throw down your weapons. Trust me on this. You really don't want me and my men to have to come in there and take them off you. Surrender quietly and I guarantee you a fair hearing."

Ranuk snorted.

"Surrender quietly and I guarantee he'll have us hung, quartered and burned."

Gorm considered his blood brother's words for a moment before speaking up, softly, but with real authority.

"Nobody here is thinking of surrender, Ranuk. Whatever the outcome of this day's events, this is to the death, now."

He glanced around at each of his friends in turn.

"Agreed?"

Their faces were uniformly pale and tense. Nobody said anything, but each of them nodded their agreement.

"Good. Blunt, do you want to give it one more try? At worst it may buy us just a little more time to prepare."

The blacksmith smiled at his young friend. The lad had matured so much in such a short time; it was just a shame that it was all going to be for nothing. All they could realistically hope to do now was die bravely and with honour.

"Why not?" he said, taking hold of Jennah's left hand and squeezing it gently as he turned to the flap.

"Wud duh yuh min, Uruk?" he called out in reply to Arak, bluffing brazenly to the last.

Arak, however, was not to be fooled and offered them an explanation as to why.

"Listen, you twisted piece of shit, Lord Malroth would never say 'thank you'…and he certainly wouldn't say it in a Lumbeygan accent, abscess or no. Oh, and you forgot to hide the bodies of the two guards you cowardly bastards murdered. Bit of a dead giveaway, my invisible friend."

Gorm told the others to move back, away from the entrance, while he snatched a brief glimpse of the opposition through the hole the bolt had bored through the canvass. He considered the likelihood of another bolt striking the exact same spot to be negligible, but still held his breath as he peered through the tiny portal.

"Perhaps two dozen experienced fighters, backed up by maybe as many more armed, camp followers. They're roughly halfway down the slope, just above the ridge, and the rain has been falling heavily for over an hour now, so it's going to be slippery as Haletosys out there. I can see only one crossbowman. He's about thirty-five yards distant, in the front rank and slightly to our left. He's kneeling, but has already reloaded his weapon. He's not very smart, though."

"How d'you make that out?" Ranuk asked him, out of

professional interest.

"He's wearing a bright red strip of cloth around his head to hold the hair out of his eyes. Take a look Jennah and see if you think you could kill him with a single shot. We will have no second chance, but if you can take him out the remainder will have to come to us. I see there's also a more powerful hunting bow than mine over there behind the bed that Blunt can use. Once you've killed the crossbowman, the pair of you will have to kill or disable as many of the attackers as you can in the initial charge. Ranuk and I will have to deal with the rest hand to hand. Five yards before they reach us, drop your bows, grab a sword and shield and cover our flanks. We'll take the brunt of the charge in the centre."

Jennah merely nodded as she stepped up to the hole in the flap, while Blunt retrieved the second, larger bow. The herbalist stared hard at her target for several seconds before stepping back, picking up Gorm's bow and looping the string she had loosed back over the knock. The blacksmith selected an arrow carefully and handed it to her to notch on to the chord. Taking a deep breath, she gripped the weapon and drew back the chord and attached missile until the knuckle of her right thumb was level with the lobe of her right ear.

"Gorm, when I say 'now', you lift the flap for two seconds, no more. The rest of you, overturn that table and crouch behind it. When my arrow kills him there is no telling in which direction his bolt will fly."

Reassured by her air of confidence, the others did as she suggested. She waited until all but Gorm was safe behind the raised barrier of the table.

"Ready when you are." The Delirian informed her.

The herbalist sucked in another breath, held it for one second...and in a perfectly clear and steady voice said: "Now!"

The triangular gap as Gorm tugged on the flap was still barely three inches wide when the arrow hurtled through it.

Blinking the rainwater out of his eyes, the kneeling crossbowman caught a flutter of movement in the region of the entrance flap a millisecond before a circular disturbance at the center of his field of vision ended his life. He toppled forward in the mud, driving the arrowhead that had pierced his right eye out through the back of his skull. Arak and the others looked on in

197

disbelief as the crossbow bolt skittered away harmlessly through the mud. Now it was Gorm's turn to call out a warning.

"Arak, you snivelling scumbag, if you want us you're going to have to come up here and take us, one by one…and make no mistake, if you are foolish enough to choose that option it is going to cost *all* of you very, very dear."

His words hit home immediately and some of those at the back of the crowd, still hypnotized by the body of the crossbowman kneeling lifelessly at a bizarre angle in the blood-soaked mud, began to drift away soundlessly, lest Arak detect their desertion and turn his wrath upon them. They need not have worried, for as far as Arak was concerned, this business was personal, now. Malroth and Norvul were evidently either captive or dead and if the marauders were to remain together, it had become his responsibility to provide the glue that would hold them in place. He beat on his shield with his sword and called along the line to his most experienced fighters.

"You hear that, men? That spawn of a toad up there had the nerve to threaten *us*! So, I'll tell you what *we're* going to do. We're going to kill those cowering bastards, whoever they are. We're going to rip out their hearts and eat them while they're still beating! We're going to drink their weak as ditch water blood! We're going to stamp their crushed bones in to the mud and piss on their rotting carcases! Lock shields! We advance!"

And with a great roar of rage the twenty most seasoned killers amongst the group hammered the pommels of their swords against the wood of their circular shields, formed themselves in to two ranks of ten men each, overlapped the edges of the shields and began pushing steadily up the slippery slope towards Malroth's yurt.

Realising from the man's angry response that Arak and the more seasoned marauders were not about to be intimidated by his threat, Gorm looked at the others and informed them in a commanding voice way beyond his years:

"Time to show ourselves, my friends. Blunt and Jennah, I want you to aim below the shields for their legs. Difficult targets, I know, but it is our best hope now of slowing them down and spreading uncertainty and fear. You may only have time for two or three arrows apiece, so go for near the center of the shield wall where they are less likely to be wasted. Ranuk, you and I will stand shoulder to shoulder and deal with those that get through. Watch for them coming in from the flanks at the edges of the shield wall."

Ranuk nodded, grimly.

"Shoulder to shoulder...and, if it should come to that, back to back at the last, brother."

"Ahem."

Blunt laid a great hand upon one shoulder of each of the young warriors.

"You cannot allow any of us to be taken prisoner, either. We all know what that would mean. If it looks as though we will be overwhelmed, then you must take my life, Gorm and then fall on your sword. And Ranuk, I trust you to do the same for Jennah."

Gorm and Ranuk glanced uneasily at one another for just a moment, before nodding their agreement.

"If such a terrible thing becomes necessary, then it will be done. You may both depend on it." he assured the blacksmith and the herbalist.

"Now each grab a shield from that rack and make sure you have a sword to hand."

He stooped and dragged the cloth from Malroth's severed head, plunged his left hand in to the thick curls of dark hair and held it aloft, much to the distaste of his companions.

"Ranuk, sever Norvul's head and do likewise."

Ranuk stared at his blood brother as though he had taken leave of his senses.

"What for? He's already dead?"

"Because when it comes to intimidating a belligerent enemy who outnumbers you, two heads are better than one."

And with that Gorm turned and threw back the entrance flap with a flourish he kept for just such occasions, and the four of them strode outside in to the early light of day to keep their appointment with destiny.

CHAPTER 47

The front rank of the shield wall had advanced to within twenty-five yards of Malroth's yurt by the time Gorm and his friends stepped outside and took up their defensive positions. As they braced themselves to face the onslaught, Gorm raised Malroth's severed head high with his left hand to make sure the attackers could see it. Certain he now had the marauders full attention, he lifted **Skullsplitter** high above him with his right, so that the weapon attracted the available light to its gleaming surfaces, reflecting the distant, dying flames with a bloody and unholy glow. Ranuk kept his own sword in its scabbard to enable him to hold Norvul's head above his own with both hands. Faced with this macabre and unnerving spectacle, the advancing ranks paused awkwardly, uncertain now whether or not to proceed. Their disembodied former leaders appeared to be glaring down at them with disapproval, and the burnished sword of the Gods was quite unlike any such weapon they had ever seen. Taking advantage of their hesitation, Gorm called out loud enough to be heard by everyone in the marauders' camp:

"I hold in my right hand the mighty sword of the Gods, the magical **Skullsplitter**, with which I have just slain Malroth of Eebollah in mortal combat. I am Gorm…the Avenger…come to seek final and bloody retribution for the sacking of the village of Nurk and the slaughter of its inhabitants. All those of you who took part in that terrible raid, prepare to die a violent and most gruesome death!"

As muttered exchanges continued amongst the experienced fighters and armed camp followers ranged across the slope, Blunt noticed that his hands were shaking, his palms sweating, his legs trembling and his bowels threatening to embarrass him. The moment of truth he had feared his entire life had finally arrived and he knew that he was going to die. Would he find the courage to die with honour, he wondered, or would he dishonour his friends and disgrace himself by attempting to flee the slaughter once more, like the coward he had always assumed himself to be. He turned to glance at Jennah, standing on their opposite flank, alongside Ranuk. She was so beautiful, so composed, so brave, he thought.

Her mouth was tight lipped and her features strained, but her hands were steady and she displayed no physical manifestation of the fear she must also be feeling. Sensing she was being watched, the herbalist turned her head towards him, met his wondering gaze and smiled.

'I love you.' she mouthed silently, and in that moment the blacksmith felt his own fear evaporate and an extraordinary sense of fatalistic calm descend upon him. He returned her smile and mouthed: 'I love you, too.', before returning his attention to the angry mob paused barely the length of a tall tree-trunk away.

"Jennah and I will bring down as many of them as we can in the initial rush, but when the inevitable clash of shields comes," he informed his companions, "their axemen will attempt to embed their blades in the top edge of our shields and haul down our defence, to enable the swordsmen to lunge at us with their blades. Plant your feet firmly, watch for the axes and be ready to raise your shield and hold it at a tilt, angled backwards to protect your head, then stoop swiftly and thrust below their shields with your own blade. Push hard, strike cleanly and withdraw your weapon, ready for the next opportunity...and may mighty Grun be with us all."

Although both Blunt and Jennah were crack competition archers and first rate hunters of food for the table, neither had ever loosed an arrow at a human target until the herbalist's execution of Norvul a few minutes previously, and were thankful now to be excused an initial killing spree courtesy of the locked shields that faced them. The nervous fighters behind those shields now resumed their advance at Arak's threatening insistence, as he pointed up the slope with his sword and yelled:

"Kill the interlopers!"

"Whad'e say?" the marauder with the oversized helmet and rusting, tin-sheathed teeth asked the fighter next to him, as they resumed their increasingly dogged trudge up the slope through the cloying mud.

"Dunno, mate. Sounded like 'kill the antelopes'." his companion replied.

"Why'd e' call them antelopes?"

"Buggered if I know. Maybe he..."

Their conversation was interrupted painfully as the pair of

archers at the top of the slope released several rapid volleys of arrows in to the rows of exposed legs below the shield wall with devastating results. Three of their first four arrows struck home, one caught in the lower edge of a shield, piercing but not passing right through it. Every arrow loosed in the third and fourth volley found a flesh and bone target however and within seconds the front rank had been reduced to disarray, men toppling over and screaming or hopping about in agony, clutching at a pierced ankle, shin or shattered kneecap.

The cursing fighters in the second rank began to trip over or collide with their wounded comrades from the front rank, and several of those following behind turned and ran, slipped or slid back down the muddy, churned up slope. Enraged by the accuracy of the fire from above and the desertions of the cowardly camp followers below, Arak screamed foul-mouthed abuse and threats of even greater violence at the writhing wounded and those attackers still on their feet, encouraging (for want of a better description) the depleted and now ragged ranks to continue forcing their way up the slope.

As Blunt dropped his bow and reached for his shield and sword, he was astonished to be elbowed aside from behind by a short, helmeted man in a mail shirt, clutching a shield and also brandishing a sword.

"Room for one more in this pathetic excuse for a shield wall?" a familiar, laughing voice enquired.

"Broos?"

"Who else were you expecting, you great lummox?"

The great lummox turned to alert Jennah and saw a tall, unnaturally thin and similarly armed and armoured man standing alongside her, gesturing lewdly in his direction with a two handed, two fingered salute.

"Relf, too?"

"And a dozen more mean and moody lads from the village. Couldn't pass up the opportunity of a good scrap like this. Besides, the missus really wants that bloody horse of hers back in one piece. But more of that later, eh. Time to concentrate on the task in hand, my big, fat friend."

The inevitable clash of shields, when it came, was much

diminished, but none the less brutal for that. Seeing the numbers of the opposition swollen suddenly by the addition of heavily armed and experienced looking fighters, several more of Arak's men had deserted and only a hardcore of angry marauders arrived at the yurt to press home their ragged assault. Gorm and his friends had heeded Blunt's advice however and the front rank of the charge broke up in confusion as they were impaled on the low, lunging blades of the defenders in a frenzy of brutal blood letting. Axes rained down on raised shields and the attackers heaved and their own blades came slashing in, gashing skin and puncturing mail as Gorm yelled above the yelling and screaming:

"Take two quick steps backwards and brace yourselves."

"Murdering bastards!" screamed Disuhn, laying about her wildly with a wicked looking meat cleaver, before tripping and disemboweling herself with her own weapon.

Gorm's perfectly judged order proved to be the correct one, as the attackers own weight and momentum sent them toppling in an undignified tangle, rendered off balance and suddenly defenceless by the unexpected withdrawal of the wall they had been assaulting. What followed was a brief but brutal massacre, as the marauders were slaughtered without mercy. Arak was the only attacker to remain on his feet throughout, battering his bloody way through the interlocked shields with brute strength and frenzied energy. He might even have turned the tide of battle in that instant had it not been for the quick thinking of Jennah. Realising that the demented marauder was about to smash his way through their rank at the weak point she represented, she took several more steps back from the melee, retrieved her bow and, as he turned and swung his sword at Blunt's unprotected flank, put an arrow clean through his right ear and deep in to his skull at almost point blank range, ending the last vestiges of resistance.

Blunt grinned relievedly at her as Arak dropped to the ground beside him with a final grunt of exhaled breath and a mouth full of bloody saliva.

"I think that makes us even."

Ranuk, sweating profusely and drenched in other people's blood, winked encouragingly at the herbalist.

"Nice arrers…again. Remind me never to get on the wrong side

203

of you."

Blunt, equally blood spattered and still perspiring heavily, slapped his thigh suddenly and roared his relief in the form of near hysterical laughter.

"And thank Grun for Broos, Relf and the lads from Impettigoh!"

Ranuk was amazed.

"You know all these guys?"

"No, I'm just bloody good at guessing the names of bands of complete strangers." Blunt informed him, sarcastically.

Ranuk looked peeved by the response.

"I only asked."

Gorm, meanwhile, had spotted a movement by the entrance to a soaking, but largely intact yurt, down near the shore. Lard, weighed down by saddlebags laden with booty and food, was attempting to sneak undetected to a small boat drawn up half out of the water on the shore of the lake. He was dragging a very reluctant, screaming teenage girl by the wrist, which rendered the possibility of his undetected escape negligible. The grim faced avenger of Nurk and its inhabitants tapped Jennah on her shoulder.

"I have need of my bow and the straightest arrow in the bag."

Puzzled by the request, Jennah turned to face him and caught sight of the fleeing Lard and his not overly enthusiastic female companion, who had given up screaming in favour of attempting to bite the hand that dragged her. The herbalist nodded towards the pile of corpses before Malroth's yurt.

"Gorm, take a good, long look; its over." she reminded him, sympathetically, before nodding in the direction of the struggling girl, who had now sunk her teeth deep in to Blunt's wrist.

"And the tub of Lard is not going to get very far with that one in tow. She'll turn the boat over before she'll allow him to get away with her."

"Over? Not yet, it isn't. Nor for me." the young Delirian replied, his tone singularly lacking in any milk of human kindness.

Jennah shrugged her shoulders and handed over the bow and an arrow without another word, while the rest of the little group looked on in silence. This was no longer their fight, but she recognized from the set of his bloodstained face that Gorm had unfinished business with the fleeing thug. Accepting the proffered weapon from her, he fitted the notch of the projectile to the chord, drew it back to the full extent of his arm, took aim and visualized its proposed trajectory as he called out in a voice more than loud enough for the fleeing marauder to hear:

"Fat and spineless murderer of women, children and babes in arms, let the girl go and turn and fight me! This is your first and last, undeserved chance to die like a man, for you gave no other any such chance."

Breathing heavily with the exertion of shouldering the weight of the bags whilst dragging his struggling captive, Lard paused for an instant as though recognizing his description and giving serious consideration to Gorm's exhortation. He glanced back at the girl as she fell sobbing to her knees and released his vice-like grip of her arm, before hurrying on towards the boat. At seventy yards the steel broadhead of the arrow passed clean through the back of the lumbering marauder's bloated neck, piercing the jugular and puncturing the carotid artery. The butcher of Nurk staggered on for several paces before collapsing head first in to the shallow water at the edge of the lake, still several paces short of his means of escape. Gorm lowered the bow wearily and stared without emotion at the grotesque corpse as it swayed gently in the shallow, windswept water.

"A promise is a promise, Lard."

CHAPTER 48

A lone magpie perched on the bloodied hand protruding from the carpet of mist that had settled over the shore of the lake. The bird shuffled nervously from foot to foot as it scanned its silent surroundings. Nothing moved amongst the smouldering, fire-blackened remains of the settlement, save for an occasional wisp of acrid smoke; it was as though Nature had attempted to sweep all evidence of the battle under the carpet, but had missed a bit here and there. A shadow passed over the magpie and the bird tilted its gaze beyond the gathered carrion crows to the buzzards circling slowly on the thermals drifting up from the sacked settlement, impatient for the unveiling of the feast.

Ignorant of the violent drama enacted in its absence, the sun eased itself above the rim of the eastern hills, inadvertently catching the burnished surface of the ring on the finger beneath the magpie's feet. Dazzled by the sudden brilliance of the gold, the bird tilted its head, opened its beak and, with the persistence for which its kind is justly renowned, began working the ring to the end of the wrinkled, podgy finger, now shrunken somewhat in death. Having finally worked the glittering trinket free, the magpie adjusted the position of the prize in its beak and took off towards its nest.

A large, hastily assembled, unmarked cairn beside the lake gave the only clue to the whereabouts of the suppurating remains of the infamous Malroth of Eebollah and the followers who had died with him in the battle of the previous day. The pallid hand protruding from the top of the mound suggested the burial party had been none too thorough when interring the occupants. All but Malroth's yurt had been stripped of anything of value then set alight and the former settlement now reminded Gorm of Nurk as he had seen it last, though the emotions he had experienced on that morning all those weeks ago (although it seemed more like years to him, now) were entirely absent on this occasion.

"Gorm the Avenger." He mused quietly to himself, liking the sound of the title that had come to him out of nowhere, as he had stood on this very spot, facing down the advancing enemy and brandishing *Skullsplitter*. With a last look around the scene of desolation below him, the burned yurts, scorched and still smouldering forest, and final rough and uncomfortable resting place of his vanquished enemies, he turned on his heel and stepped back inside the great yurt to rejoin his friends.

They had caroused all night, eating Malroth's food, drinking his excellent, pilfered wines and mead and toasting one another noisily at regular intervals between raucous songs, ribald jokes and unlikely stories of wildly exaggerated heroism. A terrible evil had been put to the sword, a vicious cancer cut from the land, and they were high on relief at their unexpected survival, exhilarated by victory and bound by the comprehensive destruction of a common enemy. Of a sudden, life was good once more and filled with promise for the future.

"So Broosh, tell us how y'knew where to find us." Suggested Gorm, somewhat the worse for wine, to which he was as yet unaccustomed.

"Wasn't so difficult." Broos admitted.

"Naw. We used satnav." Relf butted in, before his cousin could elaborate.

Gorm frowned in to his goblet, as if expecting to see an explanation floating on the surface of the contents.

"Shatnav?"

"Yup, we sat on our horses and navigated by bloody guesswork."

Ranuk slapped his thigh and roared with laughter.

"Like it, like it."

Broos, the more serious of the cousins, shoved Relf's shoulder.

"Shuddup! I'm tryin' t'explain to 'im. We was paid a visit by a fuckin' fat merchant named Mammot and his fetchin' but foolish daughter…hmm, didn't think I'd be able t'say that, drunk… Deenah. When they told us 'f their 'ventures in the forest, my wife Lon became consherned for the shafety of that lump of a blackshmith over there."

Blunt raised his goblet in acknowledgement at the mention of his profession.

"She's got somethin' of a soft spot for the big lummox." he smirked, before adding:

"Though pershonally I am at a lossh to fathom why?"

"You tell her to keep her hands to herself." Laughed Jennah, snuggling closer to her man and placing a hand upon his broad chest to emphasise ownership.

"Big lummox he may be, but he's my big lummox."

She pulled herself up to the height of Blunt's shoulder and kissed him on the cheek, much to the blacksmith's delight.

"I've got somethin' of a soft spot for 'im, too. Iss called a shwamp. Anyhow," Broos continued, "my bold cuz Relf here agreed t'accompany me in a shearch for 'im, although Lon's real concern was for her beloved 'orse, I'm shure. She loves that fuckin' animal more than she loves me, y'know."

"And who can blame her?" giggled Relf.

Ignoring the comment, Broos turned awkwardly in his seat to regard Gorm.

"I b'lieve you 'ave named the beast Concorde, Gorm. Can't exactly shay why, but the name sheems to shute."

Gorm, mouth still full of wine and roast fowl, nodded his agreement with this statement.

"Mmmmm, s'true, fits 'im like a shoe."

"So, we s'plained the shituation to the village council and asked for volunteers t'assist us an' these twelve brave wankers agreed."

The twelve brave wankers (who were too numerous for the author to bother coming up with individual names at this late stage in the narrative) raised their goblets in wine-spilling recognition of the compliment.

"We rode as fard and as hast as it was shafe to do through the forest and were met by Concorde a couple of hours ride fr'm here. He led us to the ford 'bove the lake and we realised we'd reached the shettlement in the nick of whatshit."

"Don't wish to seem ungrateful," Ranuk interjected, "but we had the situation under control, y'know."

Gorm smiled at his blood brother.

"S'true, Ranuk…s'very true, but I'd rather have had Broosh 'sistance than not had it, if y'know what I mean? You n' I are not seasoned in battle yet…"

"Thad'll teach you t'take plenty 'f salt n' pepper with you, next time." Giggled Relf.

"…and p'raps this wus not our time."

Ranuk frowned at him.

"You think? After all, we won, didn' we?"

Gorm nodded. His head was beginning to clear and he wondered if he had drunk himself sober, as Ranuk had insisted it was possible for him to do. His tongue, which had earlier appeared to ravel up in to a scarcely controllable form as he drank, appeared to be unraveling again.

"We did, and I do, but I also think *our* time is near. When we leave here t'morrow we leave together and we pick our future battles carefully. Some of the marauders escaped through the forest and will filter out in to the four kingdoms. Our renown will grow quickly and trouble will soon come looking for us, my friend, as men who live by the sword seek to enhance their own reputation by slaying *us* in battle. So, never fear brother, there will be fighting aplenty from now on...and gold and fame and women, too. Our reputations will earn us much work from those who have need of a sword to fight their battles for them."

This all made perfect sense to Ranuk and he lifted his goblet in a toast to an exciting future with his blood brother, battling ridiculous odds against dastardly foes and emerging victorious, always.

"To the future, then...especially the women!"

The rest of them raised their goblets in response.

"To the future!"

Blunt was impressed by the maturity of Gorm's speech and realised that his own work here was done. The Delirian was no longer a boy. He was a man now, Gorm the Avenger no less, slayer of Malroth the Malevolent and would soon become a legend in his own lifetime. The blacksmith glanced fondly at Jennah, still leaning against his shoulder, finally fast asleep. It was time for them both to go home...wherever that might prove to be? In recent days they had discussed returning together to Lumbeygoe, setting up a joint venture in a peaceful settlement and building a new home and life for themselves overlooking the sea. And what of his newfound friend and unlikely saviour, Broos? He would journey home to Immpetigoh with his courageous neighbours and return Concorde to his pining mistress.

At that moment the blacksmith's reverie was interrupted by the reflected firelight winking at him from the gems embedded in the hilt of the sword at Gorm's waist. Was the destruction of Malroth and the ending of his reign of terror the extraordinary weapon's true purpose, or was that yet to be revealed to his friend? Time would tell, he had no doubt, and whatever might be expected of Gorm in the years to come, he was confident the young man would rise to the occasion. Blunt smiled to himself as he took another swig of the wonderful wine, which had become more wonderful still with each refill of his goblet. Who would have thought a perilous journey to the much feared Darklands and the Forest of Improbable Fate would have resulted in such a remarkable, life-changing outcome for them all, he reflected? Truly, Grun did work in mysterious ways, for did ever such an unlikely band of brothers share such an improbable fate?

Printed in Great Britain
by Amazon.co.uk, Ltd.,
Marston Gate.